# TIER 3

## CINDY GUNDERSON

Button Press

"Never doubt that a small group of thoughtful, committed citizens can change the world; indeed, it's the only thing that ever has."

—Margaret Mead

CHAPTER 1

"THE WEIGHT NEEDS to be a little higher up," Eric instructs, deftly manipulating the line with his fingers.

"Why?" Bentley asks, standing up to let Eric work.

"Would you want to eat food that looks like it has a weird piece of metal attached to it?"

"No, but I'm not a fish," he argues jokingly.

"True. But fish don't like strange looking things either. They can be surprisingly skeptical," Eric explains, finishing the knot. "There, try that."

Bentley and Tal have been fishing with us hundreds of times since we've been here, but it's still a learning curve when they're preparing their own lines. Especially when rotating our fishing sites.

"Dad, I got one!" Tal shouts excitedly from downstream. Grabbing the net and bucket, Eric rushes to assist. My line continues to lie still, which gives me pause. We need to hook at least three more for the week, unless Tal's catch is a big one.

"How's it going, Bentley?" I ask, watching him cast for the second time with the new weight.

"I don't think this works any better," he answers glumly.

"You can assess that after two casts?" I ask, teasing.

Rolling his eyes, he turns and casually reels it in. Not wanting to micromanage, I remove myself and begin organizing our equipment. Looks like one pole will need repairs again, but it should hopefully be a simple fix. I set it apart from the others so we won't forget to deal with it at home. Convinced that there isn't anything more I can do to be helpful, I resume my position, raise my pole, and cast. The sound of the burbling stream only adds to the general tranquility of our fishing spot this morning. Tall pine trees flank the long grasses rooted in the stream bed, allowing the early morning light to stipple the ground in dancing bronze medallions.

Fishing was not something I was familiar with before living on our own, but I've taken a liking to it. Catching food was one of the many things to which I gave very little thought back in Tier 1. Now, I often think of the hours that followed the departure of Nick's transport. Hours that quickly turned into days, subconsciously dictated by a low, throbbing panic. The elation and relief at seeing Eric and Tal again was tainted by the unknowns of our new situation. I was so wholly consumed by the goal of putting our family back together that I wasn't able to anticipate the consequences. That moment he pulled away...I don't think I have ever felt more naked.

And yet, here we are. Thriving after two hard-fought years. It took time for me to learn how to shut down my need to plan for the future. Here, there's no such thing. Not really. Unless you count the next two weeks—the next season, at most—as the future. Thinking about what my children's lives will look like in ten—or even five—years is the only thing that potentially has the power to send me into a downward spiral these days. And there's simply no time for that.

"Got one!"

The sound of Bentley's high-pitched squeal makes me jump. Eric still hasn't returned with Tal, so I reel in my line and run to him, dropping my pole in the brush.

"We did well, as usual," Eric congratulates as he sets our plates onto the smooth surface of our new kitchen table. His finger lingers on the edges of each dish, as if reminding himself of his fine craftsmanship. Smiling, I turn, not wanting to embarrass him by staring. He has the distinct ability to always sound as if there was never a doubt in his mind that we would accomplish the task at hand. If he is ever worried—deep down—he is incredibly good at masking it.

"I can't believe I caught two!" Bentley exclaims, following Eric with a clay pitcher of water, slowly filling each cup to the brim.

"Your initial assessment of my line adjustment was a tad hasty, wouldn't you say?" Eric chides. Bentley grins, but doesn't give him the satisfaction of an answer.

"Sometimes we just have to be patient," I comment, turning from the sink and drying my hands on a cloth. "Is the fish almost done?"

"Should be," Tal answers. "I'll go check."

He returns a few moments later with four fillets—crisped to perfection—and a bowl of steaming Jerusalem artichokes. Sometimes I miss the convenience of having an oven, but the flavor of food roasted in a pit cooker can't be beat. Tossing the salad one last time, I move it to the center of the table. Our sunflowers haven't gone to seed yet, so I was limited to a few blueberries and shallots to compliment the chard, but at least it's something.

The boys are silent as we dish up our food, both of them mentally and physically exhausted from our day's adventures. When they were young, we used to have to invent ways to wear them out so they would go to bed on time. I suppress a laugh, thinking of the relative absurdity of it.

"I miss yogurt," Tal says, stuffing a fork full of salad into his mouth.

"You and me both," Eric agrees readily.

"If you could only figure out how to milk a deer, Tal," I say, and Eric snorts, nearly spitting his food out.

"What? It might be possible," I tease.

"I don't miss it that much," Tal chuckles.

"What do you miss, Bentley?" Eric asks, and I hold my breath.

Chewing for a moment, Bentley's eyebrows furrow. "Kids."

I exhale. That was his answer last time, as well. I guess I was secretly hoping it would have morphed into something else. The yogurt problem? I can at least pretend to be able to solve that, but peers? Friends? I've got nothing.

"I miss talking to the researchers at the lab," Eric says, nodding. I purposefully take another bite to prevent myself from saying something unhelpful. Thinking of the parts of our experience that aren't ideal makes me uncomfortable; I don't enjoy being reminded of my lack of control. But, I also recognize the importance of validating the boys' feelings...so I let Eric do it.

Bentley yawns.

"Time for bed already?" I ask, and he nods, finishing his last bite of fish. After clearing his plate to the sink, he moves next to my chair and wraps his arms around my shoulders, his chin barely able to rest on the top of my head.

"Goodnight, Mom," he says as I rub his back, then exits to the washroom to brush his teeth.

"Are you off, as well?" Eric asks, motioning to Tal.

"Almost. I think I want to add one more part to the separator first."

I nod. "We'll clean up dinner. You better hurry, there's probably only a half hour of good light left."

Scooting his chair back, he washes his hands and heads out the door. Eric stands, gathering the utensils and moving them to the sink.

"Do you think their tinkering will ever amount to something?" I ask, scooping the last of the salad onto my plate. "Did you want any more of this?"

"No, go ahead, thanks," he answers. "I don't know. Honestly, I barely understand what they are even up to. They both have such mechanically orientated brains. Maybe if I had spent more time working with my hands as a kid..." Eric trails off.

"I don't think even an infinite amount of experience would have helped me. I just don't have a vision for it like they do," I admit.

"We were conditioned for a different world," Eric sighs, beginning to wash the plates with the newly pressed soap. I stand, setting the rest of the dishes on the counter next to him, and lean against his strong back, my cheek pressed against his shoulder blade.

"I think we've adapted fairly well," I say, breathing him in. He turns, pulling me to his chest. Not for the first time, my brain registers that he smells different here. At least, different than I remember. But who knows what I actually remember at this point.

"I certainly wouldn't change anything," he says slowly, his heart steadily beating in my ear.

"Do you ever wish we—"

"No. Never."

## CHAPTER 2

My hands are deep in the dirt when it happens. The normally silent sensor dings, nearly giving me a heart attack. Pulling myself up off of the ground, I brush off and run to the house.

"Eric?" I call, searching around the perimeter. Realizing that he is likely in the middle of scraping a hide, I rush inside for better lighting. Though I prefer to receive new information together, there's no way I can wait this time. It's been too long since our last communication. Sitting down at the table, I pull up the message and begin to read.

*Kate, Eric, Tal, and Bentley,*

*I'm sorry it's taken me so long to connect. While I don't think I am at risk of being caught communicating with you at this point, I have been so consumed with my responsibilities that I haven't had a moment to get in touch. I know, it's a lame excuse, but I think you'll let it pass when I fill you in.*

*First things first, how are your supplies holding up? You were in good shape last time we talked. I hope that's still the case. Not that I could do anything if they weren't, but it always makes me feel better to hear it.*

*Now, to explain my absence. You won't believe it, Kate, but Jessica and I now have TWENTY representatives supporting our integration initiative. That last piece of info that went public seemed to be the tipping point for individuals in Tier 1. I am finally seeing the light at the end of the tunnel. Tamara and I have started another round of conditioning trials. We don't have a perfect solution yet, but the more results I see, the more I am convinced that integration is the only option. I know we're all on the same page here, but it's exciting to see proof in the data.*

*Beth and Leah are thriving. Getting into trouble as always. The other day, Leah whacked Beth on the head with a spoon and I had to physically pull them apart—you should have seen the fire in Beth's eyes. Wish I could give more details. Send word when you can.*

*-Nick*

The dull ache in my chest, always present in some quantity, heightens as I read the last paragraph. If Nick succeeds in integrating...no. I can't allow myself to get my hopes up. Re-reading the message, I focus solely on the societal progress that is being made through sheer grit and determination. Nick is truly a force to be reckoned with.

I quickly respond, giving him a breakdown of our current resources—proud to recognize that we have been incredibly prudent. Sending a few descriptions of the boys' latest adjustments to their water filtration system, I again express my gratitude for his surprise technological gifts. How he was able to sneak it all in with our supplies is beyond me, but I can't imagine the boys' lives without it. So far, they've made progress with remineralization, but nothing groundbreaking enough to announce. Likely, scientists in Tier 1 have already surpassed this tech anyway, but I would never tell Tal and Bentley that.

"What are you up to?" Eric asks, startling me.

"I didn't even hear you come in," I say, my hand flying to my chest.

"Sorry," he chuckles, "the door squeaked like it always does. I wasn't trying to sneak up on you." Noticing the sensor in my hand, he stops short. "Did we get one?"

Nodding, I slide it across the wooden surface to him so he can read Nick's message. He washes his hands, then pulls a chair back from the table and sits next to me. I can't help but scrutinize his face as he scans the text.

"Wow, I'm impressed," Eric admits. "Based on how resistant the Committees were to making everything public, I can't believe it actually happened."

"They agreed to his conditions. Did you really think they wouldn't comply?"

"You really didn't question whether they would?" he asks, incredulous.

"We're here, together, aren't we?" I laugh, snatching the sensor from his grip and snapping it back on my wrist. "If they were willing to do that, I guess I assumed they were serious about all of Nick's other terms."

"You're still an optimist," he accuses, and I gently smack his shoulder from across the table. "All I'm saying is that it took them nearly two years to release the full resource numbers and inform the patients that had been treated without consent. I think I'm justified in being skeptical."

"I'll give you that much," I say, rising to chop vegetables for lunch. "Were you out working on that skin?"

"It's all done," he announces proudly, crossing his arms behind his head and stretching his legs.

"What is Tal hoping to use it for this time?"

"New shoes."

"Didn't he just finish his last pair a month ago?"

"Turns out, when you're twelve, you grow a lot," Eric laughs.

I grin, turning and scrubbing a carrot under the slow stream of water from the tap. When its orange skin is gleaming, I set it to the side and pick up the next one.

"Hey," I say, turning my head, my hands still working autonomously, "we have enough ashes for more soap. Can you ask the boys what herbs they want this time and then have them gather enough for about eight bars?"

"Sure," he responds, standing. "Should I go get them for lunch?"

"That would be great. I'm going to pull out some chapatis to eat with the jam."

"We still have more? I thought the boys ate them all," Eric says, looking surprised, but pleased.

"I never put them all out on the table at once," I admit, grinning. He crosses the space between us and pulls me close, kissing me softly at first, then with more intensity.

"Are the boys—" I start to ask, taking a breath, but Eric cuts me off with another kiss. His rough hands tenderly search the soft skin of my lower back. Setting the carrot down on the counter, I turn off the faucet and blindly reach for a towel to dry my hands. As I am lifted off the floor, my legs wrap around Eric's waist as he walks to the bedroom. The soap can wait.

I stare as Eric dresses next to my side of the bed, his back muscles stretching as he lifts his shirt above his head. His body has adapted well to the lifestyle we have here. All of us have physically changed in some ways, but Eric's lean, chiseled musculature is what stands out to me the most. Sometimes I mourn that Eric was sterilized during his time in Tier 2, but at least there is a silver lining. With no procreation restrictions here, I would have loved to have had more children with him. The inherent risks involved with pregnancy and childbearing might not have been enough to dissuade me, so this has saved me from myself in a way. Still, I sigh, imagining what could have been.

Eric kisses me before he walks out the door to find Tal and Bentley. I stare at the ceiling, breathing deeply and soaking in the last few moments of relaxation. Eventually, I force myself to leave the comfort of my blankets and jump back into the demands of the day.

Back in the kitchen, I linger near the window, anticipating Eric's return with the boys. I am waiting for the slow, consistent pace of life here to become so commonplace that it doesn't register as something to be grateful for. But it hasn't happened yet. These moments of silent reflection—so few and far between in Tier 1— seem to be sprinkled throughout each day here. There are definitely days when we are rushing from dawn until dusk, but they are few and far between. And even then...the rhythm is subtly different.

After finishing with my meal preparations, I lie down on the bench cushion and prop my feet up, allowing the hems of my cotton pants to slip to my knees— another beautiful, momentary respite from the work still to be done this afternoon. The room brightens as the sun peeks from behind the clouds. Perfect timing. We will be able to make the soap tonight if that keeps up.

I am grateful every day for the care Nick took in finding this location. I doubt the Director would have been quite so generous. From what Nick told me before we arrived—and what we've been able to gather since—this used to be a distribution center in Tier 3, which is why it has so many basic amenities. Eric framed out new rooms for us and built furniture, making it practical and cozy. Detoxified soil, well-water, septic system, and solar panels—all of the necessities, really. Though we don't have a battery complex, it's not overly inconvenient to save the tasks that require energy for sunny days. It does get old having to take cold showers in the wet and gloomy winter months, but I can only imagine how much worse it could have been. Even just the thought of how close we were to never seeing Eric and Tal again...I am more than happy to deal with cold showers.

The door abruptly squeaks open as Tal and Bentley fall over each other in a rush, trying to be first inside the house. Eric follows, a smile still on his face, and I blush as he meets my eyes.

"Alright boys, that's enough. Wash your hands, and let's eat," Eric instructs gently.

Watching them jostle one another at the sink, I give up on attempting to create peace and order, instead resigning myself to the seat at the end of the table. The lid to the jar of elderberry jam sticks a little, but I eventually get it open and place a spoon into the rich, purple jam. The boys take their seats hurriedly and immediately lunge for the food.

"Nope! Hands down," Eric commands, taking his seat. "What are you grateful for, Tal?"

Sighing, Tal slumps back into his seat. "I am grateful for a deer skin so I can make new shoes."

Eric nods. "And you Bentley?"

"I am grateful for a sunny day so I can charge my reading light," he says.

"How many times are you going to read that book?" Tal scoffs under his breath.

"I'm *making my own*, I'm not reading that one again," Bentley shoots back, his eyes flashing.

"You're making your own book?" I ask.

"I just started," he answers, clearly trying to downplay it. "I found a box of paper in the storage shed."

"I think it's great," I comment, shooting a pointed look in Tal's direction. "What's it about?"

"It's just a field journal. I'm keeping track of the arsenic levels in all of the water samples we test," he says casually, scooping jam onto his chapati bread.

My jaw drops in surprise, and Eric beats me to my next question. "Since when are you testing arsenic levels?" he asks. "This area is detoxified."

"No, it's the perfect way to assess water pollution," Tal explains, speaking quickly. "Even if this area was detoxified at some point, there are certain places that have higher levels of contamination, which means there has to be some source that is continuing to alter the soil chemistry. The most likely culprit is groundwater. And we need those counts to assess if our system is working."

"Should we be worried about our water supply?" Eric asks, looking genuinely concerned.

"No," Bentley assures us. "I test the well regularly and it's always below dangerous levels. Arsenic is commonly occurring in the earth's crust, so it's not like we can avoid it completely."

"Can we eat already?" Tal asks, annoyed.

I meet Eric's sidelong glance and suppress a smile, dishing up greens onto my plate as a distraction.

"Yes," I say, "dig in."

The boys gratefully lean forward and fill their plates. The next few moments are blissfully lacking in commentary, filled only with the sound of clinking, chewing, and swallowing.

"Can you pass me the water, Tal?" Bentley asks.

"Please," I correct, and he mimics me in an especially silly voice, causing everyone to laugh. Dinnertime is pleasant here. It's not a means to an end like it used to be, rather a moment to be enjoyed. A time to be present.

Our kids' choice of hobby is foreign to me, and I'm not convinced that it's actually leading anywhere useful, but I can't help but get a kick out of their enthusiasm. I am constantly shocked by what I don't know and what they do.

Sensing that they are finishing up, I break the silence. "I'm definitely going to make the soap tonight since I'll have access to the burners, so please bring in your herbs as soon as you finish."

"I'll trim the lavender, you get the sage, okay Bent?" Tal instructs, his mouth still full of food. Their arms move quickly, obviously attempting to salvage as much after-dinner time as possible before bed.

Bentley nods. "Then meet back at the lab?"

Tal sends him a thumbs up as his dishes clatter on the counter and he scoots out the door.

CHAPTER 3

TAL AND BENTLEY are off hunting pheasants while Eric and I put in the next planting. My shovel sinks pleasantly into the rich compost, and I lift pile after pile into the empty wheelbarrow. When it's full, I push it over to the potatoes, mixing the compost into the tilled soil before heaping another layer around the tall, leggy shoots. Incredibly, these mounds will be nearly four feet high by the time we need to harvest.

Eric is kneeling nearby, carefully laying the carrot and radish seeds into neat rows. It looks like it's going to rain later this afternoon, so the seeds should get a quick, solid start. To my right, I notice a few bright green seedlings emerging from the soil, and a grin creeps across my face.

"What are you so happy about?" Eric asks, amused.

"My lettuce re-seeded itself and it's already sprouting," I say, childlike energy bubbling up in my chest. "Can you believe that? I love watching things grow."

"I've noticed," he chuckles. "If you're finished with the potatoes, would you mind starting on the beets?"

"Sure," I say, moving to the next section of the garden and turning it over with my trowel. A sound catches my attention, and I sit up on my knees, my head pointed in the general direction of the noise. Though I can barely hear them, I eventually see two small figures running toward us from the woods. Eric, noticing my concern, follows my gaze.

"What are they doing back so soon?" he questions under his breath, lifting to his feet.

"They seem to be worked up about something," I comment, continuing to stare.

A few moments later, when they are finally within earshot, we are able to understand what they've been yelling from the tree line.

"We saw something!" Bentley shouts and Tal—though out of breath—reiterates his brothers' concern through wide, troubled eyes.

Eric motions for them to calm down, and they both double over in the grass near our feet.

"Breathe for a minute, then you can tell us," I instruct, growing more concerned by the look of their flushed faces and the lack of pheasant.

"We saw something," Bentley repeats, his voice a normal volume, but still gasping for breath.

"We understood that much," Eric says, "but what do you mean by 'something'?"

"A person," Tal says, still sucking in air as he rolls to his side. "There was someone in the trees."

Eric and I freeze, both of us searching the boys' expressions.

After collecting his thoughts, Eric asks calmly, "You saw a person?"

"Yes! They were in the trees watching us," Tal explains, exasperated by our obvious lack of understanding.

"Describe them," I command, my brows furrowing and mind racing. Who could possibly be out this far? Is someone in Tier 1 attempting to keep tabs on us? But why? It would make no sense to waste human resources like that.

"We were walking past, and I saw eyes inside of the bush—" Bentley starts.

"Wait, you only saw eyes?" I cut in.

"Yeah, but—"

"How do you know it wasn't an animal?" Eric asks.

"Dad, they were *not* animal eyes. And besides, what animal would have large eyes that are colored, not brown? I haven't ever seen green eyes on a wild creature, have you?"

I think for a moment. "No," I admit, "I don't think I have."

"So what happened next?" Eric prods.

"We stared at each other for a moment, then I said 'Who are you?' and the eyes got wide, then disappeared. I ran around the bush, trying to find the person they belonged to, but they were gone. Then we rushed back here to tell you guys."

I am flummoxed. What—or who—could this possibly be? My brain circles to the same possibility of someone from Tier 1 here to observe, but then again rejects that conclusion. It is much more likely that the boys misunderstood what they saw...but I don't want to be the one to accuse them or kill their story.

"Can you take us there?" I offer instead. Perhaps we will find animal tracks, or other evidence that will put this to rest.

The boys immediately turn on their heels and beckon for us to follow them. I gently place the package of seeds in my hand on a flat stone, then run after them, trying to keep up. Eric, walking next to me, takes hold of my hand and leans in.

"It had to be an animal, right?"

"I don't see how it could have been anything else. Though I am anxious regardless. If they thought it was a human eye, it must have been large. And so close to them..." I shudder.

"I know," Eric says, his voice low.

We walk in silence, but the tension in Eric's hand communicates everything I need to know. We are both reliving that moment from last summer. Hearing Bentley's shriek from the field, a sound so foreign that it pierced me with terror before I even knew what had caused it. Running through the grass to find Tal with an axe raised high over his head, his arms shaking with adrenaline. The mountain lion hissing and spitting, ears lowered against its head. Bentley. Eyes closed, lying on the ground. Blood soaking through his shirt.

I blink, focusing on the grass in front of me to force those images to recede from my conscious brain. That remains the singular incident requiring us to break into our emergency medical supplies since we have been here. Had Nick not been available that night on his sensor, who knows if we would have been able to patch Bent up properly. *They are fine*, I remind myself, refocusing on their ruffled heads in front of me.

"Here!" Tal shouts, pointing into the thicket ahead of him. Eric carefully pushes into the underbrush, stepping lightly and inspecting the ground. Bentley stands close to me, and I put my arm around his shoulder.

"Well," Eric says finally, "I don't see anything. No footprints, no broken branches, nothing." His face appears above the shrubs, and he begins to extricate himself, displacing branches of goldenrod as he moves toward us. "The ground is actually quite soft back there, so I'm surprised there aren't any prints. Though, if an animal stepped in just the right spots, they might miss the bare mud," he concludes, brushing his hands on his pants. "Sorry guys, I wish I had a better answer for you."

"It was a person, Dad. Probably really smart if they didn't leave prints," Tal huffs.

"We aren't saying you're wrong, Tal, just that it's very unlikely," I explain. He nods—but makes it clear that he isn't in agreement—and we start back toward the house.

Later that night, after tucking the boys into bed, Eric and I escape to the yard to watch the stars. While there wasn't an inordinate amount of light pollution in Tier 1, the sky certainly didn't ever look like this. I immediately search for my favorite star—a bright, warm blinking light in the northeastern sky. It comforts me to see it there night after night, reminding me that we are somehow a part of something much, much bigger.

Eric sighs as we settle into the hammock together—yet another product of the boys' creativity, handiwork, and engineering. Instead of wasting the old fishing supplies, pieces of fabric, and hide that weren't utilized in other, more important projects, this hammock was born. Initially, I was wary about it holding our weight combined, but Eric seemed to think it was sound, and he was right. I snuggle close to his chest, enjoying the warmth from his body in the cool night air.

"I think you should accompany the boys when they hunt," I say softly.

"I've thought about it. I know we've become complacent...but at the same time, it's sometimes a practical reality that they have to go on their own."

"Do you really think there are times where you *couldn't* go along?"

"During planting and harvest it will certainly cut our time short."

"True," I admit. "But if there's nobody to plant and harvest for..."

"Kate, the chances—"

"I know. I'm being dramatic. That just scared me," I whisper.

He pulls me closer and I can feel his chest, rising and falling with his breath.

"I'll go with them from now on."

CHAPTER 4

"Mom, don't do that," Tal complains, jumping as I enter the shed.

"Sorry, it wasn't my intention to startle you," I apologize, laughing under my breath at his terrified expression. Bentley and Tal are hovered over a series of tubes and beakers, intently focused.

"Any luck?" I ask, moving toward them.

"Shhh," Bentley instructs and I attempt to be silent in my approach. Watching from a slight distance, I observe Bentley adding something to the test tube on his right—the liquid settles and then begins to trickle into a series of containers connected to a significantly larger receptacle. Once it drains, both boys relax and begin cleaning up the work station.

"Can I talk now?" I ask.

"Yes," Bentley answers matter-of-factly, wiping up excess liquid with a cloth.

"What did you try this time?"

"Tal made a solution—I think it's too complex to describe," he explains.

"Too complex? As in, you don't think I can understand it?"

Bent grins sheepishly, but doesn't give any more information.

"Well, at least I know your opinion of my intelligence," I tease. "Do you think it will be successful this time around?"

"Of course I think it *could* work, otherwise I wouldn't have tried it," Tal says.

"Alright, alright!" I say, holding up my hands in defeat. "I'm just trying to learn more about what you're doing," I sigh, moving toward the door.

"Mom, sorry," Tal calls, running after me and pulling on my arm. "It's just frustrating because we've run so many trials and still haven't found the winning combination. One day, our water is going to run out, and if we—"

"Wait," I cut him off, placing my hands on his shoulders. "Do you somehow feel responsible for creating a clean water supply for us? Is that why you are always out here working on this?" I ask, incredulous.

Tal and Bentley both nod, their expressions deadly serious.

"Guys, no," I respond, my body deflating as I pull them close. "Dad and I are responsible for making sure that we have enough. You don't need to hold that burden. We love watching you experiment, but in no way do we expect you to solve this problem. Of course, we absolutely believe you're fully capable of doing so, but we don't *expect* it. We have enough filtration supplies to last for a long, long time—"

Tal cuts in, "But even you said that those filtration tabs don't actually get everything out. We're still constantly being exposed to contaminants, which means we're going to be susceptible to DNA damage. We don't want you and Dad—"

"Tal, Dad and I have been exposed our whole lives. While I do believe that if that exposure were halted, we would definitely see some benefits, I don't think they would be life-altering at this point."

"But for me and Tal..." Bentley muses.

"Sure, yes. For you and Tal, I'm sure it would make a significant difference. But so would a lot of things! We can't live our lives constantly worried or disappointed that we haven't progressed past a certain point. We have to learn to be grateful for where we are— accept any potential consequences—and then do all we can to improve. There's no magical, elusive endpoint. We just keep moving forward."

Tal nods, but I'm not sure whether he agrees with the sentiment or not.

"Did Nick get in trouble for putting this equipment in our supplies?" Bentley asks softly, and it takes me off-guard.

"I—I don't know. I guess I hadn't thought of that."

"It doesn't seem like lab equipment would be necessary for survival," he argues.

"No, definitely not," I agree. "I guess I never questioned whether he had clearance for that or not, I just assumed it was on his list of conditions, but—"

Bentley shrugs—obviously done with the conversation—and walks past me, letting in a burst of sunshine as he passes through the door. Tal laughs at his abrupt exit and my disoriented expression at being cut-off mid-thought.

"I'll try not to worry about the water," he agrees, then pats my back and follows his brother into the light.

The rain moves in swiftly that evening, hitting the tin roof with force, the noise almost deafening. The rise in humidity chills me, and I find myself putting the boys to bed dressed in nearly three full layers of clothes. I lie between them, holding their hands, and listening to the cacophony above us. Moments like these remind me how delicate life really is. The natural flow of this planet is powerful, yet somehow—in the day-to-day hum-drum—I convince myself that I'm above it. Arbitrarily separate and immune. The pelting drops strike an ancient chord within me, appropriately realigning my prideful assessment of my own importance. Slowly, the storm begins to calm, and the thundering above us lessens. When it becomes a soft pitter-patter, Bentley turns his head.

"Mom, what will I do when I grow up?"

"What do you mean?" I ask, buying myself time to think of an answer.

"Well, I can't really pair and have a family, right? There isn't anyone to pair with. What will Tal and I do?"

I shift my head to look at Tal who is already breathing deeply. Letting go of his hand, I roll to the side so I can look him in the eyes.

"Bud...I wish I had a good answer for you," I murmur, gently brushing a lock of hair from his forehead. "The truth is, Dad and I...we don't really know what the future holds for any of us. Our goal was to be together again, but we didn't really think beyond that. We didn't get the chance to. Everything moved so fast, and nothing was within our control."

His eyes are wide, reflecting the dim light that enters from the hallway. "Do you think we'll ever see Beth and Leah again?"

My stomach clenches, and I have to physically remind myself to breathe. "I—I wish I could say yes, Bent, but..." He reaches for me and my eyes sting as his arms wrap around my neck, squeezing me tightly.

"You did the best you could, Mom. I know that."

After holding him for a moment, I extricate myself from his arms in near desperation and escape to the hall. Leaning against the wall, I allow my body to slide to the floor as I bury my face between my arms and knees, and softly sob. If only I could be so sure.

CHAPTER 5

"Hey girls," I coo, watching their legs kick in excitement as I pick them up out of their crib, placing one on each hip.

"You feel soggy!" I tease, and they both giggle as I tickle their ribs. "Let's get you changed."

Laying them on the floor, I quickly grab the cloths before they wriggle away. It's almost an impossible task with how quickly they are moving now. I allow Beth to think she's escaped while I wrestle Leah to the floor. Her contagious giggles ring through the room as I pin her legs with one hand, attempting to remove the snaps on her current diaper with my other. Eventually, I succeed, only to realize that Beth has disappeared.

"Where's your sister?" I ask smiling, gently pinching Leah's chubby thighs. She squeals and flips over, swiftly scooting to the other side of the room. "I'll be right back, I just need to find that little stinker," I assure her.

Walking out of the room with the wet cloth still in my hands, I scan the hallway. No Beth. Moving into the living room, I assume I will find her near the toys, but she isn't there either. Light from the hallway catches my eye, and I follow it. The front door is gaping open and panic rises in my chest. Frozen, I stare into the morning sunlight, a silent scream on my lips.

"It's just a dream," Eric whispers over and over, rocking me in his arms as tears stream down my cheeks in an unending torrent. As I slowly become more present, the terror begins to subside, and I am able to breathe normally again. *It felt so real.*

"I'm sorry I woke you," I say eventually, lifting my head and looking up into Eric's eyes.

"No, it's okay. I was already up."

"You were? Why?"

"One of the clotheslines had come loose and was snapping against the house in the wind. The sound woke me. When I came back in, you were crying in your sleep." He pauses, searching my face. "What was it?"

"The girls," I sigh. "I love hearing from Nick, but...*every time.* That wound is opened right up again. It's not like I would prefer never hearing from him—it's definitely preferable to know that they are thriving and doing well—but that desire to be a part of their lives...it never goes away," I admit, looking down at my hands.

Eric lifts my chin with his hand. "Nor should it," he assures, his eyes intense.

I nod as he pulls me close. "Every time I dream about them, they're babies still. Eric, they are almost three years old now and I can't even envision them—" I whisper, my voice breaking. Eric holds me close. He strokes my hair as I softly sob, grieving the loss of a childhood I won't ever have the opportunity to be a part of.

I wake to a quiet house. Eric is still passed out next to me, but the sun is high enough in the sky, I know the boys must be awake. I slip out of bed carefully, throw on my long cotton shirt, and walk out into the main room, closing the bedroom door softly behind me.

Though the boys are nowhere to be found, they have left breakfast in their wake. A pot of oatmeal sits on the burner—bowls and spoons tossed in the sink. I glance through the window and find the warm morning sun turning everything into gold, making it nearly impossible to be annoyed at the mess. A soft mist rises from the grass—the dew evaporating in the gradual morning warmth. Across the garden, Tal and Bentley take turns tossing rocks into cans on the opposite side of the yard. I don't know what competition they have going today, but even from here their body language communicates that they are quite excited about it.

Scooping some oatmeal into a bowl, I pull the carton of blackberries from the cold storage and sit at the table. I catch myself staring at the dark display of my sensor. Normally, in the days following a new message, Nick responds promptly. We usually get at least a few notes back and forth before we both return to our separate realities, and then—months later—the cycle repeats again. I shake my head and use my spoon to add the berries to my bowl.

As I eat, I ponder the unanticipated anxiety in awaiting his response. Am I antsy simply because he's taking longer than usual? Or am I heaping my own expectations onto a possible response? Despite my continual mental reprimands, I know I've allowed hope to take root, if only just barely. If Nick gains enough traction and integration is instituted, we could make a strong case for inclusion. That would mean I could be potentially involved in the girls' lives. Maybe not as their mother—I wouldn't want to cause trauma —but maybe as an aunt?

That also means I would see Nick again. I search my feelings, taking another bite of oatmeal. It would be fine if he was happy, right? *More than fine*, I chastise myself. Hopefully he has paired at this point? I haven't had the courage to ask...though he does mention Jessica in every message. Slight nausea hits my stomach, imagining another woman raising the girls. *No.* I am *grateful.* That's all. I force the thought through my brain, pushing out the insecurity and doubt. Even though it will be difficult to get used to seeing him in a new life, it would be exponentially more devastating to find Nick alone and unfulfilled. I shudder, imagining how that meeting would feel on his end.

The bedroom door opens and Eric walks out, his hair disheveled.

"Good morning," I greet him, grinning.

"Hi," he yawns, stretching his arms behind his head. "Where are the boys?"

"Out in the yard, tossing rocks."

"Sounds about right," he smiles.

"They made us breakfast," I say, motioning to the oatmeal.

"Well at least they're good for something," he teases.

"I have the blackberries here at the table if you want some."

"Perfect."


After breakfast, we dress and head out to the yard to join Tal and Bentley.

"Who won?" Eric calls, and Bentley responds by doing a little dance, pointing to himself. Eric laughs, giving him a thumbs up. "I need you boys to come help now," he adds, and they obediently come running.

Out of breath, Tal asks, "Can we try again for pheasants today?"

"Tell you what. If you can help me repair this fence, then I'll take you out this afternoon."

"Yes!" Bentley exclaims. "What do we need to do?"

Eric launches into his instructions, the boys nodding in attentive acknowledgement. I turn and begin walking my typical route around the pond, checking the nests of the ducks who roost there. Sure enough, there are a few eggs in each. I gently lift them into my basket. There hasn't been a drake around for a few weeks, but our luck likely won't last much longer. And I certainly want new ducklings for next year, so I'll just have to stock up while I can. Pausing, I roll one egg—slightly heavier than the others—in my hand. I'll have the boys check these with light, just in case.

Making my way back slowly—my boots sinking in the mud every few steps—something catches my eye. Picking it up, I realize it's a small piece of string, almost like a shoelace. It doesn't look like anything we own, but it could have been left here in years past. Maybe turned over in the rain? After rinsing off the mud in the pond, I wring it out, and put it in my pocket. You never know when something like that could be useful.

With the fence repaired, the boys get ready to head off on their hunt. Assessing the state of the yard, I realize with satisfaction that I'm caught up on most of my projects. I'll be busy next week when we harvest the green beans, but until then...

"Would you guys mind if I came along?" I ask.

"You're going to come?" Bentley responds excitedly.

"I was thinking about it," I laugh. "If you'll have me."

"That would be great," Eric says. "Family hunt! I love it."

"You can use my gun, Mom," Tal says.

"No, it's okay, I don't need to shoot, I can just help. I don't want to take away your fun," I assure him.

"Maybe you could at least take one turn," Eric teases, knowing that I have zero desire to actually do any shooting. He chuckles as I send him a derisive, sidelong glance. Pulling out my backpack, I place a few plums and carrots into the outer pocket, then fill up the bladder with cool water. The empty shelf in the pantry reminds me I need to make more granola bars, but I want to wait until we harvest the oats. While we do already have some in storage, it makes me nervous to break into those until we have more to replace them.

"Do you need me to prep anything for dinner before we go?" Eric asks, breaking my train of thought.

"I was thinking we could just cook up a few eggs and vegetables along with the leftover jerky. Does that sound alright?"

"Sounds great, that will be fast and easy," he says, giving my hip a swat. "I'm glad you're coming."

The boys lead us down a well-worn trail into the brush. They have a few favorite spots for pheasant hunting, but I'm not sure which area we're headed to now. Not shouldered with the responsibility of being the leader, I relax and enjoy the beauty of the woods around me. Here in the deep shade of the trees, the late summer air is cool on my skin, and I can almost taste the decomposing wood as I breathe in.

Bentley pulls out a silver bar from his pocket and a smile spreads across my face. "What are you doing, Bent?" I ask.

"Just taking a picture," he answers, holding the small display in front of him. "Those trees are really beautiful."

"They are," I agree. I don't see him use the imaging display often, but I know he always has it on him. Eric and I grappled with whether we should allow the boys to even know it existed when we first found it in our supplies. Pictures are opinionated and biased, which is why Berg never supported wasting resources in providing access to imaging technology. Everyone in Tier 1 knew it existed for security and certain scientific purposes, but we also recognized its limitations. Images create false memories and can be altered to manipulate our perceptions and moods. Why distract the mind with potentially false information when we can offer it experiential truth?

In the end, Eric and I decided that the risk in our situation was low. Could viewing those images potentially create future problems for the boys? Perhaps. But with such little access to technology in general, we couldn't make a good enough argument to keep it hidden. Experiencing the magic of reliving something through a picture is a guilty pleasure we are currently willing to provide.

After we walk for a time, the trees open to a small meadow. Tal and Bentley lead us to a log behind a particularly tall bush, dense with leaves and branches.

"Let's watch from here," Tal says, crouching down. "If they're in the meadow, we should see some sign within a few minutes."

I sit next to Eric and watch the boys do their thing. Eric doesn't jump in once with instructions or advice, and witnessing their independence makes me proud. Eventually, they seem to be convinced that this is, indeed, a good location. After getting themselves situated and in position, they sit completely still. Waiting.

After what seems like an interminably long interval of silence, Bentley's head perks up. Tal slowly lifts his rifle, pointing it toward the edge of the meadow to our left. My body tenses, not knowing when to expect the shot. Just as I begin to relax, he pulls the trigger, and I jump. Lightning quick, Bentley springs to his feet and runs into the field as Tal lowers his gun to the ground.

Bentley returns quickly, a gorgeous pheasant dangling from his grip. The umber feathers on its back reflect rosy iridescence in the sunlight. My eyes widen as he immediately takes charge. The boys still haven't said a word, communicating silently as they work. Tal pulls out a bag and begins stuffing the feathers into it, almost as quickly as Bentley is plucking them from the bird's warm skin. Bentley holds out his hand expectantly, and Tal hands him a small knife. Expertly, Bent makes an incision behind the sternum—careful not to cut too deep. Reaching inside the bird, he pulls out the entrails and windpipe and hands them to Tal who quickly wraps them in leaves and moves a few feet into the brush. Without pausing, he digs a small hole, buries the organs, and returns with hands full of grass. Bentley stuffs the inside of the bird and presses the two sides together, then places the carcass inside a clean sack and attaches it to his belt.

My jaw is hanging open, and—realizing this fact—I quickly purse my lips together. Not quickly enough for Eric to notice, though. He laughs and pats my shoulder.

"Where to next, boys?" he asks, his eyes smiling.

As the sun begins to set, four birds hang from the boys' belts. Each time, they had followed the same routine—switching responsibilities depending on who made the kill. While hunting is still not something I relish, I am truly in awe of my children. Having the opportunity to observe their attention to detail and mastery of each skill was a true joy. How did they become so adept? So fearless?

Eric holds my hand as we walk, the colors of the trees becoming full and vibrant in the quickening twilight. Suddenly, movement catches my eye and I pause. My eyebrows furrow as I squint— holding perfectly still—hoping to locate the source of my distraction. Nothing. It must have been the wind or a falling leaf. As my shoulders relax, another flash moves through the bushes, and this time I'm sure it is something abnormal.

"Boys," I say softly and they turn, their gaze following my outstretched finger. Zeroing in on a cluster of small trees, Bentley moves slowly around one side while Tal moves to the other, gun drawn. Turning, Eric is nowhere to be found. I remain standing in place, not sure what I can do to be helpful at this point.

Suddenly, the brush explodes with movement and I jump back, startled. Recovering, I quickly dash forward, attempting to determine the source of the disturbance and suddenly nervous that I may have put the boys in danger. Before I can get too close, Eric appears with something wriggling in his grasp. Some*one*. A small, gangly thing—dirty and struggling against his captor for dear life.

"Whoa, it's okay," Eric says gently, while still maintaining a strong grip around the child's shoulders. Bentley and Tal follow, the gun still lifted. I catch Tal's eye and motion for him to put it away. The last thing we need is someone accidentally getting shot in all the commotion. As I watch Eric try to contain thrashing arms and legs, my mind reels. Is this who Bentley saw the other day? Who could possibly be out here? And why? Why would any human be so far out from the boundaries? How long have they been spying on us? And how have they survived on their own? *Are they lost or on their own?* Recognizing this familiar pattern—a spiral of unknowns—I close my eyes and force myself to breathe, lowering my shoulders and relaxing my neck. We will figure this out, I just need to be patient.

Opening my eyes, I find Eric using his arms as restraints across the child's chest as he patiently waits for the kicking to slow. It doesn't take long for the child to tire, and eventually, all fight has seeped out of the small body, leaving a slumped over pile of skin and bones.

"We aren't going to hurt you," Eric repeats softly, "I'm going to loosen my grip. If you try to run, I will have to restrain you again and I don't want to do that, okay?" He cautiously lowers his arms, still keeping them looped loosely over the child's shoulders. "Better?" he asks, and the child nods, finally looking up. Immediately upon gaining a better view of the child's face, I recognize that it's a little girl. She can't be more than eight years old, judging by her height and facial structure. Although, based on how skinny she is, she may simply be malnourished.

"Hi," I say with a hesitant smile. "I'm Kate, what's your name?"

Her eyes are wide—fearful—and she doesn't respond.

"Do you understand what we are saying? Nod if you do, no need to say anything," I assure her.

She slowly lowers and then lifts her head, not meeting my gaze directly.

"Great," I say, relief evident in my tone. This would have been impossible if we weren't able to communicate verbally. "I have so many questions for you, and I'm sure you have some for us, but I wondered...would you like something to eat first?" As soon as the words leave my lips, her head snaps toward me, her eyes almost pleading. Reaching into my sack, I pull out a plum and carefully hand it to her. She snatches it from me, savagely ripping into it with her teeth and nearly swallowing the pit. As she licks her fingers, I again ask her name. This time, she answers.

"Wild Rose," she says slowly. "Bu' people jus' call me Rose."

"Rose, that's beautiful," I say, moving a step closer. "How old are you?"

" 'leven," she answers and I try to disguise my shock by coughing into my elbow.

"Eleven, wow. Tal over here is twelve and Bentley is ten, so you are right between them."

Bentley looks confused, obviously noticing her immature speech and the fact that she is inches shorter than him. I mentally will him to keep his comments to himself and am grateful when his mouth remains shut.

"How did you get all the way out here?" Eric asks and Rose turns to him, her eyes flashing.

"This is m' home," she spits indignantly. "How did you get all the way out here?" she asks, mimicking his voice. Feisty, this one. I almost laugh at the expression on Eric's face, but think better of it.

"Your home?" Eric asks. "Do you live by yourself?"

"I live wit my family," she answers, shrinking into herself and looking at the ground. That response makes me nervous. Is she in a dangerous situation? Judging by the state of her clothes, she has either run away or her parents aren't very functional.

"Rose, we have been all over this area and have never seen another person, let alone another house. I am worried that you are in trouble. Can you show us where you live?"

"I cain't do that," she says slowly, shaking her head back and forth. "It's aginst the rules."

As she speaks, a gap in her smile screams of a missing tooth. I desperately hope that it's developmental delay and not because of decay or injury.

"Rose, we can't let you go in this condition. We need to make sure that you're okay. If you can't take us home, can you at least come to our home so we can help you clean up and give you more to eat? It's nearly dark. You'll need a safe place to sleep tonight. Then we can talk about potential options?" I ask.

Her eyes again light up at the mention of food, but then quickly darken again.

"I cain't stay long, I hafta bring food to my little brothers an' sisters. They real hungry too," she explains, twisting her hands together.

"Okay," I agree, nodding. "Let's get back and then we can figure this out. Are you alright to walk on your own?" I ask, noticing Eric's look of protestation, but waving him off. "Look at her, Eric, she isn't going to get very far on her own."

He sighs, then lowers his arms. "I'll walk in the back, if that's ok."

Tal and Bentley quickly gather their things and begin to walk.

"I caught these pheasants today," Bentley says, "but you probably already know that since you were watching us."

"*We* caught them, not just you," Tal mutters, and I can't help but laugh. So much for the seamless cooperation I witnessed a few minutes ago.

"How many sisters do you have?" Bentley asks. "I don't have any sisters. Well, I technically do, but I haven't seen them since they were babies. They live with Nick. Do you know Nick?" He chatters continuously and Rose seems content to listen, never satisfying him with a reply, which only eggs him on. Slowly, her nervousness seems to fade and she begins to march with more purpose.

"Eric, what are we doing?" I whisper, matching his step.

"I don't know, this was your idea," he reminds me.

"Well I couldn't let her leave, I mean look at her. She's skin and bones."

He nods.

"Maybe we could make her a care package of some food she can take back to her family?"

"Not a bad idea," Eric muses, "but I would much rather take it and meet this 'family'. Maybe we could offer it if she's willing to let us go along?"

"After she sees us at home, hopefully she'll realize we aren't a threat. I'm worried she's not being taken care of," I admit.

"I don't think you have to worry about that, it's kind of a fact, don't you think?"

I sigh. "Yeah, I guess it is."

Rose looks back at us suspiciously, and I pick up my pace.

## CHAPTER 6

BACK AT THE HOUSE, I show Rose how to use the shower and rustle up some of Bentley's smaller clothes for when she is clean. I gingerly pick up her dirty apparel and take it to the washbasin. Though I don't have time to put it through a full wash, I scrub it thoroughly and rinse, then hang it on the line to dry overnight. Hopefully a couple hours in the morning sun will help with some of the darker stains.

The child that emerges from the washroom is completely transformed. Her shoulder length hair lies in a sleek bob, framing her heart shaped face. Her skin nearly glows in comparison to her previous, dirt-smudged self. Even in Bentley's clothes, her delicate femininity shows through.

"Does that feel better?" I ask, and she shrugs, giving me a shy smile.

Tal emerges from the pantry with a jar of jam and some jerky. "Can I give her this?" he asks. "It's my favorite snack."

I smile and nod. It's sweet watching him take such thought and care for someone he barely knows. Just for one minute, I wish I could be inside his brain—to view Rose through his lens. Was it shocking to see another child in that condition? Where does he think she came from?

"Hey Rose, want to see my room?" Bentley calls from down the hall, and immediately her eyes are conflicted, not wanting to disappoint him, but salivating over the food that Tal is offering.

"Bent, give her a minute, okay? I'm going to cook up some eggs if you want to join us."

"Be there in a sec!" he calls back.

Eric opens the door and does a double-take when he notices Rose at the table. I shrug when he looks my direction in shock.

"I hung the birds, we can finish with them in the morning," he announces, recovering.

"Thank you," I say, walking toward him and giving him a peck on the cheek. When I turn back, Rose's eyes are fixed on us. It would be unnerving if it wasn't such an innocent stare. What does she think of us? Again, just one minute inside her head...

"Do you like eggs, Rose?" I ask.

She nods, ravenously scarfing down another piece of jerky.

"Eat slowly," I suggest, "you don't want to make yourself sick."

"Anything I can help with?" Eric asks, washing his hands.

"No, thanks. Easy dinner, remember?"

He nods, smiling. "Where should we have Rose sleep?"

"What about the back storage room? There are windows in there and plenty of space to put down blankets."

"Do you think that will be comfortable? If we just put down a few of the feather comforters?" Eric suggests.

"I think so," I say. Then turning to Rose, "Does that sound okay? We can show you the room if that would help."

"Sounds fine t'me. No need t'see it now," she says between bites.

"I'll help you get blankets," Bentley offers, following Eric out of the kitchen, swinging around the wooden beam in the middle of the room on his way out.

After all three children are tucked in and the house is quiet, Eric and I begin tidying up. Normally Bent and Tal would help with that, but they were overly excited and exhausted with Rose's arrival. I didn't have the energy to enforce another expectation.

"Do you think she'll sleep okay?" Eric asks, his voice low.

"I have no idea," I admit. "You don't think she'll take off, do you?"

"I thought about that," he says, walking toward the door and pulling a rope out of the inside pocket of his jacket. "If I lock the pantry and cold room, I highly doubt she'll be willing to leave with nothing."

I smile. "Brilliant, as always. But it does make me sad that we have to hold her hostage by withholding food."

"We aren't withholding, just dictating the timing," he rationalizes, rubbing my shoulder as he walks past to secure the pantry door.

We awaken late, the sky cloudy overhead, not allowing the sun to announce the new day. Bouncing out of bed, I quickly dress and move to check on the kids. Seeing that all of them are still fast asleep, including Rose who apparently did not escape during the night, I busy myself with breakfast. Though I wasn't planning to make anything fancy this morning, having a guest for the first time in two years inspires me. I open a bucket of wheat and grind a few cups, mixing it with eggs, soda, pumpkin puree that I canned last year—using old supply containers and a water bath—and spices. On a grey morning like this, warm pumpkin pancakes will be a treat, though it's ironic that the days that inspire a warm meal are the days when we don't have electricity to make it easy. Chuckling to myself, I throw on my jacket. On my way out to the yard, I scrape some tallow from the tin into a cup and pick up the bowl of batter, taking it with me to the fire pit.

Returning to the kitchen with a plate of steaming pancakes, I am greeted by the sound of laughter wafting down the hall from the boys' bedroom. Gathering the plates and forks, I set them on the table, then find the honey and berries from the pantry. The rope securing the door has been removed, so Eric must be around here somewhere.

"Breakfast!" I call, excited for everyone to join me. The pitter-patter of feet is nearly instantaneous. I catch a glimmer of excitement in Rose' expression before her face shuts down upon entering the kitchen and finding me there. It must be so strange for her. My heart aches that she is desperate enough to put herself in such an uncomfortable situation.

"Rose, you can take any seat you would like—"

"Sit there," Bentley directs, interrupting me. "Then you will be between me and Tal."

I suppress a smile, turning back to fill another cup with water.

"They live!" Eric teases, walking through the front door, bringing a cold breath of air along with him. "When I left to check the nests, you were all dead to the world."

"There wasn't any sunshine to wake us up," Tal hedges.

"I know, it's fine. I would have woken you had there been more to do. I'll need your help with the compost rotation this afternoon, though," he says, hanging his coat on the hooks by the door. A flake of paint flutters to the floor as the fabric brushes the wall.

Tal and Bentley don't meet his eyes, surreptitiously glancing at each other while pretending to be focused on dressing their pancakes.

"What?" Eric asks, noticing their silence, and their heads snap up, innocent expressions plastered on their faces.

"Huh?" Tal asks.

"Nothing," Bentley says concurrently, returning to the task of cutting his pancake with the side of his fork.

"You know we have knives for that, right?" I ask.

"This is faster," he answers, without missing a beat.

"Guys, do you not want to help this afternoon? I know it's cold, but—"

"No, Dad, it's not that, it's—"

"—I invited Tal and Bentley t'come see my home. Whin I go back today. They're worried they won't be 'llowed to go," Rose pipes in, her cheeks flushing when she realizes that all eyes are on her.

My eyes widen. That's the most she's said since we first found her in the brush. And, why would she invite the boys? I thought taking people home was against the rules.

"I think we should talk about that," I say, taking my seat at the table. Eric mirrors me.

"First, before we eat, gratefuls," Eric says, nodding to Tal.

He sighs, lowering the fork that had previously been halfway to his lips back to the plate. "I am grateful that mom finally made something delicious for breakfast."

"Tal," Eric warns.

"Okay, sorry. I'm grateful for a morning where we got to sleep in and eat delicious food," he counters.

"Better. Bent?"

"I am grateful that I met my first friend."

Thinking quickly, I reach for my cup and take a slow drink, attempting to conceal my emotion. On one hand, it's wonderful that the boys had the chance to connect with a peer. On the other...is it only going to make it worse? Make them less satisfied with just us? A deep, unsettling feeling diffuses through me when I remember that Rose hasn't told us anything about her home. Except for the fact that she is starving, we don't know what her situation is. Does she have both parents? Is it only her family? Are they dangerous?

"Kate?" Eric asks.

"Hmm?" I answer, disoriented.

"Your grateful?"

"Oh, right, sorry. I was just thinking. I'm grateful for food on our table, and enough to share with our neighbor," I say, smiling at Rose. "Would you like to share anything? It's okay if you don't, but I didn't want to skip you without asking."

She shakes her head.

"Well, I'm grateful for new opportunities. I'm grateful for change, and that I get to grow with the people I love most. Let's eat," Eric finishes, and the children dig in appreciatively.

Not wanting to taint breakfast, I wait to broach the subject of Rose's return trip until we are cleaning up.

"So, Rose, would it really be alright for us to come with you? See your home today?"

She looks at me with shadowed eyes.

"I think she only wants us to come," Bentley answers matter-of-factly.

"Oh. I guess I understand why that would be easier. But, I don't really feel comfortable sending you without us. Rose," I say, turning my attention back to her. "Can I ask why you're so against us coming?"

"Kate and I were thinking we could bring food with us—to help you get through the next couple of weeks," Eric contributes.

Her eyes dart between us. Hopeful? Terrified? I can't tell.

"I—don' want to git my fam'ly in trouble."

"Rose, we aren't going to cause trouble for your family. I'm going to be honest, though. If you aren't in a safe situation, I will step in. If you are being hurt—"

"It's nothin' like that," she says, "we take care of each other."

"Okay, then."

She nods resolutely. "You can come if y'bring the food," she says, turning on her heel and retreating to the boys' room.

"Well that was easier than I thought it was going to be," Eric says, chuckling.


After meticulously wrapping our care package in strips of cloth, I bundle it into the top of my pack, supported by the extra hiking supplies below it. All three of the children work to finish the compost with Eric before we head out. Based on Rose's description of the journey home, we should be able to make it there before sunset as long as we move quickly. It may be too much to ask that the boys don't dawdle—especially Bentley—but they seem to be especially motivated. I am beside myself that we have been living here for so long without having any inkling that there was another habitation within walking distance. We didn't specifically have any reason to go far from our home, nor did we think that finding people was a remote possibility, but still.

*Could there be more?* The thought stops me in my tracks. Should we consider exploring and mapping more of our surrounding area? I shudder. Even thinking about it makes me nervous. Since I am already anxious trusting the navigational estimates of a child, this might not be the best time to plan other adventures. We can cross that bridge if and when we come to it. Setting my pack down, I pull my coat on and trudge out into the garden to see if I can assist in any way.

"Perfect timing," Eric calls. "We just finished." He leans on his shovel—sweat on his brow despite the chill in the air—and smiles as the children begin heading in the direction of the storage shed, their tools in tow.

"Couldn't have planned it better," I laugh. Then more seriously, "I'd really like to get going so we aren't pushing it on the way back."

"Agreed. Let me just put this away and grab my supplies," he says, gathering a few pieces of errant plant material and returning them to the pile. Hearing the door slam behind me, I infer that the kids are inside gathering their things, as well. Turning, I follow them back into the house.

I'm interested to see how they do on this long of a hike. We've hiked to our fishing spot, which is basically equivalent to what this one-way distance should be, if Rose's estimates are correct. They'll be walking double the distance with the return trip. Rummaging in the gear bin, I throw a few straps into my bag just in case. If Bentley gets tired, I may be able to use these to carry him in a pinch. If Tal gets tired...he'll be out of luck.

"We're ready!" I hear from down the hallway. Walking toward the voice, I find Rose and both boys dressed for the journey, their packs slung over their shoulders. My heart warms at the sight of Rose in one of Tal's woolen hats. Though she had a jacket on when we found her, the temperature is low enough today that she wouldn't have been comfortable with only that.

"Looks like you are," I concede, smiling. "We're just waiting for—"

"Let's go!" Eric shouts, emerging from the closet, an exuberant expression on his face. I jump at the unexpectedness of his appearance and the kids think this is hysterical.

"Never mind, looks like we're not waiting on anything," I say, smacking Eric as I pass.

"What?" he asks, grinning broadly.

With everyone outside, we look to Rose.

"Lead the way," Eric says cheerily. Without a word, she immediately tromps off into the trees, causing us to put forth actual effort to keep her pace. Maybe we won't have to rush home after all.

. . .

Hours later, Rose stops abruptly in front of us. Standing stock-still, she doesn't turn to acknowledge us. Approaching her, I gently touch her shoulder.

"Is everything okay?" I ask softly.

She nods. "We're almos' there," she mutters matter-of-factly, snapping out of her trance and looking at the ground, her body still rigid.

Rubbing her arm, I say gently, "Thank you for letting us come."

Lifting her head in response to my touch, she seems to steel herself —her hands clenching into fists—and she marches onward resolutely. We follow and, a few moments later, emerge from the brush into a large clearing. On the opposite side, a modest shelter sits near the trees. Much like ours from the looks of it, but in obvious disrepair. My heart sinks. What are we going to do if we find something unsavory here?

Thankfully, there is no time to ruminate on this thought. As soon as we approach the shelter, children come pouring out of the front door. Though they are all young, the smallest of the bunch seems to be at least seven—based solely on his height. Eight of them? Ten? I can't get a proper count with them buzzing around us like this. Bentley and Tal's faces light up. Tal turns to me, questions written all over his face. I shrug, not having any more information or answers than him at this point.

Rose, after hugging the children, turns to us. "Wait here, I need to do somethin'," she commands, then swiftly turns on her heel and races toward the steps to the porch, disappearing through the front door. The children follow after her closely—as if tied to their queen bee—and we are left in stunned silence.

"What...just happened," Eric asks, and all three of us stare at him with wide eyes. Before we can attempt to discuss it, Rose returns. Behind her, a girl and two boys hesitantly poke their heads through the distressed front door frame. Rose stops, looking back, and motions for them to follow. The girl steps into the light first, which seems to give the boys courage. All three of them linger near the step, and Rose again has to coax them forward.

"This is m'sister and brothers. They aren't really m'sister and brothers, but that's what we say," Rose explains.

"So nice to meet you," I respond gently, hoping that my smile will inspire some trust. "How old are all of you?" I ask.

Rose answers for them. "Lila is ten, Root is fourteen, and Caleb is thirteen." Bentley and Tal give shy grins, their eyes still wide at the prospect of spending time with so many children. I sigh, immediately regretting our planned return trip and wishing we could give them more time to play.

"Can we meet your parents?" Eric asks. The eyes of all three children dart sideways to Rose who looks down at the grass, hands tethered behind her back.

"Rose..." I start, but her head snaps up at the sound of her name, causing me to hesitate. She turns toward the shelter and motions for us to follow her. Bent flashes me a worried look, so I take his hand and grip it securely as we walk. I carefully guide him around tree branches, old posts, and a few broken dishes that litter the yard surrounding the entrance. As we walk up the steps and through the open door, a protruding nail nearly catches my shirt. Eric and I exchange a glance.

It takes a moment for our eyes to adjust to the dim light inside. The windows are coated with a natural film, preventing the sunlight from penetrating the interior fully. My eyes circle the room, taking everything in. While it definitely isn't in great condition, the kitchen—much like ours, attached to the main open space —is remarkably tidy.

Rose pauses when she reaches a roughly hewn table in the center of the room.

"I—I din't want you to come because...this is our fam'ly. We take care of each other." She turns to face us, twisting her fingers around the hem of Tal's coat. "We need food. Bad. But now..." she pauses, her face contorting as she continues, "Please don' make us go," she pleads, her words beginning to tumble out of her. "Mom went an' I din't ever see her again, I don' want to leave—"

"Whoa," Eric interrupts, holding his hands up and walking toward her. She instinctively pulls her arms tightly around her torso as he approaches. "Rose, we aren't going to make you go anywhere. What are you talking about?" He gently strokes her hair as her shoulders continue to rapidly rise and fall. When she doesn't answer, he asks, "Where are your parents?"

"Gone," she answers, her voice barely audible. My heart stops.

"Where did they go?" Bentley asks, his voice obviously taking Eric by surprise.

She shrugs her shoulders.

"Are any adults here to take care of you?" Eric asks gently.

Rose shakes her head, her arms still clenched.

"How long?" I ask, almost not wanting to hear the answer.

"They've been gone since I can remember. I don' know—" her voice breaks as she begins to desperately sob. Despite her obvious desire to avoid contact, she leans into Eric and he pulls her into his chest. Tal and Bentley stand stock still, absorbing this information. *Since she can remember?* Could it possibly be true that these children somehow remained alive...on their own? How? And why? And what possible reason could there be for them to even be out here in the first place? Questions swirl in my thoughts, and the most disconcerting realization is that there may not be anyone to answer them.

## CHAPTER 7

"WE CAN'T JUST LEAVE them like this," Tal asserts, following us out into the fresh air. Through the door, we can hear the children gratefully digging into the food that we brought for them. I am already certain that we didn't bring enough.

"I know, Tal," Eric says, placing a heavy hand on his shoulder. "Just let us talk for a minute so we can figure this out."

Tal nods anxiously and moves to join Bentley, who is tossing sticks at a makeshift target.

"He's right," I sigh. "I can't leave here knowing that these children are fending for themselves. What have we gotten ourselves into?"

"I know, I feel the same way," Eric agrees. "But what are our potential options?"

"Bring them home with us?" I suggest. "That's the only thing I've come up with so far."

"I thought about that, but we don't have room—"

"We could build another shelter—"

"I thought of that too, but what about our supplies? It seems that we have plenty now, but that has to last us for...well, who knows how long. For the rest of Tal and Bentley's lives? If we divvy that up between..." he trails off, running his hands through his hair.

"I know, Eric. It won't last long, especially as all of these kids become adults. But I don't know what else to do. We can build another shelter, and we would have more hands to help, so we could grow more food and hopefully not need to dig into the rations as we get better at it."

"But if we have more harvest years like the last—"

"I don't think we will. This year everything seems to have gone well, right?"

"Kate...you're ignoring the fact that these kids..."

Again, his voice peters out, and I look at him questioningly, not following. What is he not saying?

Eric lowers his voice. "They're Tier 3, Kate. It's not like we would be bringing in children with...a similar mindset. And they haven't even had *any* role models, their conditioning—" He catches himself, turning from me, shoving his hands in his back pockets. When he doesn't continue, I move close and wrap my arms around his waist, holding my body to his back. His chest expands as he takes in a slow breath.

"I'm not trying to say—"

"I know," I confirm softly.

"It's just—"

"I know, Eric. It scares me, too. And I know you feel the pressure of having to provide for us already, let alone these other children. I have no idea what kind of issues these kids would be bringing with them, you're right about that, too. But I can't in good conscience—"

"I know, me neither," he agrees, turning toward me and pulling me to his chest.

"So what do we do?" I murmur, my breath warming his shirt, continuing to rapidly search my mind for possible solutions. I have no experience with Tier 3 in the first place, and these children have basically raised themselves. Who knows what extra trauma they have experienced in this situation? But...they did *raise themselves*. They survived and somehow took care of each other. I wouldn't have ever expected that to be possible.

"Eric—"

"Maybe we stay," Eric says, both of us speaking over each other.

"What?" I ask, wondering if I heard him correctly.

"We could stay for a day or two. Give us more time to think. I could help fix up the place a bit and help build up their food stores. It would also give us the opportunity to observe and have a better idea of...what we'd potentially be getting into."

"I think it's a great idea," I say, "I just don't know logistically...where *would* we stay exactly?"

"We can make a shelter if need be. I brought some extra supplies in my pack."

"You did?"

"Always prepared," he answers humbly, smiling.

Bentley and Tal catch my eye. They are huddled together near a large pine tree, their heads close together as if in serious conversation.

"Should we put them out of their misery?" Eric laughs, and I nod. "Boys, you can come over now," he shouts, motioning for them to join us. They nearly tumble over each other as they run in our direction. Eric squats to their level before speaking.

"What do you boys think about all of this?"

"How are they surviving?" Tal asks seriously. "They don't have any resources or help."

Bentley nods, his eyes pleading for answers.

"I honestly don't know," I answer, shaking my head. "Dad and I are absolutely as shocked as you are."

"We have to do something," Bentley adds quietly, and Eric places a hand on his shoulder.

"I know, bud. We came to the same conclusion. But doing something is going to require sacrifice on our part. Are you willing to do that?"

They both nod excitedly, their expressions eager.

"Alright, then," Eric says, resuming an upright position. "Tal, you and Bent need to scout out a good spot for a shelter." He barely finishes his sentence before both boys march purposefully to the edge of the clearing.

Eric grips my hand, and we move toward the building.

"Do we think this idea is going to go over well with Rose?"

Eric chuckles. "Doubtful? But here's hoping."

*CHAPTER 8*

INSIDE, the children are winding down—some licking their fingers, a few still picking at the salted meat in the center of the table. They turn our direction when we enter the room and it's like looking at a macabre painting. Not one of them moves.

"Thank you," Rose breaks the awkward pause softly, her eyes wide and innocent. When she speaks, the children seem to relax.

"Did everyone get enough?" I ask, wondering at the lack of leftovers. Their heads nod in unison.

"I'm glad," Eric says, moving toward the table. The children scatter—like ripples reacting to a thrown rock. He leans his hands on the table and lowers his head to meet Rose's eyes.

"Rose, you and your...family have done an incredible job looking after each other. We are more than impressed," he admits genuinely. A small smile plays at the corner of her lips as she listens, and she links her hands behind her back, her chest protruding proudly.

"While we have no doubt that you are capable of continuing on like this, we can also see that it hasn't been—nor will it become—easy," Eric continues. "Kate and I can't in good conscience leave you here alone," he finishes glancing around the table.

"What d'you mean?" Rose asks, alarm evident in her tone. "You can't call—"

"We aren't going to call anyone, Rose," Eric assures her, standing to his full height. "I know you're worried about losing your family, and I can't speak to what happened in the past. I only know that we promised we wouldn't cause trouble, and we plan on keeping our word. But, we also can't have you starving out here."

Rose stares at him, unmoving.

"Would it be okay if we stayed the night?" he continues. "We have supplies for our own shelter, you wouldn't need to worry about us. But if it's alright with you, we'd like to be here a little longer, at least. It would give us some time to help you find food and figure out what will be best moving forward."

"What's best is for you to leave us alone," Rose replies flatly. The older children tense instantaneously, but the younger ones lower their heads, almost in disappointment.

"Rose," I say moving next to Eric, "we don't want to infringe on anything that you've built here. We aren't going to tell you what to do or how to do it. But, we *are* adults. We have been educated, and we have experience. We simply want to do what's right. We can help," I suggest, pausing. Then more forcefully, "Now that we're here, I think we have a responsibility to help."

Rose's eyes flit between the young children's hopeful expressions, then motions for the older three to join her in a small huddle at the end of the table. They whisper to one another, the room silent except for their lowered voices. Eventually, their shoulders move apart and Rose turns to face us.

"Okay," she agrees. "But we don't have to do anything unless we want to."

Eric nods. "Sounds good to me. We'll be outside if you need us. In the morning, I can take you and anyone else who would like to come along on a scavenging run. Hopefully show you some more food options you may not have considered." Smiling, he turns and reaches for me, and we exit the shelter together.

Tal and Bentley wave to us immediately as we enter the yard, obviously eager to show us their camping spot. The sun hangs low in the evening sky, illuminating the meadow in soft, golden light. The chill of this morning still lingers, but the sun has taken some of the edge off. Clouds hang ominously on the horizon, and I am nervous about rain hitting again overnight, knowing how exposed we'll be. While I'm sure Eric has the supplies we need, I don't relish the idea of waking up wet and cold. Eric, seemingly in tune with my thoughts, squeezes my hand and pulls me along.

"We cleared the ground, Dad," Bentley announces proudly.

"I can see that," Eric answers with a chuckle. "You've done well."

Bentley beams, and Tal approaches to help Eric remove the cuben fiber shelter—another gift in the supplies from Nick—and retractable poles from his pack. Thankfully, this model is fully enclosed and any worries about weather slip from my mind. The boys quickly work together and a small, silver tent materializes within minutes.

"I know it won't be as comfortable as at home, but at least it will be cozy," Eric muses, tying the fly into place.

"Looks perfect," I say gratefully.

"Here, Bent, can you inflate these pillows and lay out our blankets?" Eric requests, handing him a small bag with neatly folded mylar sheets. He slowly climbs through the opening and begins to exhale rapidly into a slim, flat, rectangular package.


The air becomes frigid the instant the sun goes below the horizon, and we all scramble into our blankets, closing the shelter behind us. Within minutes, I am much more comfortable, and Eric reaches up to open a vent in the top of the tent. Not surprisingly, Tal and Bentley are asleep nearly instantaneously, but I have a harder time quieting my mind.

"What are you thinking about?" Eric asks, pulling me close.

It takes a moment for the words to coalesce. "I can't stop wondering if there are more of them out there," I sigh finally.

"Tier 3?"

I nod against his chest. "How could Berg, in good conscience, leave children alone out here to fend for themselves?"

Eric doesn't answer.

"You do think they knew, right? How could they not?"

"They knew," he agrees. "I have to believe that they did everything they could. If these families were actively fighting—"

"We wouldn't have done anything different."

Eric is silent.

"If we help them—"

"We are perpetuating a gene pool that has been deemed a threat to our survival as a species. Expressly deviating from our beliefs and even my life's work," Eric finishes.

That last sentence hits us both hard. "Exactly."

"And yet..."

"We can't not help them."

Eric brushes his fingers along my temple, tracing my face. "Sleep. We'll figure this out in the morning," he assures me. Trusting his words, I close my eyes and drift.

CHAPTER 9

WAKING, I roll to my back, my shoulder stiff from being pressed against the ground. Though the earth is soft and spongy here, it's not nearly as forgiving as our bed at home. Registering the silence around me, I survey the tent and find that I am the only current occupant. Checking the sensor, I am shocked to find that it's already eight in the morning. The boys probably left hours ago to find food and I must've slept right through their departure.

Pulling the sheet off, I sit upright and begin to dress in an extra layer of clothes. It's warm now, but as soon as I zip open the door...I know I'll be grateful for the added protection. Sure enough, the cool, damp morning air hits my face, shocking me into alertness as I step from the tent. A low mist hangs heavy in the yard, magnifying the incredible stillness. Breathing deeply, I jump —my adrenaline spiking—as a sparrow flits above my head and breaks the silence. Just the push I needed.

Walking determinedly, I climb the steps and knock on the door. There isn't any audible movement within the house, and I'm about to turn back when the latch clicks. Rose answers the door hesitantly.

"Is everyone still sleeping in there?" I ask, mostly joking, but honestly beginning to wonder. I don't know why I assumed they would keep the same schedule as my boys.

"No. Ev'ryone is off with Eric."

I nod, still separated from her by the screen. "You didn't want to go?"

Her eyes lower. "Someone needed to do the chores."

"Well that was very kind of you to stay back. Can I help?"

Her posture immediately stiffens.

"Not that I think you need any help," I hedge, "I am just...kind of bored," I admit, shrugging my shoulders.

She searches my expression. "Okay," she says finally, pushing the door on its hinges. Entering the house, I wipe my shoes on the threadbare rug, trying to remove excess moisture. Though it makes me uncomfortable, I can't quite bring myself to take them off here.

"Put me to work," I command, stretching my arms to the sides. "What can I do?"

"I'm used to doing all the reg'lar chores," she says slowly. "I don't really know what else—"

My head involuntarily cocks to one side. Is it just me, or is her speech improving? I shake it off.

"How about you just show me where your cleaning supplies are and I'll start somewhere," I offer gently.

Nodding, she starts toward the kitchen, and I follow. Under the sink, she shows me a pile of rags—mostly pieces of old clothing, from the looks of it—and a tall, glass jar.

"What's this?" I ask.

"Vinegar."

Ah. That explains the smell I noticed yesterday. "Is this what you use to clean?" I ask, and she nods. "Where do you get it?"

She picks up the jar and points to a shimmering, gelatinous disc floating on the surface of the pale liquid. "She makes it," Rose says simply.

I nod, taking the jar from her and standing up. "Do I need to pour some into another jar to use it? I don't want to hurt her."

"You won't hurt her. But I like to pour some into one of these—" she says, reaching for a glass bottle on one of the shelves, "—and then add water. Otherwise it's strong."

Her speech is definitely becoming more refined. Could it simply be from spending time with us and hearing our pronunciation? Handing me the bottle, along with a ladle and funnel, she spins on her heel and returns to her task of cleaning out the fire bed. Dumbfounded, I follow her instructions. Though I theoretically know how vinegar is made, I've never actually seen it first-hand. How do these children know how to do this? And where are they getting the alcohol to start a new batch?

I gently tip the jar and allow liquid to trickle into the bottle, careful to avoid hitting the mother. Rose says it won't cause a problem...but I'm not totally sure I believe her. When the bottle is a third of the way full, I replace the cloth covering the top of the jar, return it to its spot under the counter, and ladle water from a bucket into the bottle to dilute the solution.

Taking a few rags along, I move into the living area. Though the room is bare bones, it doesn't look like it's been wiped down in a while. Finding a few pieces of clothing hiding under the table, I search the rest of the room and throw the discovered sticks and leaves out into the yard. Using a rough broom I noticed in the kitchen, I sweep the floor and push the dirt out onto the porch. Placing a folded rag over the mouth of the bottle, I invert it, allowing the solution to soak the cloth. After scrubbing the table, I move to one corner of the room and begin washing the floor on hands and knees. I'm going to need more rags, I think, observing the black residue on the cloth.

My mind is abuzz with questions and possibilities. These kids know far more than we gave them credit for. As far as I can tell, they haven't had any resources set aside to make their lives easier. Everything they have, they have worked for and created. I'm not convinced that a Tier 1 individual in the same situation would see such success.

A small rustle behind me catches my attention. Rose is standing in the door frame.

"Am I doing it right?" I ask, lifting my hands from the floor and sitting upright on my knees. Her face lights up with a rare smile.

"Yes," she answers shyly.

"Can I help you with something else?"

She shakes her head. "I—" she pauses, looking at her toes. "I wondered if I could ask you some questions."

"Sure, ask away," I say, returning to my task.

She moves next to me and begins dusting the long shelf below the window that sits halfway up the wall.

"What is it like?"

"What is what like?" I ask, clarifying.

"The world. Out there. With the people. You came from Tier 1 right? I don' really know what that means, but I remember my Mom talking about it. She said that they—you—were better than us and we had no place there anymore. That's why we came here, because they were sure that Berg was going to..." she trails off and we both scrub in silence for a moment. "They were right," she finishes, her voice barely audible.

The timeline suddenly snaps into place in my brain. That's why they're here: Berg was going to kill them. I take a shaky breath.

"I'm so sorry, Rose. I can't imagine what your family has gone through. I'll try to explain it the best I can, but feel free to stop me if you need more details, okay?"

She nods.

"The Tier system was created initially because we truly didn't have resources after the Crisis. Do you know about that?"

She nods, but looks unsure.

"Our predecessors built a selfish and volatile society where people fought for what they wanted and gave no thought to others, nor did they think about the way their actions were affecting the environment around them. The earth became polluted and unsafe, and eventually most of the human race was wiped out by a really dangerous virus. Nobody was ready for it. They were weak, sick, and exhausted, making them all susceptible. Berg had to step forward to use the genetic information they had to save what was left of our kind. To utilize resources most efficiently, they created the Tier system."

"The Tier system was created to save us?" Rose asks skeptically, her eyebrows furrowed together.

*To save the best of us,* I think, but don't say it outloud.

"Yes, let me explain. There weren't enough resources for everyone and a decision had to be made in order to prevent *more* fighting and death. It was voted that people with the highest chance of success—of living and surviving—would receive what they needed. Any excess was then distributed to the next groups who were more likely to survive than others, and so on. As other measures were put in place and the population self-regulated over the years, those became officially Tier 1, Tier 2, and Tier 3."

"We're Tier 3," Rose states, matter-of-factly. Her face falls as she makes the realization. "So that means we weren't supposed to survive."

"Not necessarily, it just means that you didn't have the highest chance of survival. Those numbers don't guarantee success or failure. There are some members of Tier 1 and Tier 2 that don't live as long as predicted, just like I'm sure there are members of Tier 3 who live longer. It isn't a perfect system, but it's the only one we had."

"So how did we exist? So many years later?"

"Well, we've continued to progress and heal. That means that we have more resources now than we had then, and there is much more to go around in Tier 2 and Tier 3. Do you remember anything about your life before you came here? Did your parents have service assignments?"

Rose shakes her head. "I've only ever lived here. My Mom only ever lived here."

That's right, I think, trying to pull pieces of information from that conversation with Nick so long ago. *Nick,* I sigh heavily. The timeline is fuzzy. I have a vague memory, but nothing tangible enough to go off of.

"But they told stories," she adds, her voice lifting.

I lift my eyes from the swatch of floor in front of me, realizing that she has finished with the ledge and is staring at the dirty window. Those are next on my list.

"What kind of stories?" I ask, egging her on.

Her eyes seem to be exuding light as she speaks. "Stories of their life there. My grandparents served by growing food, building equipment, making supplies, jus' everything. They were so strong and knew how to do everything. At least that's what Dad said. That's where my Mom learned it." Her eyes darken suddenly. "I don' remember half of what she taught me," she admits, shame evident in her tone. "Lila, Root, and Caleb—they remember some things and all of the skills we know put together gives us a lot to work with. But I—" she stops, pulling out a well-worn chair from the table and slumping into it. Is she crying? Her shoulders are shaking and she places her face in her hands. Setting my supplies on the floor, I stand and go to her.

"Rose, what's wrong?" I ask, placing a hand gently on her shoulder, rubbing slowly, attempting to console her.

She doesn't answer right away, but eventually she lifts her head, sniffing. "I don' know how much longer we can do this," she whispers. "The wine is almost gone, we don' have any more salt, which means we can't preserve anything. Things are breaking left and right and I don' know how to fix 'em—" sobs begin to violently escape her lips. Years of undue responsibility coming to a painful head.

"It's okay, Rose, you don't have to be strong for me. Just let it out," I whisper, rubbing her back.

Eventually, her sobs turn to soft whimpers and her breathing begins to normalize.

"That's a lot of responsibility you've been carrying all these years," I comment, and she turns her face to mine. "Can I finish my story?" I ask.

She nods, wiping her nose on her sleeve.

"So, the Tier system was created," I review, pulling out a chair and sitting next to her, our knees almost touching. "The years went on, more resources became available, more people survived, and our population grew. Eric and I were both born in Tier 1, and we had Tal and Bentley there, too." My heart clenches as my tongue naturally wants to continue with the names Beth. And Leah. Taking a deep breath, I continue, "But now, things are changing again. We have been successful enough that there isn't as much need for the structure that currently exists. Berg argues that the Tier system is still absolutely necessary for building a society that won't fall into the same mistakes of our ancestors. But, Eric and I have already seen it begin to deteriorate into just that."

Rose looks at me quizzically. "What do you mean?"

"Well, our family is here because...because we weren't willing to do what Berg wanted," I finish, searching for the right words. "We have been kicked out, just like your family. And there are others, too. Not that have been kicked out—at least not that I know of—but others who are in agreement that things need to change. We've seen leaders unwilling to change their perspective..." I trail off, not sure whether to continue. "But who knows, maybe it is changing now. We've been removed for a couple of years now. Sometimes I get information from a friend in Tier 1 and it seems like things are moving in the right direction. Our job in Tier 1 is—was—to make things better, to improve society. Eric and I didn't succeed in that. Maybe someone else will and, someday, we can all go home," I say hopefully, my throat constricting.

"That's a lot of responsibility you have been carrying all these years," Rose quotes, her voice a perfect mirror of my own, and a laugh bursts out of me.

"But I'm an adult! That's different," I insist. Both collecting our thoughts, we sit in silence. Rose, still sniffing slightly, cleans her fingernails with a small piece of wood she found sticking out from the table's edge. I can't help but inspect my own as I watch her.

Noise outside in the yard catches our attention and we stand, both moving toward the door. Children seem to be pouring out of the woods, excitement and broad smiles on their dirty faces.

One little boy dashes to the door at top speed. "Rose! Eric foun' us new roots and berries. There are tons of 'em!" he announces, grabbing her hand and pulling her through the screen to the porch. I follow, waiting until the door slams before I push it open again. Rose is unwillingly being pushed along in the middle of a gaggle of children, and I stifle a laugh. Eric, along with Tal and Bentley, are moving toward them with a line of rabbits and birds strung between them, and the excitement in the clearing is palpable.

Stepping down to the grass, I walk to Eric and embrace him as he sets down his load.

"Tough morning, hey?" I tease.

"This makes me look good, but it was mostly the boys. The other kids were great, too, they just needed to know where to look. I think they had exhausted their favorite spots," he muses, turning his head to observe the raucous behavior.

Returning his gaze to mine, he kisses me.

"I had a good conversation with Rose," I say.

"Really? She said more than two words?"

"She did," I nod, looping my fingers in my pockets. "From what I gathered, I think she may be open to help. These older kids have been carrying a heavy burden."

Eric nods. "I can only imagine. What are you thinking?"

"What are *you* thinking?" I shoot back at him, not wanting to be the one who suggests it this time.

He sighs. "I think we need to bring them home with us," he admits.

I nod in agreement, throwing my arms around his shoulders. "I know it will eat through our resources, but I don't see another way. We can...figure something else out. I can send a message to Nick when we get back and see what our options are. Speaking of which, I still haven't heard from him," I digress. "I also want to find a way to see if there are any other groups like this stuck out here. He's going to get sick of me bugging him."

"Seriously, Kate? We can't handle saving any other groups," Eric says incredulously, placing his hands on my hips.

"I know! I just mean, we could work with Nick to see if there are any. Then decide what to do."

"I know what that means," he mutters.

I smack his arm and he laughs. The children fight for our attention now, wanting to use the morning's spoils to make lunch.

"Use it," Eric calls, "but don't waste. We can save the rest."

Rose flashes me a worried look, and I assure her with a wave.

"We need to meet with the older children," I say to Eric when she turns.

"After lunch," Eric promises, then gives my hand a squeeze and walks—with a definite skip in his step—to join Tal and Bent in the group.

CHAPTER 10

FROM THE WAY the sun hangs in the sky, it looks to be about noon when we finally sit down with Lila, Root, Caleb, and Rose. The younger children are all happily playing ball with Tal and Bentley. Tal was absolutely floored that they didn't know the rules of freeze tag, and Bent jumped at the opportunity to teach them. Watching his excitement struck home the intense sadness in my heart over the lack of socialization for the boys in our current environment. While the butterflies in my stomach are alive and well over potentially taking responsibility for these children, I can already see the positives of having a community of sorts.

Rose sits on the floor between Lila and Root. Her fingers twist and untwist as she watches us nervously.

"How are you all feeling about the next few months to a year? Living how you're living, I mean," Eric asks gently.

Almost immediately, their eyes drop to the ground, but Root recovers quickly.

"We are doin' good—" he starts with a feigned strength, but Rose cuts him off.

"Root, I told her. It's okay. She knows we need help and...I think we should listen t'what they have to say."

Though his face turns slightly pink, Root relaxes slightly and nods.

Hesitantly, I begin. "I can't properly express how amazed we are by your success here. We truly have no idea how you have been able to keep everyone alive on your own, and your knowledge and expertise is impressive." I pause, allowing my words to hopefully sink in. "Rose let me know that you have all been really nervous about the future, especially since you are running out of the few supplies you were given. I know change is never easy, but we would love to offer help. If you'll take it."

Lila's eyes flash slightly, but she reigns in her emotions before speaking. "What help are you talkin' bout?"

"Kate and I would like...to invite you to live with us," Eric stammers.

All four of them stiffen, but Rose reaches out, placing a hand on Caleb's arm before he can speak. She pulls them into their characteristic huddle while Eric and I watch and wait. This one seems to take much longer than the last few we have witnessed. I guess it's understandable, considering that we have asked them to completely upend their lives. Eventually, they stand and turn to face us.

"We would have to leave our home," Root says matter-of-factly.

"Yes," Eric answers.

"Do you have enough for us?" Lila asks.

"Well, that depends on what we're talking about. Do we have enough beds? Not yet, but we can easily remedy that. Especially if we all work together. Do we have enough resources? Yes, for now. We will have to make a plan to solidify our supplies for future years," Eric answers. Before we came into this meeting, we both agreed that it would be best to be completely up front with these four. They have earned the right to be treated as equals.

Lila nods, seemingly satisfied with Eric's response.

"It's...hard to depend on someone. To change a way of doin' things that has always worked for something...that we don' understand," Rose explains.

I nod. "It's hard for all of us, Rose. You're not alone in that. And we can't promise that it's going to be easy or perfect. The only thing we can promise is that we will always work with you to solve whatever problems come our way. We'll be in this together," I say.

Looking at each other, the children seem to reach a silent agreement. Rose turns to us and her smile, though hesitant, completely transforms her face.

"Okay. Let's go," she agrees simply.

"Alright then," Eric says, wrapping an arm around my waist. Nobody moves.

"What d'we do now?" Lila asks, and I can't help but burst into nervous laughter. Somehow we're supposed to have these answers, but the ridiculousness of what we're doing is so overwhelming that I can't think past the next second.

"We'll head home with our boys now," Eric says. "Give you time to pack up the things you need. Then, in a couple of days, we'll come back and help you all make it over to our land. You'll have to camp out on the floor initially, until we can build an extension to the shelter, but that shouldn't take too long."

They nod, still unmoving.

"Let's go tell the others," I suggest, and everyone seems grateful for a task to push us away from this uncomfortable juncture. The children stumble over themselves as they leave the room. At least I now know it's not just Tal and Bent that struggle to do things in an orderly fashion.

Eric moves to follow, but I pull him back into an embrace. Wrapping my arms tightly under his arms and across his strong back, I press myself into his chest.

"This is right," I say, my voice a whisper.

"It is," he answers, moving his fingers through my hair.

"And we can pull it off?" I ask, laughing nervously.

"We can," he assures me, and gently tips my face toward his. As he kisses me, warmth spreads through my limbs and it centers me. *We can do this*, I think. We have to do this.

## CHAPTER 11

BACK HOME, the boys fall asleep immediately after snuggling into their soft blankets—a far cry from the sheets we used the night before. My hips ache for a soft bed. Eric and I put away only the items that absolutely need to be dealt with and leave the rest for tomorrow. We're too exhausted to be thorough.

As we stumble into bed, I realize that I haven't sent a message to Nick yet. I am still unsettled about the fact that I didn't ever receive a reply from him. Quickly pulling out my sensor, I type a quick note:

*You're never going to believe this. We found a group of Tier 3 children who have survived on their own. On their own, Nick! For years! They are in a fairly desperate situation at this point, so we are working on it. How is everything progressing there? Any news? How are the girls? Finding these kids has shaken me a little bit. What else is Berg hiding?? Do they know that not all Tier 3 popula-*

*tions were eradicated? Are there more? Eric and I (well, I guess more "I" than Eric) feel compelled to find out the answer to that last question. Any maps of the area (specifically where old Tier 3 settlements were) that you can send would be helpful. Thanks, as always.*

--Kate

Turning it off, I slide it across the floor—not even bothering to charge it—and give in to sleep.

Morning comes much too quickly, and my eyelids are still heavy with sleep when I know it's time to get going. Without checking, I know Eric is already up. The emptiness of the bed beside me seems to penetrate the air, and a feeling of panic surges, taking advantage of this lonely moment. *What have we done?* How can we possibly care for so many children with the resources we have? Forcing myself to take a deep breath, I close my eyes and relax my head on the pillow. It takes a good minute or two to compose myself, but eventually, I am able to leave the safe-haven of the sheets and begin my morning routine. Any fears are pushed away for the time being, and I trust that the intensity of them will pass.

Walking into the kitchen, I find a full plate of sweet potato hash on the table. Three other place settings are in the sink already. From my vantage point, I can barely make out the boys lugging a wide, wooden beam toward the house—with Eric's help, of course. I can only assume they are already deep in preparations for the addition that will be needed on the shelter. For once, I am grateful that Eric didn't ask for my opinion. I don't have the brain capacity to engineer something of this magnitude right now. Nor is it my forte.

As I enjoy my breakfast, I think of Rose. My perspective on these perfectly salted potatoes has forever changed after my chat with her the other day. Was it only yesterday? Despite my ability to remain positive in our current situation, there has always been a part of me that took pride in our level of sacrifice. Each time we have gone without something, or worked to create something that would have been handed to us in Tier 1, I have revelled in our resourcefulness. Our ability to do without. And here these children are...Well, our level of sacrifice seems slightly pitiful.

Taking my last bite, a thought occurs to me, and I quickly exit the room, still chewing. Scanning the floor, I find the sensor that I hastily tossed out of the way last night and power it on. No new messages. I wait for a moment, giving it time in case it hasn't fully connected to the network yet. Still nothing. With a message like this, how could he not at least send an acknowledgement? It's kind of a huge revelation. Maybe he's out of town? My eyebrows furrow as I place the sensor around my wrist.

"Hey," Eric calls, his shirt drenched in sweat.

"Hey," I answer with a wave. "What are you guys up to?" The sun is shining brightly today, an unexpected treat, considering the past week.

"I thought we'd get a start on things. At least get the basics in place. Check this out," he says excitedly, motioning for me to follow. "If we put a door here, we can build a small hallway that will lead to two bunk rooms—one for the girls, and one for the boys —about this size. That way we can utilize this exterior wall, and the piping for heat runs right here, so that should be easy to tap into on both sides."

"I love it. Simple and effective," I comment.

"The best part is we can put in *triple* bunk beds," Bentley adds.

"I'm not completely sure on that, Bent," Eric chuckles. "But I think it would be fun if it works."

"Is there anything I can help with?" I ask, "Otherwise I can go do some food rotation so that we can make a plan for rations."

"Do that," Eric nods. "In a minute I might need you to help me lift this piece, but I have to notch it first. I'll come get you when it's time."

"Sounds great," I say, pecking him on the lips.

Besides the few moments when Eric needs my assistance, I spend the rest of the day calculating and planning. I'm impressed with our ingenuity, yet again, as I see the physical numbers in front of me. We have used less than half of the expected resources during our time here. Granted, I think Nick was generous in his estimations initially, but we have also put tremendous effort into making things last. I am grateful for both of these things now that our lives are going to dramatically change.

Checking my wrist for the thousandth time today, I see it is still blank. Not able to hold back any longer, I type another message.

. . .

*Nick? Hey, just making sure that last message came through. If you haven't seen anything, let me know and I'll re-send. It's not like you to take so long to respond with something like this. Sorry if you're busy and I'm bugging you! Talk soon.*

*--Kate*

Leaving the resource shelter, I begin to trudge back to the house, lost in thought. Halfway there, my step becomes lighter as I remember my purpose: to share with Eric the resource numbers I've tallied. Knowing how much we have available has lifted a weight from my shoulders and I hope it will do the same for him.

## CHAPTER 12

MY SENSOR DINGS and my eyes fly open. Eric and the boys left yesterday to bring the children home, but they didn't return by nightfall. We assumed there would be some loose ends to tie up, but I am hopeful they will return today. I never sleep well when Eric's gone.

Rubbing my eyes, and with my heart pumping, I bring the sensor display into view. It nearly blinds me in the darkness. A single line of text appears.

>*Who is this?*

Who is this? Terror grips me. Could someone have gained access to this line? Hacked into our communication? Nick assured me it was completely secret and secure, but who knows how much technology has changed in the last two years. Is Nick messing with me?

I highly doubt he would let a practical joke like this last more than a minute and I don't see anything else coming through. My initial response is to answer, but if it's someone from Berg...I don't want to cause Nick any trouble.

My mind flicks back to my message, horrified at the thought of anyone else seeing it. We've become so cavalier, not coding anything or being the least cryptic in our speech. Anyone who has read that message will know that something isn't right. Why would someone in Tier 1 be talking about finding Tier 3 children? I start to panic. Discarding the thought to play it safe—at this point, that would only breed more suspicion—I go with honesty. And cross my fingers that it's either Nick playing a sick joke...or a friend.

*This is Kate. Who's this?*

My hands become clammy as I wait.

Ding.

*>Kate? Kate who? This is Jessica.*

Jessica. That name sounds familiar, but my brain is having trouble placing it. *Jessica.* Where do I know it from? Tamara...and Jessica! She's the woman from the council that is helping Nick. Emotions swell within my chest. At least I know she has similar priorities. But why would she have access to his messages? And if it was serious enough for her to be living with him, why didn't he say anything about it? I almost spit those words out in my head. I freeze, horrified at my reaction. Am I jealous!? Did I somehow think that Nick would be single forever—pining for me—while I live out my life with my family? Bile rises in my throat as I recognize the truth in this thought. No. I refuse to allow myself to react negatively if something has gone right for Nick.

*But what about the girls. Is this their new mom?* The thought nearly bowls me over with its intensity. *No.* I will not jump to conclusions. And they would do well to have a female figure in their lives. I trust Nick, I remind myself. Having a pair would explain all of this. If Nick was out of town or something and she was somehow alerted to this message...I'm not sure why a secure message would be visible, but mistakes happen all the time. He could have forgotten to log out?

*Hi Jessica, I'm an old friend. Where is Nick? He is helping me with a project.*

Ding.

*>You haven't heard?*

Heard what? Immediately my mind jumps to Beth and Leah. What if something happened to one of them? Is that why Nick isn't home? I am lightheaded and the space between us is suddenly intolerable. I ache to be back.

*I haven't heard anything. What is going on?*

Ding.

*>I don't think this is something we should discuss over message. Can you call? Or stop by?*

I wish.

*That's not an option, unfortunately. Thank you for the thought. Please just fill me in.*

Ding.

*>Nick's dead, Kate.*

My heart stops. *Dead?* That's not possible. There has to be something going on. Maybe this is Berg—intercepting our communication and punishing me for my insolence. Is this even really

Jessica? It's not real, I'm sure of it. Steeling myself, I begin to type.

*If this is some joke or an attempt to hurt me, it won't work. I realize that I wasn't allowed to have contact with anyone and I will leave Nick alone. Please don't drag him into this.*

The sensor is dark for a long time. I am frozen on the edge of my bed, sweat drenching my shirt, my breathing shallow.

Ding.

*>Are you the Kate that Nick was talking about in his presentation years ago? Were you paired with Nick? Are Beth and Leah your daughters? Have you been communicating with Nick this entire time? You're alive? Are you doing okay? You found Tier 3 populations there? How is that possible?*

My brain is overwhelmed with the questions. This doesn't sound like Berg, which means...

*WHO IS THIS? AND WHERE IS NICK?*

. . .

Ding. This time almost immediately.

>*This is Jessica. I was there at his presentation, when you were still paired. When his research was just beginning to make waves. His information really touched me and, after a deal was reached with Berg, I have been working with him ever since. I am at the house for the time being. To take care of everything until we can figure out what to do. Nick is gone, Kate. I am so so sorry to have to be the one to tell you. He died four days ago in a car accident. The computer malfunctioned.*

No, no, no, no, no, this can't be true. This can't be true. I involuntarily repeat this in my head over and over again. Like a loop that can't be broken. The sensor clatters to the floor and I follow it, dropping to my knees on the woven rug that covers the rough concrete. Collapsing in on myself, I hyperventilate, squeezing my arms tightly around each other. Hoping that I can somehow press hard enough that the hurt will disappear. Nick can't be gone. He is making so much progress and he is such a *good man*. A leader that we need in Tier 1, someone who truly wanted to make a difference and who was forcing needed change—

I freeze. Time seems to stand still as a thought crystallizes in my mind. Cars don't malfunction. I mean, they do, but it's extremely rare. What are the chances that Nick, of all people, would experience that. How convenient that *Nick*—a revolutionary in his own right—would suddenly have an accident. Wiping my nose and tears on the backs of my hands, I search on my knees for the sensor. Finding it, I turn it over, barely able to stabilize it with shaking fingers.

>*Kate? Are you alright? Are you there?*

I dry my hands on my shirt.

*I'm here. I'm not alright, but I'm here. Jessica, I'm choosing to trust you. Because Nick must have trusted you. I don't think this was an accident. The chances of a car malfunction in Tier 1 are extremely slim. Nick was pushing boundaries. This doesn't seem right.*

I spent so much of my life fighting against the idea that I had a choice. That there could be alternate paths moving away from any situation. But in this moment, I use the word "choosing" purposefully. I want to take ownership.

There is a long pause, and I almost jump when the sensor finally dings.

>*I know it wasn't an accident.*

How? How does she know?

.   .   .

Ding.

>*I am choosing to trust you, too, Kate. Truth be told...I am terrified to talk to anyone in Tier 1 at this point. I am going to send you some of Nick's files. Will you please read over them? Some Committee members will be here soon and I need to have things in order. Do you have a time tomorrow night that we could discuss?*

Committee members? My heart is pounding.

*Sure, I'll read them. And anytime is fine. I'll keep my sensor close, just send a message when you can.*

Ding.

>*Beth and Leah are safe.*

Tears begin streaming down my face. This time, I don't even attempt to pull it together before responding.

*Thank you.*

. . .

Waiting just in case another message comes, I sit stock still, staring at the display. When nothing appears, my shoulders finally collapse and my hands drop to the floor. Leaning my head against the side of the bed, I close my eyes, allowing all of my emotions to wash over me. Nick. *Nick,* I scream internally, my mind and body in shock. Sadness, guilt, regret, anxiety, and horror take turns terrorizing my heart. The pain is too intense.

"Eric, I need you!" I shriek into the darkness, my voice organic and raw, even to my own ears. Too overwhelmed to do anything else, I curl up on the rug—pulling my legs to my chest—and sob.

## CHAPTER 13

ERIC'S FACE begins to take form through my blinking eyes. Why is he above me? My shoulder aches and the pain tethers me to the information I received...days ago? Hours ago? How long have I been lying here? Tears spring to my eyes as I frantically scramble to my feet. Interpreting my distress, Eric grips my arms and helps me up, pulling me to him.

"Kate, what in the—" he is saying when my body slams into his, knocking the breath out of his lungs. I am so glad he is here. I needed him so badly before, and his presence now brings comfort to my aching heart.

He strokes my hair, silent, waiting for me to speak. When my breathing returns to normal and the weight on my chest momentarily lifts with the physical release that accompanies tears, I pull my face away from his shoulder and meet his eyes.

"It's Nick," I begin, thinking that I can finish the thought, but my voice catches in my throat and I can't speak.

"Kate, what about Nick?" Eric asks soberly, concern evident in his expression.

"He—he's gone," I splutter before sobbing afresh. "It—it was B-Berg," I stammer through stilted breaths.

"What do you mean? *Berg killed Nick?*"

I nod, but then regret the accusation. "I don't actually know anything, Jessica and I—"

"Who's Jessica?" he asks.

"She's been working with Nick, she was the one who gave me this information," I say in a rush. "We both think it wasn't an accident and—"

My mind suddenly jumps to our conversation. I let go of Eric abruptly and grip my wrist, checking for the sensor. It's there. Pulling up the display, I find a link to a folder.

"She sent me his files," I sniff. "I need to read them. She says there is information there that we need to discuss. That she can't talk to anyone, but the girls are safe," I recite quickly, my dialogue completely disjointed. I'm not sure if he's even able to follow this.

"Take as much time as you need," Eric says softly. "I left the kids in the yard. I didn't know if you had plans for meals, but we'll figure something out."

The kids. How had I forgotten about them?

"I can—"

"No, just get in bed and read. I'll take care of it," Eric states and his eyes assure me he is serious. I nod and crawl under the covers, propping myself up with his pillow behind mine.

"Are you sure?" I ask weakly.

"Positive. We can talk tonight after you know more."

"Tell the kids I'm sorry."

"There's nothing to be sorry about. They are so excited to see everything here that they won't even notice," he assures me as he moves toward the door. With his back to me, he pauses in the doorway.

"I'm so sorry, Kate," he whispers, then closes the door behind him.


The file takes a minute to open, which gives me time to collect myself. It seems that as soon as I am able to calm down, another thought or memory sends me reeling again. The first time a message from him came through on this sensor, it gave me much-needed hope. Even though I haven't seen Nick in years, just knowing that he existed centered me. Made me sure that things were going to be okay, that the Tier system was going to transform into something better. I was so sure that Nick could make that happen. Now, who is going to continue his work? Who has enough leverage with the Committee to exert that kind of pressure? And who will want to take that on when they see where it got Nick?

Sighing, I tap on the folder and begin scrolling from the beginning.

. . .

### *Entry #22*

*It's done. I dropped them off this morning and it was quite literally the hardest thing I've ever had to do in my life. Upon arriving home, I let Beth and Leah take their nap with me in my bed and I was able to fall asleep for a few minutes at least. The grief I feel is actually a pleasant distraction from the constant fear of fallout from Berg. I don't have a guarantee that this is all going to work out in my favor. I promised Kate that I would care for Beth and Leah, but...what if I'm not around?*

I had no idea he was worried about repercussions even then. I was worried, but he seemed so sure of himself. And then when nothing happened, I just assumed everything had worked itself out. From his messages, it seemed like compromises were continuing to happen on both sides, plus, the terms he had initially set out were being met.

The next several entries contain technical information on new subjects and trials. While I'm sure it's interesting, my brain can't even process basic charts right now. I continue to scroll until I see something more personal.

### *Entry #47*

*My sensor dinged first thing this morning, and I thought I was dreaming. The first piece of information has been released to Tier 1. While I think Berg could have been more liberal in what they selected to be disclosed, at least it's something. Carole insists that this has to be done gradually, and who am I to argue? As long as it gets done, I am satisfied. Their announcement included resource numbers from a few years ago and the real Tier 3 numbers from about halfway through the decline. Though they aren't recent, Tier 1 individuals don't know that. It's a start. This will get conversations going and hopefully prepare people for the information yet to come, and the more intense conversations we will need to have soon. Hopefully very soon.*

Moving through the next entries, I fully expect to see an update, but there's nothing. Just more comments on methods in trials, interesting patients, and such. Jessica's name is mentioned more than a few times. I cling to each, allowing them to reaffirm my belief that she is a friend.

### Entry #83

*It's been three months and no new information has been sent out. I'm figuratively pulling my hair out here. I understand that new numbers can't be sent out yet, but we could definitely begin discussing reversal patients. The Director has assured me that we will be holding a briefing with patients in the next week or so, but I'm not holding my breath.*

Nick didn't tell me any of this. He always gave me the impression that things were moving forward in exactly the ways he had initially lined out. Why didn't I think to ask for details? Why did I assume that Berg was going to do things *our* way? I read on.

### *Entry #91*

*Tamara and I got our first results back. Our rubric focused on skills and attitudes that are most likely to affect future progress (and hopefully appease the concerns of the Committee). These include: resiliency, flexibility, creative thinking, and problem solving. In each group, participants were informed that they would be conditioning in diverse company (mixed Tier 1, Tier 2, and reversal patients). In only one group was this actually true. Compared to the control groups, there was a slight bias effect seen in the non-diverse groups, but in the singular diverse trial group, the results were through the roof. Beyond statistically significant. They consistently out-scored the other groups in all areas, and here's the best part: the results were significant regardless of whether a Tier 1 or Tier 2 individual was responding. Can you believe that? I can't wait to share the results and begin our next set. Come to think of it...maybe I will follow Carole's lead and introduce this information slowly. Give the Committees time to adjust to a new mode of thought.*

Of course. These were the trials he was working on. Technically, I knew he was studying multi-Tier relationships, but I didn't quite understand what information he was looking for. Those results are mind-blowing, considering everything we've been taught in Tier 1. If having mixed company is able to improve us in those ways, what else have we been missing out on by being segregated? My mind buzzes with possibility, but—as exciting as it is—I am too curious about the rest of the entries to stop and consider the possibilities.

## Entry #102

*The Director called today. Our first briefing will be Friday, and I am oddly nervous. Though it wasn't me who ordered the treatment, I was the one who physically carried out the procedures. Are patients going to lump me in with the Committee on this one? Technically...I am still on it, though I haven't gone to a meeting in weeks. Seems pretty pointless when they won't discuss real issues when I am there. Maybe someday I won't be considered a threat?*

They made Nick do the briefing? Not surprising that they would refuse to publicly take responsibility. Yes, Nick performed the reversal therapy procedures, but he had nothing to do with withholding information from patients. He had nothing to do with sending patients for treatment without disclosing procedural information. I am seething as I read on.

## Entry #109

*I think we've officially hit everyone in our Territory. Every patient I treated knows. Some opted not to discuss, but at least they now understand what to look for in potential symptoms (since not all of them were completed using my new procedure). Many of them have asked to be re-treated to avoid this, but I can't take that risk yet. I hate to make people suffer needlessly, but I can't give away any information until this process is complete. Knowing Berg, they would somehow find a way to record everything and refuse to meet the remaining terms of our deal. Patients will just have to wait. Now that I have a vested interest in getting patients on the list for treatment, I anticipate Carole stretching it out just to make me uncomfortable. I hope—for their sake—that I'm wrong.*

More scrolling. More trials. More run-ins with Berg. Then my throat catches.

### *Entry #126*

*I witnessed a conversation at the girls' conditioning today. People are discussing the most recent release and it is giving me hope. I'm not sure if everyone feels the same as these two women, but from what I overheard, they were very much in line with my own thinking. The real doozies will hit within the next few months: the extent of our excess resources, and the potential side effects of reversal therapy. Once that happens...I won't have any excuse anymore. I'll have to present my procedure and hope our society has changed enough to protect it. Tamara will be with me this time, and that is a comfort. We will present our current research at the same time. They will have to acknowledge that it's time to consider integration. The data are clear, and we can't ignore it any longer.*

CHAPTER 14

THE WORDS of Nick's last entry haunt me throughout the evening tasks. Eventually, earlier in the day, I had to get out of bed to keep from going completely crazy. Though I am physically here witnessing the children's excited faces as they all bed down in the hall outside of Tal and Bentley's room—spilling into the now-cramped living space—I am numb. None of it touches me. Time seems to float around me in a fog. Almost as if I am watching my own life from far, far away.

*I'll have to present my procedure...they will have to acknowledge that it's time to consider integration...* Is this why he died? Did he share his reversal procedure and then they didn't need him anymore? The thought that Berg was plotting against him—just waiting for their information—makes me sick. This is literally what the Tier system was set up to avoid: seeking for personal gain, power, and control. And without Nick—without someone who is willing to stand up to them—how will it ever change? Will we have to go to the extreme measures of our predecessors? War? Revolution? I shudder at the thought. That can't be the only way.

"Mom?"

"Huh?" I say, finally hearing a small voice cutting through the thick wall of my thoughts. Somehow, I find myself standing in the kitchen. My disconnected arms continue to wash dishes as I slowly turn to face Bentley.

"I've been calling you and you didn't answer," he says sheepishly.

"I'm sorry, I've got a lot on my mind and...I'm not at my best right now."

"I know, Dad told us. About Nick."

"He did?" I ask, the shock of it coming out of his mouth hitting me full force.

Bentley nods, and tears spring to his eyes. He looks at the floor to disguise his sadness, but I quickly dry my hands and drop to his eye level.

"Bentley, I am so sorry," I say, pulling him to my chest. His arms wrap around my shoulders and we hold each other. Somehow, this contact loosens something within me and a small semblance of feeling seeps in. It feels good, and so necessary.

"Mom, why did it happen?" he asks, his voice muffled against my shoulder.

Releasing my grip, I answer, "I don't know. But I do have some suspicions."

"You think Berg had something to do with it," he says, his voice picking up tempo. "I do, too, but I didn't want to be the first to suggest it."

A laugh escapes my lips, despite my best efforts to hold it in. "I'm sorry, this is the worst time for laughter, but you just sound so...grown up."

"In case you haven't noticed, I am pretty much grown up," he says, puffing out his chest ever so slightly.

"You're right, what was I thinking," I say, grinning through my tears.

"So what are we going to do?" Bentley asks.

I sigh. "I don't know yet. I'm going to talk to Jessica in a bit—she's a friend of Nick's, someone who has been helping with his research and ideas. Maybe we can come up with something..." I trail off, already trying to process potential plans of action.

"Okay," Bentley says, pulling me back to the present. "Well, let me know tomorrow. I want to help." He smiles, then turns on his heel and begins marching to his room. "Oh, Mom!" he exclaims, turning back toward me. "Look at this," he says, running to my side and pulling out the imaging display. A brilliantly vibrant bluebell flashes into view and my breath catches.

"Wow, where did you see that?" I ask in awe.

"They were blooming along a log. Since you weren't there, I thought I'd capture it for you. I didn't want you to miss it."

I stare at the delicate petals, perfectly preserved on the display. "Thank you," I whisper, pulling him close.

Bentley grins and scampers off to his room.

I am left wondering at this interaction—this perfect embodiment of the outward expression of grief. One moment I am frozen inside, the next I am alive, then I am hurting, then laughing. Everything moves too quickly, it's too out of control. But trying to control it only deadens the good along with the bad. I have to let go. To feel it all. Turning back to the dishes, a resolve to never lose myself in this deepens. I am here, I think. *I am here.*

Ding.

I scramble for my sensor, half asleep. Eric breathes peacefully next to me; I try not to wake him.

*>Hey Kate, it's Jessica. Are you up?*

My heart pounds from the shock of being woken up. Taking a deep breath, I respond.

*I'm here.*

· · ·

>Sorry I couldn't respond earlier. There's a lot going on here, as I'm sure you can imagine.

I get it, no worries. Thanks for getting back to me.

>Did you have a chance to look over the files?

I did. I have so many questions.

>Shoot. I'll try and answer as many as I can.

I furiously begin typing. Not the easiest task when I don't have a full display, but I do my best.

Did Nick end up revealing his reversal procedure? If so, that means all of his terms were met. What is happening in Tier 1? How did people take the news?

>He did. The terms were met, albeit slowly, and he presented his full procedure to the region two weeks ago. People in Tier 1 are...concerned. Definitely concerned, but—excluding the patients who were treated against their will—regular members still have so much blind trust in Berg that they aren't 'concerned' enough, in my

*opinion. I think Nick expected that once the resource numbers were out and people knew the truth about Tier 3, everyone would be driven to action, to change. Berg continues to send out 'updates' that are really just words smoothing over their decisions regarding these resource numbers. Showing how rational and compassionate they have been, whilst conveniently leaving out other important details. Nick was extremely frustrated and was brainstorming how to present his newest research to the Committee in a way that would finally be heard and considered. But I think he was beginning to lose hope.*

*What do you think Berg is going to do at this point? Just keep things the same? What about the patients—you mentioned them as feeling differently than the group. Is there potential for putting pressure on Berg through them?*

*>Berg is beginning to suggest the possibility of re-splitting the Tiers. Tier 1 individuals are in more of a tizzy about that information than anything else. It's a distraction. But it's working. People are trying to be their best to potentially qualify for the top Tier again, meanwhile Berg is refusing to acknowledge the body of research that is growing for an integrated system. It's not just us fighting to be heard, Kate. As for the patients, yes, they are understandably outraged. But it's just difficult to ask people to fight against the only thing they've ever known. They aren't willing to take the risk when it comes down to it. Hardly any of them went public with their stories.*

. . .

*Wow. I can see why Nick was frustrated. Jessica, I'm going to be honest. I am dying just sitting here and doing nothing. But I can't, for the life of me, think of anything I can do. I'm sitting here—my shelter filled to the brim with Tier 3 children—with no way to help anyone. Not these kids, not my own family, not the community that I love. I know we're technically not a part of Tier 1 anymore...but in my heart, it's my home. I can't sit here and watch it fail.*

The silence stretches long enough that I wonder if she's fallen asleep. My eyelids begin to droop as I sit stiffly, the sensor held tightly in my palm.

Ding. The sound sends a shot of adrenaline through my limbs.

*>Let me think on this. I'll be in touch.*

Setting the sensor down more gently this time, I collapse into bed. Despite my exhaustion, it takes a few moments for my body to settle after being startled. Slowly, my thoughts begin to drift.

## CHAPTER 15

I DREAM OF HIM. All night long, I dream of him. His broad smile on replay—a constant loop, as if my mind is trying to make sure it doesn't let this image slip away. Tossing and turning, I try to get comfortable, but by the time the early morning hits, I'm frustrated enough that I throw myself out of bed. I may as well get started on the morning chores and try to take a nap later, rather than continue to fight with myself. Quickly pulling socks on to protect my feet from the chilly floor, I pull my hair up, throw on a sweater, and grab the flint and steel to get a fire going.

Based purely on the sunshine we had the other day, I'm guessing it will be cloudy again. Saving the solar energy for heating, rather than using it to cook breakfast, seems like a more prudent choice. Checking my sensor, I am dismayed to see that it's only 4:45. I don't want to start gathering ingredients and wake anyone prematurely—especially since there are at least four children curled up in blankets near the table. Instead, I move to the pantry and begin preparing a menu plan for the week, rotating items as needed.

After forty-five minutes or so—probably catalyzed by thinking about delicious meals—my stomach can't take it anymore, and I have to eat something. Pouring water into a clay cup and sprinkling some cayenne pepper in, I take a drink. This should tide me over until breakfast is finished.

Feeling somewhat satiated, I begin pulling supplies off the shelves to make said breakfast. Realizing that I am cooking for—how many? I don't think I even took a full count of the children the other day. At least fifteen people, including our four—I pull full canisters to the counter. Anxiety rises in my chest, just thinking about this much food being used for a single meal. There's not much I can do about it now. Transferring the ingredients quietly to the counter, I pull out a wooden cutting board and begin to slice the first of many potatoes.

My thoughts go to the girls. Even though Jessica said they were safe, panic on their behalf simmers just beneath the surface. What does "safe" mean? Are they being passed around to different caregivers? They are old enough now that a lack of consistency has got to be taking a toll on their well-being. They must know that something is wrong—and they surely miss Nick. Has anyone told them what happened? Once again, every fiber of my being craves to be there. To be able to hold them and comfort them. Even just to know what is going on and have the option of finding a way to help.

A sharp intake of breath accompanies the realization that I have cut myself. My mental distraction made me careless, and the knife slipped off the side of the potato, catching the tip of my left index finger. Though much of it was protected by my nail, droplets of blood appear through a thin slice. Holding a clean cloth to the wound, I look under the counter for a bandage.

"What are you doing, Mom?"

I jump, almost hitting my head on the counter above me. "Bent, you scared me!" I complain. "I cut myself, so I'm looking for a bandage."

"I can help you," he offers, his voice still sleepy.

"It's okay, I just found one," I say, standing and pulling off the protective wrapping. Applying it, I show him, "See? All better."

Bentley nods. Without warning, he throws his arms around me and begins to sob, his body heaving with emotion.

"Whoa, bud, what's going on?" I ask, taken off guard. "Did you have a bad dream?"

He shakes his head as best he can, with it still pressed against my torso.

"Okay," I say softly, rubbing his back, and pressing my cheek against the top of his head. Standing there, I hold him until he begins to calm down. Eventually, he loosens his grip and looks up.

"I miss him," he says simply. My heart aches as I gaze into his eyes, still shimmering with tears.

"I do, too," I answer.

"Even though he isn't here, I knew he could be. Someday. Or that we could be there," he continues. "But please don't tell Dad! I don't want him to think—"

"Bent, it's okay," I interject. "Loving another person who helped you, mentored you, and loved you, doesn't take anything away from the love you feel for your Dad."

"But what if..." he starts, then trails off, pondering. "What if I didn't get all of my memories back? With Dad, I mean?"

"Nick assured me he was thorough—"

"But we only had a few days to take care of everything," Bentley insists. "And Nick was stressed—we were rushed. What if...the reason I miss Nick so much is that I'm not as bonded with...Dad," Bentley asks, a deep shame echoing in his question.

Taking a moment to think, I pull him close again and run my hands through his hair. "I'm not going to pretend that that's not a possibility," I say softly. "Though I think the chances are low. Even with all of your memories properly restored, you still missed that time with your Dad. You grew and matured a lot during that time with Nick, and that's *not a bad thing*, Bent. Love isn't exclusive. Loving one person doesn't mean that you love another person less, nor does it mean that there's a certain amount of love that is acceptable. If there's anything I've learned the last few years, trying to deny or ignore emotions won't actually get rid of them." I lean down and meet him at eye level. "Bent, let's name what you feel."

"I feel sad," he starts. "Sad that Nick is gone and...bad that sometimes I wish he could be my Dad, too."

I nod. "Great job. Now what can we say to that? Instead of trying to hide?"

"It's good that I love Nick and Dad. It's good to miss someone I love," he offers, searching my face for approval.

"That's a great start," I say. "Do you know what else will help you process all of this?" I ask, smiling. "Food! Do you want to help me with breakfast? It takes a lot longer to prep everything for this many people."

He perks up, wipes his eyes, and energetically joins me at the counter. I don't even have to pull up a chair anymore; he's tall enough to see everything. I sigh, momentarily missing his pudgy arms, slipping pants, and childlike movements. A pang of sadness pierces my heart as I remember that I'm currently missing all of that with Beth and Leah. The loss just never goes away. Everywhere I turn, everything I do, reminds me of them.

Wiping a tear from my cheek, I hand Bentley the salt and pepper. "Can you season those for me?" I ask, pointing to the potatoes in the cast iron pot.

"Sure, Mom," he says gently, his other arm reaching up to lightly rub my back.

As soon as breakfast is ready, the children on the floor are awake, and more kids begin stumbling out into the hall, still rubbing their eyes.

"We made breakfast!" Bentley announces excitedly. Almost in unison, their hands drop to their sides and their sleepy eyes open wide in surprise.

"We don' ha' cooked breakfast," a little boy with sandy brown hair says slowly.

"Well, now you do," I say warmly.

They move quickly to the table, all except a young girl who approaches me. "Can I help?" she asks innocently, and my heart melts.

"I think I've got everything ready to go, but you could really help me by telling me everyone's names. I need to learn them sooner or later."

She beams. "I'm Reya, and this is—" she rushes, but I stop her with a hand.

"Whoa, you're going to have to go slower than that," I laugh. "I'm going to need a lot of repetition, too."

She blushes. "Okay, I'm Reya," she says slowly.

"I got that one," I confirm.

"This," she points to the boy who spoke earlier, "is Pete."

"How old are you, Pete?" I ask.

"Seven, I think," he answers.

"Are you the youngest?"

He nods.

"Reya, how old are you?" I ask, realizing I haven't been the best at predicting just by height and body size.

"I'm 'leven," she answers proudly.

She does *not* look eleven. If I had to guess, I would have said nine at the most.

I smile. "Okay, who's next?"

She slowly moves around the table and I try to repeat each name in my head three times. I know I'll still forget, but at least it's something. It seems that the older kids—including Tal—are still sleeping, but everyone else is present. Doing a quick count, there are nine children between the ages of seven and eleven. With the older four, plus Tal, that gives a total of fourteen kids. Sixteen of us total. This number takes my breath away.

Eric appears in the doorway, a smile on his lips as he observes the happiness and excitement in the children's faces. Walking around the table, he greets me with a warm embrace.

"Tal still asleep?" he asks, collecting a plate from the counter and dishing up.

"Seems like it," I answer.

"He's not asleep," Bentley says and my eyebrows furrow.

"What do you mean he's not asleep?"

"The older kids were all gone when I woke up," he answers matter-of-factly.

Setting his plate down, Eric moves down the hall and peeks into the room. "They're not there," he confirms.

Looking out the window, I search for movement in the yard. The lighting still isn't great, but I don't see any obvious signs of life.

"I'll go check the workshop," Eric says calmly, recognizing my distress. He rubs my shoulder as he passes—ignoring his breakfast completely—and slips on his boots and coat.

Noticing that the children have all but finished eating, I decide to set some ground rules. Just as I'm about to open my mouth, one child after another picks up their place setting and sets everything in the sink. Though they have a difficult time reaching, they also attempt to wash their hands. Turning the water on for them, I show them how to use the soap. Pete smells his hands after drying them and grins. Then he moves to his sleeping area and carefully folds his blanket, setting it against the far wall. The other children follow suit.

"Go ahead and get dressed for the day," I say, completely amazed by their behavior thus far. "You can play outside for a bit before chores begin. Does everyone have a coat?" A row of little heads nod in unison, then scatter to their various piles of belongings.

"Thank you," Reya says softly, then runs to join the others.

I wonder what it must be like for them. To have depended on themselves for so long, and then suddenly to have someone there to help. I'll have to remember to avoid jumping in and unintentionally stealing their hard-fought independence. I also can't help but hope it will be a learning experience for Tal and Bentley. While they have always been good about contributing, this self-reliant mentality is something completely foreign. We've never asked Tal or Bent to take full responsibility for the success of our family. While I appreciate the new perspective, there has to be a way to find a healthy balance.

The door swings wide and Eric is trailed by Tal, Root, Caleb, Lila, and Rose. Removing their shoes, they move excitedly toward the food still on the table.

"How in the world did you leave without me noticing?" I ask.

"I didn't know you were up, but I did think it was strange that there was light coming from the pantry," Tal says. His voice sounds lower this morning and it throws me off.

"That explains it," I say. "I was menu planning in there so I didn't wake anyone. We must have just missed each other."

"Sorry if w'scared you," Rose apologizes.

"I wasn't scared, just confused."

Tal raises his eyebrow.

"Okay, maybe I was a little bit nervous," I admit, and Eric laughs.

"They were out working on Tal and Bentley's experiment."

"Oh?" I ask, taken aback.

"Yeah, when we were walking back here, we were telling Rose about our experiment. She asked if we had tried adding in these seeds," Tal says, pulling out a handful of what look like tiny leaves —thin and paper-like, with a round black center.

"What kind of seeds are those?" I ask, confused. "I've never seen anything like that."

"They're from a tree in the woods," Tal answers. "These are some that Rose had with her, but she knows where to get more."

"So, what do they do?" I ask.

Rose speaks up. "We use them in our drinking water at home. You crush them and let them sit in the water, then drain it. My mom said it makes it safe."

"Huh," I say, looking at Eric. He shrugs. "So you're going to try it?"

"Yep," he answers, shoving a bite of potatoes into his mouth. "We already have the carbon filter, the sand filter, and the charcoal filter. Our main problem is that, even with those filters, the heavy metal level is still too high. Specifically iron and arsenic. We haven't found anything that will lower those. We're going to add this and see what happens."

"Wow, I had no idea that you had already added all of those other filters. You weren't kidding when you said you were seeing progress," I comment, impressed.

"Yeah, but people have known how to do all of this forever," Tal counters.

"Right, but what Berg doesn't know how to do yet is remove these metals in a sustainable way. They have chemicals that will do it, but those have their limitations, as you boys have already discovered. Unintended consequences," Eric says, looking pointedly at Tal.

"I know, I know," Tal says.

"I'm just saying, you shouldn't minimize this project. It's really important," Eric says.

"Thanks, Dad."

The other children don't say a word, their mouths filled with food.

"You can play for awhile," I say, "but then it's time for chores. We have a lot to get done."

They all nod obediently.

"The sooner we can get that addition up, the sooner you'll all have your own beds to sleep in," Eric adds. I turn to the sink to start washing dishes, though there's hardly anything left to wash. They must have licked their plates clean.

"Can we start building beds today?" Tal asks.

"I think we better get a roof up first. Otherwise the beds will get rained on."

Agreeing, the children slip their shoes back on and run into the yard.

"I don't think I've ever seen Tal and Bentley so happy," I sigh, watching them through the window.

"I know, I hope it lasts. I'm sure they're going to start getting on each other's nerves at some point."

"I'm so impressed with their behavior," I say, setting a plate in the drying rack.

"I agree. When we went back to get them the other day, their level of organization was impressive. And their willingness to leave things behind. Remember when Tal used to cry if he was ever missing his blanket?"

I laugh, remembering.

"There was none of that. If I said that something needed to stay, there were zero complaints. I have to admit, I was initially worried about what this was going to do to our family culture, but seeing that—"

"I don't think you have to 'admit' that," I tease. "You were fairly vocal about it."

"Ha, ha," he laughs sarcastically, then leans over to kiss me. "I know we haven't had a lot of time to ourselves lately. How are you doing?"

"I'm okay," I say.

"Truly?"

"I mean, as well as can be expected. I'm kind of worried about the girls," I start, but physically saying the words out loud opens a floodgate of emotion and tears begin to stream down my cheeks, my face contorting. Eric pulls me to him and my hands, wet with dishwater, soak the back of his shirt.

"We're going to figure this out," Eric murmurs.

"How?" I whisper. "How, Eric? Nick is gone. I have no control over what happens to them at this point. And our resources—"

"I promise," he states firmly. "One day at a time."

I sink into him, letting the burdens lift in his confidence, if only for a brief moment.

## CHAPTER 16

IT'S BEEN A WEEK. I have survived another seven days and slowly, I am beginning to feel a little more like myself. At least, I can see that my normal could potentially exist again. Somehow, even though I still feel Nick's loss acutely, I seem to be managing my emotions better than I have in the past. When I mentioned this to Eric, he suggested that it could be because we have had to deal with so much loss—and adjust to such extraordinary circumstances. We have honed our resiliency muscles, so to speak.

I have been mulling this idea over and over in my brain. Wasn't all of our Tier 1 conditioning supposed to accomplish this exact end result? Yet I *feel* the difference here, ironically, where we have no safety net. Where life is so much harder and less sure. Could it be that hardship and physical struggle actually build emotional strength? And not in a superficial sense, but in a true, *better* sense. Obviously, we know that our predecessors were strong. They had to be in order to put food on their tables and protect their families. However, we also know they dealt with illness and disease that have since been proven to be exacerbated by stress. Tier 1 belief is that the life our ancestors led made them sick. But what if that was simply correlation? Those early pioneers also had no education, no leadership, and no surrounding community.

Something clicks as a thought coalesces. Diversity. They had no diversity. No divergent ideas or variety in life situation. Sure, they had individual uniqueness within their groups, but life was just perpetually difficult, leaving no excess time or energy to personally grow from opportunities that may have organically existed. It was simply survival. Maslow's hierarchy of needs. What if it's actually that breadth of experience—the very recognition of what we have and what we've lost—along with unique qualities in the people around us that builds resilience? Is it even possible to have both? To be enlightened *and* struggle? Are they incompatible?

I'm stronger now because I was thrown into a new circle. I learned from Nick. Not only from his research, but his very outlook on the world. I learned from betrayal—something that individuals in Tier 1 don't normally have to experience. I grew from losing my family and then finding it again. I continue to learn how to be patient, how to hold strong and trust, and how to cope with situations that are outside of my control. What if that sadness is what actually *helps* to bring me peace? What if I need to watch myself struggle through things to trust that I can do it again in the future? Isn't that what resilience truly is?

Of course, there's always the chance that this added "stress" will make me sick eventually. But, even in that case, I'm not convinced that one absolute is better than the other. If I do die earlier than I could have, it was a direct consequence of me leading a fuller life.

Would I rather live longer, but in a more protected, less vibrant state?

I sit on a stump—the yard humming around me—staring above the heads of the children who are diligently working alongside Eric to put the final touches on the sides of the addition. The roof should be finished by tomorrow morning, if not by tonight. These children—the worst of the worst by Berg's standards. But just look at them. Despite my longing to remain in the easy comfort of blind acceptance, I'm beginning to question everything. And it's terrifying.

"Mom! Mom, you have to come see this!" Bentley shouts, tearing through the front door into the kitchen, not even stopping to remove his shoes.

"I'm making dinner, Bent. Can it wait?"

"No, this absolutely cannot wait," he insists.

"Alright, alright. Let me just put this in the pot," I say, scooping up a handful of chopped fennel. Rinsing and drying my hands, I slip on my shoes and follow him out the door. Running quickly ahead of me, he continually stops, waiting for me to catch up.

"I know where you're going," I tease. "I can meet you there."

"Just c'mon, Mom. Hurry up!"

What could possibly be making him this antsy?

"Okay!" I laugh, lengthening my stride. He opens the door to the workshop and I step inside. All of the older children are beaming.

Eric is leaning on the crude, wooden counter, smiling and shaking his head.

"What?" I ask as they stare at me.

"Mom," Tal says, pausing for emphasis.

"What?" I repeat with more agitation.

"Are you sitting down, Kate?" Eric asks softly, his eyes twinkling. Immediately, I am transported back to our kitchen in Tier 1.


*"I am obviously sitting down, Eric."*

*"No, I mean mentally. Are you mentally sitting down."*

*"ERIC! Just say it already!"*


Tingles shoot up my spine. My eyes fill with tears unexpectedly, the gravity of the moment adequately expressed in such a simple question.

"Tal, what is it?" I ask, my voice barely a whisper.

"It's clean," he says simply, holding up a beaker. My eyes dart between him and Eric. Back and forth, not knowing how to respond.

"I tested it, Kate. The arsenic levels are below 10 micrograms per liter."

"I don't even know what that means. Someone please explain, and use normal words," I snap, then realize how my tone is being interpreted by the kids. "Sorry, this is just a lot to take in," I apologize. "I know you are trying to tell me something important, but I'm not understanding. Can you explain it to me?" I ask, keeping my tone kind this time.

Bentley steps forward before anyone else can answer. "You know that Tal and I have been using different filters." I nod, and he continues, "But, we couldn't ever solve the heavy metal problem. I tried varying the pH levels when applying different treatments and it helped a little, but never got them down to a number that was truly safe. The truth is, the chemical treatments that Berg has used up until now are not very effective—I mean, they are in the short term—but considering the negative side effects they aren't sustainable. They cost a lot to manufacture and, as our population grows, that simply won't be an option. Plus, we are obviously still being exposed to a lot of this stuff since cancer levels are still high, even in Tier 1."

"Though Dad's research should significantly help with that," Tal adds, grinning at Eric, who nods in appreciation.

"Rose had the idea to try these seeds, and I'll admit, I was skeptical," Bentley says, and I have to actively work to hold in a laugh. He is so confident and verbal, it's staggering.

"They were both skeptical," Rose accuses, folding her arms in front of her chest.

Tal grins and shrugs his shoulder, looking intensely like Eric.

"But, they worked," Bentley blurts out excitedly. "And when I saw that they had decreased levels, I had the idea to introduce microbes in a new way."

"How?"

"Through the roots of plants," he explains. "Along with the seeds, that's how we got the levels so low. I think they're working together."

I turn toward Eric. "Do you think...?"

"The science is sound. Something in the seeds must work as a coagulant. An extremely effective one. There will need to be a lot more testing, but they've definitely got something to go on here. We've been removed from Tier 1 for a long time, so there's a chance they've already found a solution, but my guess is that with everything else going on, their focus has been elsewhere."

I nod. "Has this been replicated?"

"Not yet," Tal admits. "But we just started another batch. We'll have the results in another five days or so."

"Okay," I say smiling. "I think I need to message Jessica. Pretty amazing work everyone."

I watch their faces light up and then realize that I still need to finish dinner. Exiting the shop, I nearly skip back to the house. If this is truly something that Berg hasn't figured out yet, this will be revolutionary. If it can be replicated. And tested. I breathe. Right. Don't get ahead of yourself, Kate. But...if all of that happens, they will *have* to at least consider the importance of integration. This discovery was made with Tier 1 and Tier 3 working together. Different skill sets, different eyes.

Placing the marinated rabbits and potatoes in to cook, I wash my hands. The problem, I realize, is that no result we achieve here will be satisfactory to Berg. It wasn't tested on top of the line equipment or Tier water supplies. Being able to lower rogue, possibly contaminated, water won't be that impressive. But how could we gain access to any of that now that Nick is gone. And that whole situation is a mess I can't possibly—

My body jolts. Would it work? I quickly pull up the display on my sensor.

*Jessica, I have an idea...*

CHAPTER 17

"ARE we really going to do this?" I ask Eric, my heart pounding.

"I think we have to. Don't you agree?"

I nod. "I'm just scared. It seems like so much could go wrong."

"It could. But so much could go wrong at any time. This seems like a risk worth taking. Especially if it means—"

"Don't say it," I say dramatically, pressing my fingers to his lips. "I can't get my hopes up. I'm actively shoving down any thoughts of the future and just focusing on right now. I can't handle it otherwise."

Eric sighs and puts a hand over my shoulder. The darkness seems to penetrate my skin as we lie side by side. This is the first night with all of the children being in actual beds and it feels a little surreal. The triple bunks did, indeed, work out and the kids couldn't be more thrilled. There was a lot of talk about swapping places each night so that each of them could have a turn on the top. Not everyone has a mattress yet, but at some point we'll go back and grab the few they had at their old shelter. In a few months, we should have enough feathers to sew the last few. I remember thinking that the fabric Nick sent was overkill, but now I worry it won't be enough. The children need new clothes, and that need will only increase as they grow. These thoughts solidify my resolve to go through with our plan. There are so many reasons why apathy and complacency aren't a viable game plan at this point.

I've been messaging back and forth with Jessica for weeks, nailing down final plans. Eric and I will be leaving in the morning to hike into Tier 2. That seemed safer than going directly into Tier 1, where the security is much tighter. From there—if we don't get caught and taken into custody—we hope to meet up with a group in Tier 2 that Eric is familiar with. People who also want change and will hopefully be willing to help us. Then...it's up in the air. Talking with them, we can brainstorm and figure out a way to fulfill our main objectives: Prove that Nick's death wasn't an accident and continue his work, and present our bioremediation research. Really, they are both part of the same goal. We want to make a case for integration and, though neither of us will say it out loud, a case for our family to be included.

Jessica, for obvious reasons, was not able to provide us with transportation, but she was successful in getting us maps. I was shocked to see how close we actually are to the southwestern boundaries of Tier 2. A five day journey at most, as long as the weather holds.

We do have to cross through a small mountain range, which is slightly disconcerting. But besides that, the terrain should be fairly navigable. Thankfully, my sensor has GPS, so Jessica will be able to see our location at all times, and hopefully that will prevent us from getting lost.

"How did you get introduced to this group in Tier 2?" I ask Eric, breaking the long silence.

"One of the guys worked with me. On the farm. Back then, they were hyped up on talk of revolution. I'd be surprised to find out that they've actually done anything about it, but since they agree that the Tier system is outdated, it seemed like our best bet for allies. At least they'll be sympathetic to our cause." Eric says, his voice growing sleepy.

"Sorry, I don't mean to keep you up," I say, tracing my fingers across his chest.

"You're not," he murmurs, his breath on my cheek. My breathing quickens. "We've been so busy lately" he continues, "and you've been grieving. I didn't want to add to your mental load, but...I really miss being close to you."

"I know, I miss this, too," I say.

"You know I'm not talking about "this" per se. I mean, talking is great, but—"

I laugh, "Yeah, I got the message." Throwing my legs over his, I roll onto his chest and kiss him deeply. Taking a breath, I add, "Truth be told, I was a little nervous to make any noise with kids sleeping right outside our door."

"They aren't there tonight," he whispers.

I laugh as he gently throws me into the pillows. *I am happy*, I think. Happier than I ever was before, not despite my struggles, but *because* of them. As Eric's lips crush against mine, I succumb to the moment and live.

CHAPTER 18

FINISHING OUR BREAKFAST, the house completely still, we gently set our dishes in the sink. Initially, I was extremely nervous about leaving the children here, until I remembered that they've been taking care of themselves for years. As we begin to slip on our outerwear, a noise in the hall startles us. My head snaps up.

"Boys? What are you doing up?" I ask in a whisper.

Bentley looks chagrined, having been the one to knock into the wall and cause the disturbance. In the dim light, I can barely make out their silhouettes, but it looks like they are each carrying something.

"Uh uh, nope. There's no way—" I start, but Tal cuts me off.

"Mom, just hear us out," he whispers.

"But—"

"Please, Mom."

I look at Eric, and he nods.

"Fine," I agree, "but don't think I'm going to change my mind."

They shuffle closer and, sure enough, they are both carrying full packs.

"We don't want to have an ending like Rose," Bentley blurts out.

"What do you mean?" Eric asks.

"Their parents—they left to go get help and they never came back. If you never come back...we want to never come back with you," Bentley asserts.

Eric sighs.

"Dad, we've spent too much time apart already. We're just going to worry about you the whole time you're gone, and who knows when you'll be able to get back to us. I'm sure you'll be worried about us, too, right?"

"Of course, but—" I begin.

"But we could be together and then nobody would have to worry. And we could be helpful, I'm sure of it. We won't weigh you down. We're great hikers, and we packed everything we'll need for up to a week. Dad taught us how to do that. We'll carry our own weight, I promise," he finishes, his eyes pleading.

My hands drop to my sides and I turn to Eric with a questioning look.

"I mean, they have some good points," he says, a grin playing at the edge of his mouth.

"But what about the other kids? They don't know this house as well as you do."

"I know," Bentley says, "we thought of that. We took the older four around yesterday and showed them all the chores we normally do, how to use the solar power, how to access water when the power isn't working, all that stuff. We even talked about how to ration and find a few necessities in the woods. They've done some of that with us already, so it wasn't hard. We also talked with the younger kids and told them what is off limits. Just so none of them get into something they shouldn't."

I have to admit, I'm impressed. And slightly horrified that they were working on all of this behind our backs and we had no—

"Wait, is this why you packed the larger shelter?" I ask Eric accusingly. "You said it was because—"

"I know, I had my suspicions—watching these two sneaking around the last few days. I didn't want to say anything, but thought I should prepare just in case."

I roll my eyes dramatically. "Fine! I guess I'm outnumbered. But if anything happens to you..."

"It won't, Mom," Tal says, grinning from ear to ear.

"Well, eat some breakfast and—"

"We already did," Bentley answers. "Let's go."

At a loss for what to say next, I throw my hands in the air good-naturedly and head out the door, the boys following closely behind.

. . .

By evening, we have almost completed a full twenty-two miles of our journey. Eric and I calculated that if we make at least eighteen miles each day, we will arrive mid-day on day five. It would be ideal to cross over at night, so either we will need to wait for a few hours...or if we push it, we could potentially get there on the evening of day four. So far, that's looking well within reach. Day three will be our mountain pass, so we accommodated our estimates for the elevation gain and more taxing terrain. We only need to travel 13 miles that day to make it. If we can get most of the easy stuff out of the way, and partially cross into the pass tomorrow night, it will give us more of a cushion, even if we don't make it early. Plans have been set in motion and it would not be ideal to show up late.

The boys have already set up the shelter while I am pulling out meals from our packs. The boys really did an excellent job with their preparations. Somehow, they knew to only pack prepared foods. Or maybe those were just the easiest to grab. Whatever the reason, it was exactly what needed to happen. With so much travel, the last thing we want to have to do at night is cook dinner. Nor do we want to attract any attention as we approach the Tier 2 borders.

Sitting on the grass feels like heaven. My legs ache. Though we hike regularly, we haven't pushed ourselves this hard in a long time. As I chew on my jerky, I relieve my hamstrings and my back in a series of stretches. The boys follow suit, and soon we are all lying on our backs on the cool earth.

"I could go to sleep right here," Tal announces.

"I wouldn't recommend it," Eric says. "Lots of critters out here at night."

Bentley's eyes go wide. "Our tent isn't very strong, something could easily break it," he says nervously.

"We'll take precautions, just like we always do."

"You brought the tree bag?" Tal asks.

"I brought the tree bag," Eric confirms, pulling it out of his pack. "Anything smelly goes in here, please. That includes nasty socks."

I groan as they begin to peel their socks from their sweaty feet.

"Don't worry, I'm sure we'll be able to wash these...in about four days," Eric chuckles.

"Do we really have to put our food in there with those?" I shudder.

"I brought compartment bags, I'm not a complete heathen," he says, pretending to be offended. The boys toss over their socks and he zips them into a smaller bag, then places it in the big one. "Anything else?" he asks. "Tooth cleanser? Soap?"

The boys rummage through their packs and pull out both items, tossing them over.

"Let's brush our teeth first," I suggest, and it's the boys' turn to groan. Pulling out a bottle of water, we walk for a good five minutes from our camp before stopping to brush and go to the bathroom. Returning, we place the items in their own zipped bag.

"Great, that should do it," Eric says, loading the last of our food in with the rest. Standing, he ties a cord to the bag and then tosses it over a high tree branch, securing the cord with a series of knots to a neighboring tree.

"Now, I'm going to collapse," I announce, crawling into the tent.

"It's not even fully dark yet," Tal laughs.

"Don't care, I'm out!" I say. Though they tease, they are also layered in thermal wear and cuddled up in their sheets within minutes. It won't take much to get us to sleep tonight. Especially because we know we have to do it all over again tomorrow.

## CHAPTER 19

"My legs are getting really tired," Bentley says, not whining, but stating facts.

"Mine, too, bud," Eric agrees.

"How much farther do we have to go?" Tal asks, slightly out of breath.

Eric stops in the brush. "I think part of the reason we are all struggling right now is the elevation gain." He reaches into his pack and pulls out a filtration bottle. "There's a stream over there. Let's take a break, get a drink, and reassess the situation."

We all nod gratefully, slowly pulling off our packs and finding places to rest. Eric trudges to the small bank and dips all of our bottles in. We've been lucky. We have found fresh water every few hours and that has made the journey significantly less stressful—on our bodies and our minds. Still, he refills our storage containers each and every time, just in case our luck runs out.

Finally sitting, I'm able to more fully take in our surroundings. Though still green, the grasses, shrubs, and trees around us have begun to feel foreign. Unfamiliar leaves, flowers, and detritus bring an exotic energy. I know it's not necessarily more beautiful than what we have at home, but right now, it seems so. What is it about the 'new' that makes everything seem more exciting?

Recognition of a bottle approaching my face breaks my train of thought.

"Want the first sip?" Eric asks. "It's icy cold."

"Definitely, thanks," I answer gratefully, bringing it to my lips. He wasn't kidding. I can practically trace the path of the chilly liquid as it travels to my stomach. I shiver.

"Right?" Eric acknowledges, grinning.

"That's crazy!" I gasp, handing the bottle to Tal.

The boys have an equally gratifying reaction to the cold mountain water.

"The good news is that we're going to follow this stream to the top of the pass. The bad news," Eric says, adjusting his pack, "is that it's going to get a lot colder as we climb. I was hoping to get a couple miles farther today. Tomorrow is going to be our hardest stretch, so what do you think: should we go farther now, which would give us less ground to cover, meaning we could hopefully go slower, or should we rest now so we get more sleep before taking that on?"

"It's not that late, is it?" I ask.

"Not incredibly late," he answers, "but there will continue to be elevation gain and rockier terrain. It could take us an hour to make it."

"Can we get there before dark?" Tal asks.

"I think so," Eric nods.

"I say we go for it," Tal says, gripping the straps on his pack. "I think we'll still get plenty of rest if we push. And I'd rather walk less tomorrow."

"Bentley, do you agree?"

He nods hesitantly. "I'll do my best."

"How about I carry your pack?" Eric offers. Trying to be strong, Bent initially refuses his offer, but as we all stand, his arms struggle to lift it back onto his shoulders. When Eric reaches over and swings it on top of his, Bentley doesn't resist. I reach for his hand, and we push onward.

Consciousness dawns to the sound of odd bird calls. Beautiful, but none I recognize. Morning light is diffused through the tent fabric, making everything seem hazy. My nose is cold, which makes me hesitate to move from the warmth inside my sheet. I pull it closer around me, just for a few more minutes of comfort. Every part of my body aches. My shoulders from sleeping on the ground, my feet—rubbed raw in places, despite my best efforts to wrap them yesterday, my hips and legs from the sharp increase in activity. I breathe, trying to relax my neck and back.

A slight rustle beside me announces that Eric is waking. I watch, waiting for him to open his eyes. When he sees me, he smiles.

"Already up?"

"Regretfully."

"I know the feeling."

"Today is going to be rough," I say, groaning.

"Only seven miles—anything beyond that is bonus."

"Seven miles, straight up."

"Only one mile straight up. The rest...gradually getting closer to straight up," he laughs.

"Is that supposed to make me feel better?" I tease.

"Let's get going," he says, pushing me out of my comfortable position.

A muffled complaint escapes my lips. "Fine," I sigh. Our chatting has woken the boys and they unwillingly stir.

"Time to get up," Eric calls cheerily. "I'll go get breakfast."

Though I dread the initial act of changing back into hiking gear, I'm more than excited about food. Especially because we saved the best food for today. Warm muesli, using Eric's microstove to heat the water. We couldn't bring much fuel, but breakfast and dinner today seemed worthy of it. I can almost feel the warm nuts, seeds, and dried fruit on my tongue. I cling to that sensation as I expose my skin to the outside air.

. . .

"We're at mile six," Eric announces excitedly, his voice coming in fits and bursts. The boys and I are panting too hard to be able to answer, but I glimpse a small celebratory arm motion from Tal.

"Eric," I huff. "I need to take a break."

"Let's do it," he agrees, stopping in his tracks. "Does anyone need a snack?"

The boys shake their heads. Tal leans against a small, twisted pine and Bentley collapses to the rocky ground, both of their faces beginning to show signs of exposure.

"Water?" I ask, pulling their hats lower over their foreheads.

They nod gratefully. Eric has been carrying Bentley's pack since mile three. I've been carrying Tal's since mile five.

"Ready to do this last mile?" Eric asks. "This will take us over the top, and then it's smooth sailing. We can stop whenever we want after that, though the lower we go, the warmer it will be for camp tonight."

Though our breathing has returned to normal, no one replies.

"I'll take that as a yes," he says, physically pulling Bentley up from the ground. I have no idea how he still has energy to continue urging us onward, but somehow he does it.


When we reach the top, I nearly cry with joy. The relief of reaching a flat surface is so overwhelming that I find myself laughing hysterically.

"Whoa," Eric says, "keep walking and breathe deeply. I think you might be reacting a little bit to the lack of oxygen."

"I'm...just so happy...to be done," I stammer.

"I know," he laughs, taking in my euphoric expression. "Just keep moving a little bit so I don't have to worry about you."

I nod.

"Actually, let's just take it slow until we get back below the tree-line. No sense in stopping up here where our bodies aren't acclimated."

We follow Eric as he checks the map, leading us in a slow zig-zag down the other side of the mountain. Out of the corner of my eye, I see a flash of blue. Unsure of what is happening, I stop, attempting to make sense of what just happened. Tal is screaming on the ground in front of Eric, gripping his leg. I rush to him, but Eric gets there first.

"Tal, deep breaths, buddy. We can't have you passing out."

I can see that he's trying to follow Eric's instructions, but he physically can't stop shrieking. Something is really wrong.

"Tal, I need to assess the damage before it swells. Kate, can you grab the icegel in the bottom compartment of my pack?"

Of course he thought of first aid essentials. My fingers fumble with the zipper, but eventually I am able to pull out the pack and crack it. Holding it under Tal's shaking hands, Eric begins to press slowly down the length of his leg, starting at the ankle. As he moves higher, Tal's voice becomes more high pitched.

"Okay, okay. I know it hurts. Just a little further. I'm being as gentle as I possibly can."

Tal nods, his face dripping in sweat.

"Kate, can you hand my one of those chewable pain relievers? They should be in a bag under where you got the pack. Sorry, I should have thought of that first."

I again reach into the pack and retrieve the small foil packet. Pressing one of the pouches, I accidentally pop the tablet out and it falls into the dirt. Picking it up quickly, I blow on it, then hand it to Eric.

"Put this under your tongue and press down," Eric instructs Tal, and he does as he's told. Eric waits patiently while the drug takes effect. While it doesn't completely kill the pain, it at least allows Tal to breathe normally.

"Okay, Tal. I have to feel your bone right where it hurts. I'll make it quick, but I want you to take a deep breath when I count to three, alright?"

Tal nods nervously.

"One, two, three—"

Tal inhales sharply and Eric—his hand already up Tal's pant leg—presses quickly against the bone. Tal groans.

Eric's grim face tells me all I need to know. "I'm not going to mince words with you, Tal. You broke your tibia. It's displaced—I can feel the two pieces of bone and they're not properly aligned." He sighs, closing his eyes. "I haven't done this in a long time, but remember when I hurt my arm falling off of that ladder last year?"

Tal nods.

"I had to fix that and I figured out how to do it. I think we need to reset your bone and splint it. It's going to hurt a lot, but hopefully then the pain will be much more manageable and the bones will heal properly. Do you trust me to try?"

Tal nods again, his lower lip shaking, tears streaming out of his eyes. Bentley's face is nearly colorless as he watches from a few feet away. Noticing him for the first time, I rush to him and pull him to me.

"It's going to be okay," I whisper. "Dad knows how to do this."

"Kate," Eric calls. "I'm going to need your help."

With shaking hands, I follow Eric's directions. Tears stream down my face as I grip Tal's arms and hold them tightly across his chest. Tal's eyes—red and swollen—are closed, and, while the medicine has helped him calm somewhat, small whimpers still escape his lips.

"On the count of three, I'm going to pull the bone back into place," Eric says gently, meeting my eyes and giving me a serious expression that silently communicates: *This is going to hurt, hold him tight.*

I hold.

Eric pulls.

Tal screams.

## CHAPTER 20

"WE AREN'T GOING to be able to make it," I whisper to Eric, our faces inches from each other. Though he doesn't answer, I can almost hear his brain troubleshooting. "Tal's too heavy for one of us to carry him. We still have seventeen miles..."

"We could trade off," he suggests, but his tone indicates that he knows it's not a viable option. Tal's breathing is shallow and labored next to me. The shock of the injury, along with the aftermath, was too much for him to bear. He passed out before we could finish splinting his leg. My initial reaction was to wake him up, but when Eric confirmed that all of his vitals were normal—if slightly stressed—we decided to let him sleep.

"I need to send a message to Jessica," I say. Even as the words leave my lips, I feel like a coward. There's literally nothing she can do for us. Why would I put that stress on her shoulders? Yet, lying here and feeling completely helpless doesn't seem like a sustainable situation either.

"Let me," Eric says. "I have an idea."

"What is it?" I ask, taken aback.

"Is it okay if I don't want to talk about it?" he sighs.

"Not really..." I respond, slightly annoyed by his comment.

He turns away from me, which only angers me further. "Eric, seriously? I asked a simple question."

"Kate," he sighs, "I'm just maxed out and I want to go to sleep. Can we talk about it tomorrow?"

"It doesn't seem like time is really—"

"I can send a message tonight and explain it later, if it works."

"Fine," I say, thrusting the sensor into his hand and turning away from him this time. Even as I do it, I feel ridiculous, but I can't bring myself to be vulnerable. Everything is spinning so quickly out of control that I find myself becoming rigid and inflexible. Rationally, I know that reacting this way isn't helpful, but my emotions are so strong that they're difficult to ignore. My breath comes quickly as I try to reign it in. Very rarely have I felt my anger flare like this. What is happening to me? Tears spring to my eyes and, in that instant, the energy pours out of me. Crying relieves the pressure in my chest and I give into it.

Eric's hands slide over my shaking shoulders, and he pulls me close.

"I'm sorry," he says.

"You don't need to be sorry, I'm the one—" I stammer, but can't quite finish my thought.

"Shhh, it's okay. We've all had a really stressful night."

We hold each other in silence—with an occasional sob—until my breathing returns to normal. Wiping my nose and eyes on my hands, and then on my pants, I turn again to face Eric.

"Did you send it?"

"I did."

"Okay," I say softly.

Eric's fingers play with my hair as I drift to sleep.


Blinking awake, the previous evening rushes back to me and I startle, looking for Tal. He is still sleeping peacefully and I breathe a sigh of relief. Eric is gone, as is Bentley, and I quickly get dressed and step outside the tent. The tree bag is down, but I don't see them.

Rummaging through the bag, I find a quick breakfast. My body nearly revolts when I place the same food that we've been eating for three days to my tongue, but I force it down. Without new information, I have no idea what to do next. My curiosity gets the better of me, and I quietly return to the tent.

Carefully lifting Tal's sheet, I expose his right leg, finding it bruised and swollen. It looks awful. Panic rises in my chest as my mind immediately brings to life every negative outcome. Maybe the bone isn't set right and he'll never walk correctly again. Maybe it will get infected and he'll lose it. He won't be able to survive out here with only one leg, will he? Maybe the infection will spread...*Stop!* I command. Right now. That's all that matters.

Suddenly, I hear voices. They seem afar off, but one is high pitched. Could it be Bentley? Replacing his pant leg and sheet, I silently scurry out of the tent, trying to find where the sounds are coming from. After a few interminably long minutes, I see figures appearing through the trees.

It's Eric and Bentley, but there is someone else with them. A woman with long blond hair. Jessica? How is that possible? The hair on my neck prickles, and I can't force myself to move, so I stare until they get closer. Eric meets my eyes with an uneasy expression, only making me feel more unsettled. When he sees me, Bentley runs to greet me with a hug, which serves as a perfect distraction.

"You're awake!" Bentley exclaims.

"I am," I answer, laughing at the relief of having something to do. I stretch out the embrace, not knowing if I'm ready to join the discussion that is sure to happen when I resurface. Finally, I stand. Eric and the strange woman are facing me, and for some reason, it seems like I'm interrupting by joining them. Bentley runs off to find Tal.

"Bent, he's still sleeping!" I call after him, but it doesn't do much good. Hopefully it will at least make him tread carefully as he enters the tent.

Eric laughs and reaches for me.

"Where have you been?" I ask, more sure of myself now that his hand is in mine.

"I'm sorry, I got the message early this morning and I didn't want to wake you. I knew we would be awhile."

"And Bent—"

"I couldn't sneak past him. He insisted on coming. Kate," he says, motioning toward the woman, "this is Val."

"Hi," I greet her, extending my hand. Unexpectedly, she pulls me into a warm hug.

"So glad to finally meet you," she says.

Smiling—how could I not smile after a greeting like that—I turn in bewilderment to Eric.

Almost apologetically, he explains, "Val and I became good friends when I was in Tier 2. She helped me through a lot. That was my message to Jessica last night. I knew that we wouldn't have any help from Tier 1, but I hoped that if I could somehow get a secure message to Val, she may have the connections to be able to help."

"It was perfect timing, actually," Val jumps in. "I was supposed to be going outside of the city to visit another farm. Unfortunately, that means that you'll have to come with me on that run, but fortunately...we have a vehicle, so no more walking."

"Aren't you taking a risk—" I start.

"A risk worth taking," she interjects. "But we do need to hurry. I don't mean to rush you, but I don't want to raise any red flags by being gone too much longer than expected."

"Won't they be tracking your location?" I ask.

"This is Tier 2," Val laughs, "and I have a squeaky clean record. Nobody will be checking if I don't give them a reason to."

I nod. "Well let's get going then," I say gratefully. "How far to the car?"

"About a fifteen minute walk. We couldn't get it all the way up here, but we came fairly close," Eric explains. "I'll give you more details when we're driving."

We scurry around packing our things, helping Tal get comfortable. Val brought some medication that should significantly help his pain, but it hasn't kicked in. Though he is trying to be brave, the grimace on his face communicates his level of true discomfort. Within fifteen minutes, our packs are loaded and cinched.

"Kate, what do you think about me carrying Tal on my chest, with his leg extended behind me. You could support the splint while we walk?"

"It sounds doable," I say. "Since we are on a decline, you will have to go slow."

He nods. "Let's try it out. If it isn't working, we can figure something else out."

"I can help Bentley," Val offers, and I thank her.

Together, we begin the short but arduous trek to the vehicle. Eric's plan works fairly well, but it's nearly impossible to keep Tal's leg steady. Eric's gait is longer than mine and even when I try to mimic it, we still somehow get out of sync. Tal doesn't complain, though I know it can't be comfortable. Hopefully the medication is at least active in his system at this point.

Our fifteen minute walk turned into about twenty-five with our slower pace and frequent stops to readjust and rest Eric's arms, but we finally arrive. This is hardly a car, more of a utility vehicle. I had wondered how we were all going to fit, but am grateful I didn't voice my concerns.

Eric lifts Tal into the back storage area, making him as comfortable as possible. Tal's eyelids droop and he rests his forehead—slick with sweat—on his pack that Eric props next to him.

"Is he okay?" I ask worriedly.

"Drowsiness is a side-effect of the medication," Val explains. "We will get him the help he needs as soon as possible. I'm sorry we can't go straight there."

"No, no apologies needed. Thank you so much for coming," I say, truly meaning every word. I don't know what we would have done without her.

"I know it's not very comfortable back there, but I will need you all to stay in the back cab. Though I don't expect to be interrupted on the drive, I think it's safer. We have about a thirty minute drive down to sea level and then another thirty minutes or so to my agricultural stop. I will make my assessment as quickly as possible, and then it will be approximately an hour and fifteen back to my facility. I have made arrangements for us there."

We nod appreciatively and climb into the back, grateful to be sitting, even if it is on a metal slab.

"Eric, message me if you need anything," she says, moving to the driver's seat.

I look at Eric in concern. "Is she—"

"Yep. This is not a self-driving car."

My jaw drops.

"Tier 2, remember?" Eric laughs, giving me a boost.

CHAPTER 21

"OKAY, I want to hear everything. Start from when you sent the message last night," I demand good naturedly. Bentley sits at my side, stretching out his legs. Tal is already asleep across from us.

Eric puts his hands up in surrender after slumping next to Tal. "Alright, alright. Let's see...Right, so you were angry with me because—"

"Skip that part," I say, smacking his arm. "That was before the message."

He laughs. "I sent the message to Jessica—"

"What did it say?"

"Here, you can read it," he offers, handing me the sensor. Bentley stretches his head to read over my shoulder. Pulling up archived messages, I find it.

.  .  .

*Jessica, this is Eric, Kate's pair. We are in a bit of a situation. I'm hoping I have enough signal here to reach you. I need to contact a woman in Tier 2: Val Daye. She is an agricultural specialist. Shouldn't be difficult to track down. I don't know if this is possible, or if I will need to transmit the message through you. Just let me know what works best. Thank you for everything.*

*--Eric*

Her reply shows at 4:30am

*Eric, got it. I've tapped Val into this line. Go ahead and reply with whatever message you need to transmit. Hope you are safe.*

*--Jessica*

4:35am

*Hey Val, this is Eric. I know I am probably the last person you would be expecting to hear from, but I need your help. It's a long story, but my family and I have been making our way to Tier 2 and my son Tal broke his leg yesterday. He's stable, but we need help. I've attached our coordinates. I don't think there's any way we can make it to the border by our deadline without help. Please don't feel like you need to put yourself at risk—you've taken enough risk on my account already—but if there is anything you can do under the radar, please let me know. Thank you, Val, and I'm sorry to always be the one asking.*

*--Eric*

I read this message again. He said that they were good friends...remembering the energy I felt earlier and then reading this, I can't help but wonder if they were closer than that. A hint of jealousy surfaces, but I quickly push it away. How dare I make any assumptions or judgements when we were both living with false memories. Eric hasn't said a word about Nick and me, and we had children together. A deep sadness opens within me, not only for my loss, but for the realization that I haven't asked. Not once did I ask Eric about his loss, about the people he may have had to leave behind. My selfishness is staggering. Tears sting my eyes as I read the last messages in the thread.

5am

*Eric. Wow, this definitely took me by surprise. I have so many questions, but now is obviously not the right time to ask. As luck would have it, I am headed out to an assessment today. I think I can swing a pickup if you can meet me—I doubt I'll be able to make it all the way to your location. Here is my estimated pickup point based on what maps I have available. I should be able to be there around 7:45am.*

*--Val*

. . .

5:02am

*I'll be there. --Eric*

Handing the sensor back to him, I meet his eyes.

"Eric, I'm so sorry I never asked about your time in Tier 2."

This takes him off guard. "There wasn't much to tell," he says, shrugging it off.

"I think there is," I insist. "You obviously built some strong relationships, and it was selfish of me to solely focus on my own loss. When we get a chance, I'd love to hear about it."

"That would be nice," he answers softly, taking the sensor from my open hand. "Actually, do you want this back?" he asks, offering it to me.

"No, you keep it. We may need to message Val at some point."

Nodding, he straps it to his wrist and lets out a long sigh. "What do you think, Bent? Is this better than walking?"

"Five million times better," Bentley answers, and we all laugh.

"You two have been up for a long time," I say. "Why don't you try to get some rest. I'll wake you if anything happens."

"Are you sure?" Eric asks.

"Positive."

Bentley stretches out, resting his head on my lap after I pull out some sleeping materials to make a padded seat for myself. By the time we get ourselves situated, Eric is already leaning against his pack with his eyes closed. Though the vehicle is moving fairly quickly, the ride has been surprisingly smooth. I expected it to be much rougher going through the rugged mountain terrain. This thing must have some heavy duty shocks. Hopefully even these small bumps will dissipate when we hit an actual road.

It doesn't take long for Bentley to fall asleep. When everyone is resting peacefully, I find myself taking stock of our situation. Tal will get help today, which has eased my anxiety over that situation immensely. But, it has been replaced with my nervousness surrounding this new, unplanned entrance into Tier 2. We will no longer have the cover of night or the organized contacts. I assume Jessica has taken care of that, given the fact that she was in on all of the communication between Eric and Val.

But what now? I will have to trust Val. She seems organized and competent. I know Eric wouldn't have contacted her if she wasn't trustworthy. The weight of our return lands heavy in my mind. We are considered a threat by Berg. If they had any idea that we were back, or got wind of what we are planning...I swallow hard. Why did we allow our children to come? I suddenly question, but then remember Tal and Bentley pleading to not be left to the same fate as Rose.

My thoughts bounce to the children. *Are they going to be left alone a second time?* At least this time they would have plenty of resources, I argue, but I can't do that to them. We have to make it back. My mind shifts again to Beth and Leah, and I shut the door on that hard. I can't. I can't allow myself to hope that I will see them. If all goes well, we won't have any need to go to Tier 1 and I can't put them at risk. But I miss them so much it hurts. And Nick. I was so sure that he would live a long, healthy life. I still can't believe he's gone. *Is he gone?* Somehow, because I haven't seen the world without him, I keep forgetting.

Tears stream down my cheeks from the weight of it. All of it. *Why are we doing this again?* In the dark, musty storage cab, I list the reasons one by one. I remind myself what Nick was trying to accomplish—why his path was so on point that Berg killed him to stop it. I rewatch in my mind the moments with the boys and Rose in the shed. Hearing how they worked together to make the first step in solving one of the biggest problems of our time. They did it together. I remind myself how different I feel now—how alive I am in this place where I have no protection from anything. Where the loss is deeper, but the joy is higher than I ever could have imagined. I am so lost in thought that I don't even notice when our ride becomes completely smooth, signaling a return to civilization. Eventually, we roll to a hesitant stop, and voices outside snap me back to the present.

## CHAPTER 22

I CAN'T HEAR what they're saying. Val's voice is recognizable, but the most I can tell about the other is that it's likely a man. Or a woman with an impressively low register. Trying to limit my movement, I press my ear to the wall of the cab, but it doesn't improve anything. The voices seem to be growing more distant, and my body relaxes.

"She's just doing a routine assessment," I remind myself under my breath.

"Huh?" Tal asks, shifting his hips in complaint.

"Shhhh, Tal, don't move bud. Let me help you," I offer, moving gently across the floor on my hands and knees. "We need to be quiet. I think they've moved away from the vehicle, but we still need to use caution."

"Where are we?" he whispers.

"Do you remember getting into the truck?"

He shakes his head.

"Yeah, I think the medicine had kicked in at that point. Do you remember Val?"

"I basically remember seeing Dad and a blonde woman, then gripping Dad's neck and my body being really uncomfortable, then nothing else," he offers.

I chuckle under my breath. "That pretty much describes our morning," I sigh. Keeping my voice low, I explain, "Well, somewhere before the gripping and uncomfortable walking, you took some pain meds that knocked you out. We walked down to Val's—she's the blonde—vehicle, and we are on our way to Tier 2. We just had to make an unscheduled stop. And get this—" I meet his eyes expectantly, "—Val drives this truck."

Tal blinks.

"She actually drives it."

He blinks again. "I feel like you are looking for a reaction from me, but I don't see why this is a big deal," he whispers.

"How is it not a big deal? You've never seen someone drive a vehicle manually!" I whisper energetically.

"Mom, people drive vehicles in Tier 2 manually all the time," Tal says, and I laugh. How had I forgotten that this was his experience?

"I guess it's pretty cool for you, though," he comments, unimpressed.

I purse my lips and raise my eyebrows. "You're definitely making it feel less cool," I tease.

Tal suppresses a laugh, until he sees that my hands are moving to lift up his pant leg. "No, mom, please don't—" he pleads, then leans his head back in defeat when he recognizes that I'm not stopping.

"I'm not going to touch it, I just want to make sure that there aren't any signs of infection. Your skin is pretty scratched up."

"It feels fine," he argues.

"Anything would feel fine with the amount of medication you have in your system," I counter, inspecting his leg.

"It's still pretty bruised and swollen, but I guess that's normal, considering. Here, can you shift this way a little?" I motion for him to move his hips away from Eric, which he does obediently. Gently, I lift his leg, allowing the end of the splint to rest on one side of Bentley's pack.

"This is kind of uncomfortable," Tal complains.

"Well, that's because you need to lie down," I say, pulling a rolled up jacket from my bag and helping him lower his shoulders to the truck bed. "Better?"

He nods. "Thanks."

"This will hopefully bring down the swelling a little."

Quickly, I place a hand to Tal's lips as voices become audible from outside the truck. They move much closer this time, and their proximity sets me on edge. I motion for Tal to lie still. *Please don't wake up yet*, I think, looking at Bentley as his eyelids flicker slightly.

The voices are right next to the doors, probably two feet from my outstretched legs. I can't tell if Val is with them, but if those doors open, we will have a lot of explaining to do.

"No, that's alright," I suddenly hear Val say. "I can load these up on my own. I know you have a lot to get through."

"With all of these guys, we could be done in two minutes," a man argues, obviously trying to be kind.

"I appreciate the offer, really, but I actually need to rearrange some things in the back and it's going to take a few minutes. Really, go ahead, I'll be fine," she explains congenially.

I hear a few muffled responses, but eventually the air falls silent. The latch rotates, and the door swings out, filling the back with bright sunlight. My hand moves involuntarily to my face, but not fast enough. I'm momentarily blinded by the bright light, but I can feel that Val has jumped into the truck with us. Eric shifts, obviously awakened by the interruption.

"Hey, how is everyone doing in here?" Val whispers, crouched into a deep squat.

"Good," Eric answers, his voice thick with sleep.

"Caught a little nap?" she comments through a broad smile, "Good, you're going to need it. I'm going to load up a few crates that need to be sampled and then we should be on our way—" she spins at the sound of the door opening behind her. By swiftly placing her body directly in front of the open door, she is able to shield our view and block much of the incoming light. Which hopefully means that the view of our guest is shielded, as well. Even so, in that split second, all of us instinctively shrink down as close to the floor as possible. Tal's leg is the only thing sticking up above the packs.

"Hey Burke, what's up?" Val asks, slightly out of breath, but attempting to sound cheerful.

"Val, I had one more question for you before you go," he starts, but Val quickly cuts him off, jumping from the back and pushing the door closed behind her. It doesn't fully shut, but at least we're completely hidden again. Slowly releasing the breath I've been holding, I listen.

"I'm sorry, I know there's a lot more we could discuss, but I really have to get going if I'm going to get these samples processed tonight."

"I don't think they need to be finished same-day, if that's your worry," he drawls. "I was thinking we could get you something to eat? It's about lunch time and I thought you might be hungry."

"That's very kind, but I don't think that would go over well at headquarters," she laughs.

"How would they know if our assessment took a little longer?" Burke cajoles. I look at Eric, my eyes wide, amazed at his persistence. Eric smiles and shrugs.

"Burke, I appreciate the offer, but it's not going to happen. I have work to do," Val cuts in, her voice sharper than before. There is silence. "I'm sorry, I don't mean to be rude, but I really have a lot to catch up on."

"Alright, maybe next time then," Burke recovers, and the sound of his boots shuffling away allows me to fully relax my shoulders.

When the door opens this time, I'm ready for it. Shielding my eyes, I see Val push in a large crate. Moving in the shadow, I grip the edge and pull it back in front of Tal. One by one, she loads four more, and I shift them into position.

"Okay," she says, jumping in with us once again. "We need this to look full, but I think we can take advantage of it slipping around during transit to hide you guys in the event that someone takes a peek when we re-enter the city." She quickly begins strapping in the crates, forcing them to hold, but somehow look disheveled in the process. It's impressive.

"Val," I ask as she tightens her last line, "I'm sorry about that guy— Burke, I think?"

"Oh, it's not a big deal. Happens all the time," she says, flashing her eyes at Eric, a small smile playing at the corner of her mouth. She jumps out of the truck, latches the door, and in a few moments, we are trundling along.

## CHAPTER 23

"Explain," I say good humoredly when Tal has fallen back
asleep. Bentley didn't ever wake up in all the commotion. He must
be exhausted.

"Explain what?" Eric asks, his head rested against the pack, legs
splayed out in front of him. I move close to him and adjust the
pack to accommodate both of us.

"That, back there. With Val," I remind him.

"You mean the guy?"

"Yes, the guy, and her comment."

"Sorry, I didn't think there was anything to explain. Guys try to
pair with her all the time."

"Really?" I turn to him. "But she's...older."

Eric laughs. "Yeah, Kate, a lot of people in Tier 2 pair older."

"Why?"

"Because not many of them are cleared for propagation. They tend to...bounce around more before settling down. If they ever do."

"Really?" I say again, this time more emphatically.

"Yes! Why is this so shocking to you?" he asks, turning to his side. "You know the Tier 2 numbers."

"Yeah, I know, I guess I just forgot...what that actually meant."

"It's a different world here," he says simply. "You were only ever interacting with people who were actively working to improve—"

"That's not totally true, I—"

"No, it is. Think about it. Did the people with lower numbers ever show up to their appointments?"

"Sometimes..."

"More than once?"

"Rarely," I admit.

"Right. The only people who went to appointments—as far as I could tell—were those with something to majorly motivate them. The idea of making Tier 1, or staying alive for family members they love. People with kids go to their appointments. Single people, not so much," he sighs, shifting to his back.

"But Berg said that people were happy in Tier 2, happy to contribute in their own ways."

"They are in some ways. But there's a lot of apathy, as you know, and honestly, more anger and frustration than I would have guessed. I'm really interested to see if Kip's group has acted on any of their plans."

"Don't you think Jessica would have told us?"

"She may not know. I'm kind of nervous that they might have gone full radical over the last couple of years."

"Let's hope, for our sake, that they're still reasonable. Hopefully it will be validating to hear that we agree with them. And that we have proof."

"Kind of proof," Eric quips.

"Ha. Ha. It's proof," I shoot back. "And Jessica is working on proof where Nick's death is concerned. We have to change it, Eric. This isn't right."

He nods. "I know."

I listen to his breath, wanting to hold on to this peaceful moment forever. As soon as those doors open, either we are facing immediate danger, or slowly putting ourselves in Berg's way. Which means danger.

"Did something happen between you and Val?" I ask and feel Eric flinch slightly. "It's alright if it did, I just wondered. The messages...and the way she looks at you, talks to you...it seems like you knew each other well."

Eric sighs. "When I thought I was on my own, I eventually had to open myself up to new relationships. Val was often around at the farm and...she was kind. She was patient with me, even when I talked about you non-stop," he grins, raising one eyebrow at me. "I was planning to move forward with things, but that's when Nick got in touch. Everything spiraled from there."

"I'm so sorry," I say.

"No, spiraled in a good way. A really confusing way, but obviously having any hope that I could have my life back—that was amazing. It was just complicated. I hate disappointing people, and hurting them is even worse."

"Was she hurt?"

"Of course." He pauses, and I wait, the truck still rolling gently beneath us. "But I don't know what hurt her more. Knowing that we couldn't pair, or knowing that Berg had created the situation in the first place. While she hasn't been completely satisfied with her life in Tier 2, I think she always hoped that it was serving a purpose."

"Don't we all?"

"Yes, definitely, but Val...she's tender. Seeing the look in her eyes when I explained everything—seeing that hope evaporate—that's not something I will easily forget."

"What has she done since then?"

"You have as much info as I do, I haven't been in contact. I have no idea. But she is the one that helped me every step of the way, and I will forever be grateful."

"Me too," I whisper, closing my eyes and resting my head on his shoulder.

.   .   .

The ding of the sensor snaps my consciousness forward, out of the partial sleep I had fallen into a few moments before. Sitting up, Eric checks his wrist and I peek over his shoulder.

*ETA ten minutes. Get in a good position. I'll need to go through inspection, but they usually just look at my clearance and send me on my way. I'll message if there's trouble. --Val*

"Should we wake the boys?" Eric asks.

"Probably," I say. "Once we're through, it won't be long before we have to anyway. I would rather they know what's going on so we don't have to explain it in a crisis."

He nods, moving toward Bentley. Crossing through the boxes, I kneel next to Tal and gently shake his shoulders.

"Hey, we're almost there," I say softly. "Time to get up."

Tal's eyelids flutter open and he stretches his arms over his head.

"You can mostly stay where you're at, but I'm going to shift this over a bit," I say, giving him warning before moving his splinted leg. Eric and Bentley go quiet, so Tal and I do the same. Should be any moment now.

The hum of the motor changes. We are slowing down, and eventually pull to a complete stop. Through the wall, I can hear the sounds of other vehicles, but that noise makes it impossible for me to make out anything else. We just have to sit and wait.

After a few long minutes, the truck pulls forward, and I can almost feel the tension evaporate.

"Does this mean we're safe?" Bentley asks quietly.

"For the time being," Eric answers. "We aren't off the hook, yet. I'm not sure exactly where Val is taking us at this point."

"Hopefully to get food," Tal groans.

"Hopefully to get you medical care," I add. "I didn't realize you were hungry. Here," I say, tossing them a few snacks from my pack, which they attack, obviously ravenous. I haven't felt hungry all day, but it's likely because my mind has been occupied and stressed. It's settling to know that the boys aren't overcome with all of that. Again, I am blown away by the resilience of children.

When we come to a stop for the third time, my body tenses. I don't anticipate ever feeling at ease while inside the Tier boundaries. It's unlikely that Bentley or I would be recognized here—another reason why we felt it was safer to start in Tier 2—but Eric and Tal will need to lay low. Luckily, we don't really look like Tier 1 material anymore.

The latch turns and the doors open, but the light isn't nearly as garish here between the buildings. The lane in front of us seems to be empty, and Val ushers us out the back, as quickly as we can move with Tal in tow. We enter a building through an unmarked back entrance, carrying Tal the way we did on the mountain. Though, this time, he whimpers in complaint. His medication must be wearing off.

Our shoes click on the sterile white tile as we follow Val down a long hallway. Something about it reminds me of the facility we toured years ago in Tier 2, though it is much less grandiose and impressive. Is it the wall texture? I am not able to place it before I notice Val slowing to walk next to Eric. Without meaning to, I notice her graceful stride and the way her long hair swishes across her back. Swallowing, I look away.

"Tal, we are in a Tier 2 medical facility. It's after hours, but sometimes there are emergencies. A friend of mine should be waiting for us, so I'm going to go ahead and make sure that everything is clear."

Tal nods, his forehead slick with sweat. My body is beginning to ache, the stress of the day finally making itself known in my exhausted muscles. Reminding myself that it feels good to stretch myself out, I lean against the wall and rotate my ankles, stretching my calves. I smile when I see Bentley mimicking my actions across the hall.

Before I can even finish stretching my other leg, Val reappears around the corner.

"Come this way. Quickly," she commands.

She leads us down a second hall, and at the end of it, there appears to be a waiting area, though we don't get that far. She escorts us into a room and swiftly closes the door behind us. Inside, there is an examination table with a very tall man standing at the head of it. His silver hair curls around a pair of spectacles. I catch myself staring and quickly look away, though the boys don't quite have the social experience to recognize that they should do the same. I can't blame them. They haven't ever seen someone wearing glasses, and truly, I don't remember the last time I witnessed it. They make him seem...old fashioned. And friendly. Though I have no reason to, I trust him inherently.

"Tal, this is my friend Dr. Bradley. He's going to take a look at your leg, okay?"

She begins to walk toward Eric, but then stops, changing directions toward me. I assume that she is attempting to exit the room, but she pulls me aside before doing so.

"Kate, I have a few messages to send. I can use the computer in Shawn—Dr. Bradley's office. There's a mobile food distribution down the hall to the left. If I give you my sensor, would you feel comfortable using the credits to get you and your family some dinner? I'm sorry I wasn't able to get anything sooner."

I stare at her. "How—I mean, is it—what are credits?" I stammer.

"I'll explain it to her," Eric assures her, appearing at my opposite shoulder. Val nods, placing her sensor in my hand and moving into the hall. Turning, I find Bentley settled in a chair and Tal being prepped for an x-ray. I meet Eric's eyes.

"You can do this," he says.

"I don't look anything like Val," I respond.

"You don't have to," he assures me, "it's not like Tier 1. All you need to do is walk up, scan your sensor on the display, tap the icons of the items you want, and then wait for the attendant to bring them to the counter."

"Won't it looks suspicious if I am ordering an entire family meal on her account?"

"People save up their credits and buy in large quantities all the time."

"At a medical facility?"

He hesitates. "I honestly don't have experience with that, but I'm sure it happens. Go for it, you'll be great."

"I'm dirty, and—"

"Someday, I'm going to show you how I looked every day after my assignment here," he chuckles. "Just go."

Giving me a gentle push into the hall, he allows the door to slide closed behind me. Was it right or left? Since the waiting room is to the right, I choose left. Thankfully, the food distribution area appears before I can second guess myself. Adopting an aura of confidence, I approach the display, and lift the sensor.

"What are you doing?" a voice calls, and I immediately freeze. Blood pounds in my ears so intensely that I can't focus.

"Can't you see the sign?"

Looking around for the source of the voice, I find the attendant on the other side of the room. He motions at the display and I follow his gaze, seeing the lettering for the first time.

*System down*

I sigh a breath of relief. "Is there another way for me to retrieve food with my credits? It's been a long night."

He moves closer, giving me a quizzical look. "If the system's down, I can't retrieve the credits."

"I know, sorry. I understand," I say, beginning to walk away.

"What were you wanting?" he asks, moving behind the counter.

"Just a couple of sandwiches and an apple."

He smiles. "Since the system's down, it's not going to register these being removed anyway. Here," he says, handing them to me.

Surprised, I thank him and walk quickly back to the room. I knock on the door, and Eric ushers me in, looking gratefully at the food.

"He didn't make me pay," I say. "The system was down."

"Well there you go. No suspicious activity," he teases, quickly unwrapping a sandwich and taking a bite. Now that Tal is being attended to and I am able to relax slightly, my stomach begins to grumble in complaint. Eric hands me his other half. Bentley quickly joins us.

"What did I miss?"

"Nothing yet. He took the x-rays, now he's just analyzing the images as far as I can tell."

I nod, my mouth too full of food to say anything. Tal glances our direction and, picking up the other sandwich, I walk to him and sit in the chair closest to the table. He takes the food excitedly, one leg still stretched out in front of him, the other resting on a small platform at the base of the table.

"How does it feel?" I ask after swallowing.

"Pretty much the same."

"What does that mean."

He shrugs.

At that moment, Dr. Bradley turns his display toward us. "Well, the good news is that you did a fantastic job resetting the bone," he says, pointing at the break on the image. "It's close enough that I think it's going to heal nicely. The bad news is that we are going to have to cast it, Tal. Sorry. I know that's going to be annoying considering...well, Val told me that things are a little up in the air right now..." he clears his throat, not quite knowing how to finish.

"It's alright," Eric offers. "We'll find ways to keep him off his feet with plenty of rest."

Dr. Bradley nods. "I don't think there are any complications at the moment, but keep an eye on it. I'll treat the abrasions and give an osteoblast injection. I'm sure you know what to look for in the event that anything unexpected arises," he says, directing his comments at me and Eric. Turning his attention to Tal, he says, "I'm just going to send these measurements to the printer for the cast and we should be able to get you out of here in no time. Hopefully much more comfortable. I'll send you with more pain medication as well," he offers and Tal nods gratefully. As Dr. Bradley moves to the supply cupboard, Tal watches carefully. He grimaces when he recognizes that an injection is being prepared.

"Worth it, Tal," I tease. "Your bone is going to heal exponentially faster with that treatment."

He nods, blanching a little. The door opens behind us and Val moves into the room. "Time to go," she says hurriedly. "There's an emergency coming in."

"It hasn't quite finished printing yet," Dr. Bradley informs her.

"How much longer?"

"About four minutes, I would guess?"

"Too long," Val says. "Let's go. I'll come back and retrieve the cast after you are all in the truck."

I nod, quickly tossing our food wrapping in the compost bin and assuming my position behind Eric to support Tal's leg. Before we can lift him, Dr. Bradly squeezes between us and orders us to hold still. Before Tal can react, he inserts the needle. Thankfully, a low moan is all that escapes Tal's lips as the plunger depresses.

Quickly walking back the way we came, we exit out the rear of the building and pile into the truck bed. Val locks the door behind us, and again, we wait. Before my heart rate returns to normal, she is back—this time with Tal's cast in her hands.

"He thought you'd like black," she says with a smile, carefully fitting the honeycomb pattern to Tal's leg. "There may be a bit of pressure initially, but the internal compression will adjust to allow adequate circulation." She gives Tal the opportunity to open and close the cast a few times, getting used to the bivalve mechanism. "I want you to understand how to remove this if necessary, but know that you really shouldn't ever do it," she cautions.

Tal nods. "I understand."

"You're quite the trooper," she says, ruffling his hair. Bentley cringes, and we all laugh.

"What?" Val asks, puzzled at the reaction.

"Inside joke," Tal sighs, checking out his new cast.

Val shakes her head. "Glad we're at least in good spirits," she says, smiling. "Ready to hit the hay?"

"We need to do work still?" Bentley asks worriedly.

This time, Val laughs heartily. "No, sorry, it's an expression," she explains. "It means: are you ready for bed."

"Then yes," Bentley answers. "I can't wait to sleep *not* on the ground."

"My apartment isn't anything special, but I think I've found enough blankets and cots to keep you out of the dirt, at least."

"Thanks, Val," Eric says.

"Of course," she answers, slipping out the back and securing the door.

As the truck roars to life, I lower myself between Bentley and Tal. "Last stop for the night," I whisper. "You two have been incredible." I pull their heads to my shoulders and kiss them each on the forehead.

"Glad you didn't leave us behind?" Bentley asks.

"I wouldn't go that far," Eric teases.

"We're glad," I say, wrapping my arms around their shoulders.

CHAPTER 24

VAL'S PLACE is more than special. Compared to our humble living space, it feels absolutely luxurious. I am reminded what we sacrificed to live our lives together, but in the same moment, I also have the perspective to see what we've gained. Not just an intact family, but the freedom of space. The physical space, but also the mental space. I have taken for granted the simplicity of our lives. Watching Val bounce from one task to the next gives me flashbacks to my prior schedule. One isn't necessarily better than the other, but I think I prefer the flexibility we have now. And it isn't because we somehow have less responsibility, rather the opposite. The weight of being the sole providers for our family weighs heavy on my shoulders, but it seems more focused. When all of my energy and attention can be directed toward a singular goal, rather than being split in a million directions, it seems more achievable. Everything I do feeds into that. Simple.

Once the boys are settled in their cots, Eric, Val, and I congregate around her kitchen counter. She offers us tea, and we gladly accept.

"What a day," Eric comments. "We can't thank you enough for rescuing us up there."

Val waves off the comment. "It worked out great."

"We definitely got lucky, not running into any roadblocks," he says.

"Luck had nothing to do with it," Val jokes, raising one eyebrow.

I laugh, amused. I think I really like Val, which also makes me slightly uncomfortable. But I think I'll get used to it.

"So, on to the important stuff," Val continues. "What do you need to move on with this?"

I look up, surprised. Eric must have filled her in on their walk.

"I've been thinking about what is absolutely necessary, and there isn't much we can do without. I think we'll need access to a full lab setup. Berg isn't going to accept shoddy research. We need actual trial data to present this," Eric explains.

Val nods. "I figured as much. I think I have an option, but I won't know for sure until I hear back from one other person. Hopefully by the morning. I'm sorry we can't make any solid plans quite yet."

"That's fine," I say. "I'm sure a little relaxation won't hurt anyone. And I know we feel an incredible time crunch to get this done, but I'm trying to remind myself that Berg has no idea we are here. Their focus is elsewhere."

"Right," Eric nods.

"What about Nick's death?" Val asks softly.

"That...I am leaving up to Jessica. I don't see how I can possibly contribute without being in Tier 1 and that is too risky. I've made it clear that she shouldn't take any unnecessary risks either. I'm sure Berg is all over her, since she was so close to Nick and his research."

Val nods in agreement. "So, I will solidify access to the lab. My guess is that you'll have to use it after hours...I assume you already knew that."

"That's what I figured," Eric nods. "I brought everything that we'll need. Oh," he suddenly sits back, "I need to air those plants out. Do you have a bowl or pot I could use?"

Val turns to the pantry and pulls out a couple of large bowls. "They don't have drainage, but I am happy for you to punch holes in the bottom if necessary. I can get new bowls."

"Thanks," Eric says. "Actually, are there any smaller rocks outside in your landscaping?"

Val's eyes light up. "Great idea." She exits through the back door with the bowls and returns a few moments later, the bottoms covered in a layer of rock.

Eric returns to the kitchen with two wrapped packages and a bag of soil. "I can't wait to see what exactly is living in these roots," he comments, unwrapping the somewhat shriveled plants and delicately placing them in the bowls. Pouring the soil around the roots, he presses gently to keep them standing while Val pours a thin stream of water evenly around them.

"I can't believe you brought these," she comments.

"Hey, they worked in our initial trial. My hypothesis is that any plant should work similarly, but I couldn't take the risk that there is something particular to these. This is kind of a one-shot deal," he answers.

"Oh, I think it was a good choice, I'm just saying...slightly crazy."

"Slightly crazy," Eric laughs.

My nose stings and I wiggle it, contorting my mouth slightly, to keep tears from coming to my eyes. I like Val, and watching them work makes me incredibly grateful that Eric had her when we were apart. Guilt eats at me knowing that she is still alone. And that she didn't want to be.

"These should perk up in no time," Eric says, leaning back to admire their handiwork.

"The seeds are still okay?" I ask.

"Yep, nice and dry. I'll air those out tonight, too. I noticed a little bit of condensation on the inside of the bag when I checked them in the truck," Eric says.

"Well, I think I'm going to head to bed," I say. "I'm exhausted. I don't know how you two still have so much energy."

"Mine is quickly waning," Val admits.

"Thanks again for letting us stay with you," I say. "Is there anything we can help you with while we're here?"

"I'll let you know if I think of something. But honestly...after hearing everything you have been through, it's the least I can do," she says sincerely. "There are new towels in the bathroom. I'll be getting up and leaving early, so it should be open for you. Laundry is in the back. I'm sorry if I wake you."

"No, we'll be fine, thanks."

Leaving them at the counter, I walk down the hall to use the washroom. Realizing I've left my personal supplies in my pack, I wash my hands and face, and return to the living area. Planning to retrieve my toiletries, I find the makeshift bed next to the boys and can't quite keep myself from trying it out. The blankets are pure bliss compared to the sheets we have been using, and the excitement I feel to wash our clothes and shower in the morning is laughable.

Though I haven't brushed my teeth, I can't make myself get up to do it. Laying my head on the pillow, I close my eyes and—with the soft drone of voices in the background—succumb to sleep.

Feeling more refreshed than I have in a week, I dry myself from my shower and put on my last, partially clean outfit. Laundry is next on my list. Walking out to the kitchen, still pressing my hair with the towel, I find Tal and Bentley already up.

"How is the leg feeling today?" I ask.

"This cast is awesome," Tal answers, his leg propped on a stool.

"Is the swelling down at all?"

"Seems like it."

"Any pressure?"

Tal shrugs. That's the best answer I can get out of him these days. If he isn't concerned, I have to choose to follow suit. The crutch Val gave him last night is propped against the counter, so I assume he's at least been trying it out and not just hopping everywhere. The last thing we need is a sprained ankle on his other leg from overuse.

"Bent, how are you feeling?"

"Great," he says. "I'm hungry."

"That's why I'm here," Eric says, coming in through the back door. "Val got you something special."

The boys' eyes light up as they watch Eric walk to the fridge. "Check this out," he says, pulling a container from the second shelf.

The boys gasp. "Yogurt!?" they say, nearly in unison.

"And peaches," Eric announces, pulling a carton out from behind his back.

From the looks on their faces, I fully expect the boys to fall from their perches. It nearly makes me cry. Things that were completely commonplace in my childhood are once-in-a-lifetime treats in their world. I know it isn't the worst thing. In fact, it may actually be a gift, but—as a parent—the drive to provide our children with the very best of everything is all-encompassing.

188 / CINDY GUNDERSON

Determining what deserves the title of 'very best' is the difficult part.

As the boys devour their morning dessert, Eric hands me a small bag.

"I asked Val to pick them up," he says secretively.

Opening the sack, my jaw drops. "How—"

"They have citrus all the time now in Tier 1 and fairly often in Tier 2. After my time here, I knew it was coming. We seemed to be receiving orders of specialization more frequently by the month. Trade is fully open between the territories at this point."

"Fully open?" I repeat in awe.

"From talking with Val last night, it seems like a lot has changed."

I tear into the orange and place a segment in my mouth, closing my eyes. Pure heaven.

"It's been a few years, I guess," I say after a moment. "What else have we missed?"

"Well, I'm not sure how people have received the news in Tier 1—"

"You mean the information that was released because of Nick? Jessica seemed to think that people were frustratingly apathetic. Too concerned with their own placement in a new potential system to take action."

"I remember you mentioning that. People in Tier 2, however, have not taken it as easily."

"How do Tier 2 individuals even know? I highly doubt Berg intentionally released it."

"Oh, no, definitely not. You remember the hostility I witnessed here?" he asks, and I nod. "My experience was that it was a very small group who were just unhappy enough to even consider taking action. And I think that was probably true, but it doesn't seem to have stayed that way. That group more than doubled within months of my leaving. Val was saying that when word got out about me being Tier 1—which, she will neither confirm nor deny whether the rumor started with her—it only fueled the fire. People started to wonder what else Berg wasn't telling them? Who else could be living in Tier 2 without any clue about their past lives? Were people being taken to Tier 3 without consent? It caused an uproar in certain circles. That's when Kip's group became more serious about finding information proactively."

"So they found a way to access Tier 1 info?" I ask between bites.

"It doesn't sound like it was hard. It's shocking because Berg somehow thinks that everyone is completely under their thumb. How do they not see that revolution is coming?"

My heart stops and a shiver runs down my spine. "Eric. What if they do."

"What do you mean?" Eric asks, lifting his elbows from the countertop. "Why—"

"What if they are making it easy for a reason? What do you think is going to happen the *instant* a group like Kip's tries something?"

Eric blanches with sudden understanding. Running his hands through his hair, he starts moving in all directions, his motions scattered and spastic.

"I've got to get to Kip," he says under his breath, walking toward the hall.

"Eric!" I shout and everyone stares at me. Bentley is frozen with a drip of yogurt on his lip that would normally be somewhat comical in a less intense moment. "You can't be seen here."

"I don't really have a choice."

"But you still can't be rash," I assert. "I agree that you need to act, but this is not the best option."

Eric is obviously distraught. It's not like him to be so irrational.

"Val has a computer right?"

He nods.

"Use that."

"It could be traced," he argues.

"Then use the sensor and ask Val to send it. Going outside is too risky."

"I don't know, Kate, but I have to contact the group. I have no idea where they are—they don't even know I'm here yet, given all of the adjustments we had to make. If they make any move—"

"I know, but just because we suspect Berg's motives here doesn't mean that something is suddenly going to happen this second.

Breathe," I say, and watch his chest expand obediently. "Message Val, and I'll message Jessica. We have to organize. Fast."

Eric slides around the counter and begins flicking his fingers furiously on the sensor. I hope we're not too late or we won't be making it home as planned.

## CHAPTER 25

"It's all set," Val assures us, handing Eric the key. "There won't be any interruptions."

"Dad, we want to come," Tal calls from the couch.

"I know, but it's going to be most of the night—"

"We both took naps this afternoon," Bentley argues. "And what else do we have to do? We can sleep all day tomorrow."

Eric looks to me.

"Don't ask me, I'm not a part of this little endeavor," I hedge.

"Fine, you boys can come," he acquiesces. "But you have to do exactly as I say if anything unexpected happens."

"We will, promise," Bentley says excitedly.

"Tal, do you think you can handle it?"

"As long as I get another dose of pain meds, definitely," he laughs.

"I seriously can't believe you're doing as well as you are. That was a terrible break," I comment.

Tal shrugs. "It feels a lot better now."

Again, that comparison of pain and joy. Is he happier now that he knows how bad he could be feeling? And is he stronger for it? Incredible how I seem to find this juxtaposition everywhere now that I'm tuned into it.

Considering what I'm about to do, I am surprisingly at ease. Somehow Eric's errand feels more risky to me, even though I'll be the one who's visible.

"Are you ready?" Val asks.

"Me? Definitely," I answer confidently. There's some part of me that has been itching to worm my way into Eric's prior life. Though missing out on this part of Eric's life hasn't especially bothered me, now that I have the opportunity to experience it in some way...Well, my excitement for carrying out these tasks seems disproportionate to a typical response under similar circumstances. Meeting Kip is ultimately more exhilarating because Eric met him first.

"Comfortable with the location and directions?" Val confirms.

I nod, taking the boys' dishes to the sink. The boys have already made their way to the bathroom to change in preparation for their outing to the lab with Eric. He must have followed them because the kitchen is now empty besides me and Val.

"Sorry I can't come with you," she says. "I still think it's best for me to maintain my regular routine. With everything happening in Tier 1...I just don't want to give anyone a reason to pry."

"Absolutely, and I agree. You don't think anyone will find it odd that some woman they don't recognize is walking down the street?"

"No, it happens all the time. This area is populated enough that people don't necessarily have a general knowledge of the people walking the neighborhood. Kip knows you're coming, and that's all that matters."

I clench my jaw. "Do you think they'll hear me out?"

"That...I can't tell you. There's as much prejudice here toward Tier 3 as in Tier 1. Maybe even more so because we're closer to it," she admits.

I flash a tense smile before backing to the door and slipping on my shoes.

"Hey, Val," I say. There are so many things I want to express to her and the sheer magnitude of my emotions causes me to hesitate. She waits for my words expectantly.

"I just wanted to thank you for everything you've done for us—"

Val shrugs off the praise, "No need. This is a cause I happen to believe in and I'm more than happy to be a part of it."

"I know, but I'm actually thankful for much more than this."

Val tilts her head, looking at me quizzically.

"Thank you for helping Eric through his time here."

She looks taken aback—maybe even slightly uncomfortable—which I completely understand. I haven't brought it up because it makes me squirm a little just thinking about the relationship they built in my absence. But it needs to be acknowledged.

"I honestly haven't given him much opportunity to share his experiences here, but I am trying to be better about that. Based on what I do know, and what I'm witnessing now, I can see that you were a beacon for him. And I want you to know that I love you for it."

Val's eyes shimmer and she blinks, tucking her hands in her back pockets. "Thank you," she says softly. "Good luck, Kate," she whispers, then quickly retreats down the hall, almost running into Eric as she turns the corner.

"Is she okay?" Eric asks as he approaches.

"I think so," I answer, but secretly, I worry that I've upset her.

"The boys are almost ready. We'll be heading over soon."

"I can't wait to hear about it. They are going to lose their minds when they see a normal lab setup."

"I know. Although I hope I'm not building up the moment too much in my mind. They probably won't even react, and then I'm going to be disappointed," he muses, looping his arms around my waist.

"Oh they'll definitely react," I assure him.

He kisses me softly. "I'm glad we came."

"Me, too."

"Even if this doesn't work the way we expect it to, I would have always regretted not taking some sort of action."

I nod. "We're kind of making the same mistakes all over again, right?"

"I don't think they are mistakes," he says smiling. "Berg is in the wrong, Kate, and this time, I'm absolutely positive about that."

I tip my head, giving him one last kiss, then step through the door and down the steps to the street.

## CHAPTER 26

KEEPING MY FACE LOWERED, I navigate the streets of Tier 2 according to the directions loaded on my sensor. The fact that everything is familiar, but not totally recognizable, is eerie. The neighborhoods are similar to ones I've seen in the past. It's been constant sunshine since we've been here, and it makes me feel exposed. I've become accustomed to the grey, misty skies of our home.

I wonder how Rose and the other children are doing. It's extremely unsettling not to have any way to contact them.

Ding.

I glance down at my sensor and see a message from Jessica. Since I'm walking straight for a while, I decide to quickly peek at it.

>*Kate, we found something. A friend of mine was able to gain access to the computer program of the car Nick was in when he*

*died. There was a directive uploaded to the car about an hour before his trip started. We haven't been able to piece it together yet—the car was such a mess after the accident, it's amazing the computer was even partially intact. I just wanted to keep you updated.*

I don't even need to see physical evidence of that directive, I know what it was. How Berg ever had the hubris to—I take a deep breath, realizing my hands are clenched into fists. *This is not the time, Kate,* I remind myself. I need to go into this meeting calm and in control. My sensor directs me to turn left at the next intersection and, within minutes, I am standing in front of a door. Without hesitation, I climb the steps and walk inside.

Upon entering the foyer, I am ushered into a room humming with conversation. Immediately, I am concerned at the sheer number of people here. Can I really be sure that they are all trustworthy? If even one of them is here on false pretenses, I'm in trouble. While this realization sends my heart racing, I am also fully aware that there's nothing I can do about it at this point. I have to meet with them. I think of Nick, walking into the Committee meeting that night and risking everything...I can do this. I steel myself and take a seat near the back.

This seems to be a community building of sorts, but it can't be currently in use. The offices surrounding the common room are empty, with only a desk and chair to fill the space; there aren't any visible displays either. I scan the attendees, trying to find someone who fits Kip's description. My eyes lock onto a burly man near the front of the room, in heated conversation with a younger man seated next to him. *That has to be him,* I think. I am proven right when he stands to address the crowd moments later.

"Thank you for being here on such short notice," he drawls, commanding the attention of the room. "I know we are all ready to take action and, as a Committee, we plan to make a final decision today. Some new information has come to light and, in the interest of full transparency, we wanted to present that today and hear your thoughts before moving forward."

Around me, people react to this in varying ways. Some nod at the idea of taking action, while others look positively predatory at the mention of new information. The energy in the room is palpable. I have no idea what I've just walked into. I'm about to address complete strangers with absolutely no read on their goals or ideals.

"We have a visitor today, and to respect the safety of her family, I won't be introducing her by name. You know who you are," he invites, searching the crowd. "Please go ahead and come up."

He doesn't know what I look like, I realize. I stand and his eyes snap in my direction. His smile is kind as he beckons me to the front.

"Thank you," I say, shaking his hand.

"No, thank you," he whispers. "Nice to finally meet you. I had the privilege of hearing about you daily from Eric," he chuckles.

I smile nervously. "I don't know if 'privilege' is the right word," I shoot back, before turning to face the crowd.

Summoning my confidence, I make a last-minute decision. I have to gauge the attitudes of these people before presenting my information. I am going to get nowhere if this isn't a collaborative process.

"Hey," I begin, "before I get into everything that I have to offer, I would love to ask a few questions. I'm not sure how much information Kip has given you—"

"None," someone calls out.

"Okay, none, perfect," I say, and this seems to get a small laugh. "Let me give you a little more. Kip's right, my family is taking a huge risk by being here in Tier 2, so I hope you'll forgive the anonymity. I have children and, while I would be open to taking more risk with my own life, I'm not necessarily open to doing that with theirs."

I see a few nods and hope that mentioning the fact that I have children will earn some credibility.

"I am Tier 1—" I pause, noticing a low rumble erupt from the group at this revelation. I sense Kip rising behind me. At least I know where we stand on this one.

"I know," I continue quickly, "that probably makes me one of your least favorite people right now, but let me explain. Berg forced a...difficult...situation on my family a couple of years ago, and while we attempted to go forward with their protocol, it proved to be too much. My pair and I concluded that we needed to go in a different direction and...Berg didn't approve. They used reversal therapy—" I pause, turning to face Kip. "Is everyone here familiar with reversal?"

Kip nods, his face grim. Apparently this is another unpopular topic. "Okay, just checking that I don't need to explain that procedure," I say to the group. "So they used reversal therapy to actually split our family apart without our consent."

At this, all sound in the room ceases and every eye is trained on me. "To make a long story short, we had help from a friend who advocated for us and we were eventually able to live together again...outside of the Tier system."

There is an audible intake of breath.

"That's why it's risky for us to be here, because we aren't supposed to exist anymore." I let this sink in, slowly pacing across the front of the room. "So, now that you know a little about me, back to those questions. First, I would love to hear from you about why this group exists."

I scan the room for someone who is interested in sharing. It takes a moment, but I see a hand rise above the heads near the back. Pointing, I invite the woman to stand.

"I can't really speak for everyone, but my understanding is that we are meeting because we see things happening in our society that aren't fair or justified. Maybe they used to be, but we don't believe that they are anymore. I have personally brought this up with Tier 2 leadership—and I know others have been following due process for years. We haven't seen any indication that things are going to change. So we are banding together to find a solution."

"I love it, thank you. Unless someone else wants to add anything..." I again scan, looking for hands, but don't see any, "...that leads me to my next question. What solution are you seeking? What is your ideal situation?"

"Can I answer that one?" Kip asks from behind me.

"Absolutely," I say, backing up so he can take the floor.

"My ultimate goal is full integration, but I know we don't all have the same opinion on that," he says, acknowledging a few particular individuals in the crowd. "It has been obvious for years that our resource levels are high enough to support an integrated system, but now that we have seen the actual numbers...it is completely ludicrous that we aren't moving in that direction already. And before you give any criticisms of this solution, I'll tell you, I've heard them all already. I realize that integration could be putting us in danger of repeating the past, but as far as I can tell, we're repeating it already. I'd rather have the freedom and opportunity for all of us to progress together if that's the case. If the Tier system isn't creating the peace and sustainability it set out to create, then why continue with it?" Kip finishes, sitting back down.

"I think Tier 1 needs to pay for what they've done, for all that we've suffered," a man shouts out and I see heads nod in agreement.

"I can understand that," I say quickly, trying to avoid another outburst. "And thank you Kip for explaining." I pause, collecting my thoughts. "When I was in Tier 1, I worked as a health consultant. Have any of you met with one of those before?" Again, heads nod. "Okay, great, some of you know how that works. So I had limited interaction with Tier 2 individuals and then one of my patients actually made it into Tier 1. I took her aside one day and asked a ton of questions about her life in Tier 2, because I realized, even with the years of experience talking to Tier 2 individuals, I actually had no idea what your lives were like. I had no idea what it felt like to be in Tier 2. Her information was eye opening for me. I'm guessing that none of you have had the opportunity to talk with someone from Tier 1 in depth?"

"I talked with your pair," Kip speaks up again. "It was definitely eye opening for me," he admits. "He thought about things so differently. Kind of frustrating, actually," he laughs and a few other people chuckle around me.

"Right, fascinating that we have such different perspectives on the world based on what our experiences are. Sir," I say, directing my attention to the man who called out earlier, "when you say that Tier 1 should pay, have you thought about 'who' in Tier 1 is the problem?"

He doesn't respond.

"I can guarantee you, the problem is not with individuals in Tier 1. They have been conditioned to be loyal to Berg. Everyone that I interacted with there was kind and unselfish," again, a low grumble begins to rise under my words. "But they are also misguided," I finish. "They are being lied to, just like you. The problem is with the Committee, and even then, not every single individual in leadership is to blame. I have been corresponding with one Committee member who is actively fighting this fight in Tier 1. Your fight. There are at least twenty other members who are working with her for integration specifically, supported by research originally initiated by another Tier 1 leader. Because each Tier is isolated, it is so easy for us to believe that it's 'us vs.

them', but I'm here to tell you that it's not. We are in this together, and I'm here today to help find an answer that will be amenable to all of us. Not just me and my family, not just you in this room, but everyone. Tier 1, Tier 2, and Tier 3."

"We heard Tier 3 doesn't exist," a woman says loudly and others murmur in agreement.

"Oh they exist," I assure them. "Shall we get started?" I ask Kip. He nods, and pulls up his display.

## CHAPTER 27

"My last point," I say, concluding my presentation, "is speculation, but we believe it to be valid, nonetheless." I shut down the display and sleep my sensor. "With all that's happened—all of the information I've shown you—do you think there is any chance that Berg is not aware of you or groups like you?"

Eyes dart back and forth, but nobody answers.

"They haven't done anything to stop us from meeting. We've been discreet," Kip pipes up.

"That's exactly my point," I agree. "Look at the level of intelligence Berg has, why have they allowed you to keep meeting?"

Again, the room is silent. "I bring your attention again to the action Berg has taken in Tier 1. They—in order to receive vital information regarding reversal treatments—released information to the general public about action against Tier 3, use of reversal in Tier 1 without consent, and true resource counts. Yes, they justified every action on their part, but they *knew* that this was going to cause an uproar regardless of their explanations. Which is why, prior to—and during—the dissemination of this information, they released their plans to create new Tier divisions. Personally, I don't think they were ever intending to announce that as early as they have—another piece that confirms their true intentions in my mind.

"Instead of calling for change, Tier 1 individuals have been distracted with qualifying for this new Tier system. And, throughout all of this, Berg has done nothing in Tier 2. Don't you think that's a little odd?" My voice gains intensity as I continue to drive this point home. "If Berg was truly trying to create a new set of scientifically justified Tier divisions, don't you think they would have given that information to Tier 2 at the same time? Or, on the other hand, if they weren't ready for you to have that information, wouldn't they have made it more difficult for you to get it? If they were worried about unrest in Tier 2, don't you think they would have programs in place to deal with the feelings that they know will be dredged up with this kind of information?"

Everywhere I look, people consider these questions with furrowed brows. "I don't think Berg wants to squash a rebellion in Tier 2," I say finally. "I think they are begging for it." As these words leave my mouth, it's as if a shockwave passes over the crowd, causing a collective intake of breath. Turning on my heel, I take the open seat next to Kip, my body finally relaxing as I realize that I've finished my assignment. While it wasn't difficult to physically stand and present the information I've accumulated over the last two years, it's still stressful for me to be in front of people—especially people who technically hate me, or at least what I represent.

And it's not like I've had a lot of practice, living alone in the woods.

It takes Kip a moment, but he eventually stands. "Thank you," he says contemplatively. Then, shifting positions, he asks, "Just so I'm clear...you think that Berg *wants* us to take violent action against them?"

Remaining in my seat, I answer, "Think about it, Kip. If your group—or any group like it—creates a disturbance, it will feed directly into their dialogue. That 'the Tier system needs to be redistributed', that 'our excess resources don't suddenly justify distribution to all'. If they can prove that Tier 2 is dangerous to the peace they have created...it won't take much to convince the rest of Tier 1 that you aren't worth saving. Especially when that means more open slots for them in the new system."

"But I'm confused," Kip says, more aggressively this time. "You say that Tier 1 individuals are kind and selfless, yet you think they would condone action against us?"

"Only if they were convinced it was for the benefit of society as a whole. So don't give them any reason to think that," I assert, thoroughly spent and tired of trying to prove my point.

"Let's hear what you think," Kip says, opening up comments to the floor. "I know this is a lot to take in, but I also know you've probably got a lot of opinions, so shout 'em out."

"I don't think Berg is capable of wiping out Tier 2, but even if they tried, we could mobilize against them," one person shouts.

"Even if we could get our points across, how would we ever get them to listen?" another person contributes. The discussion moves back and forth—arguments in agreement with my points, and arguments against. After a few minutes, Kip raises his hands, asking for silence.

"I hear you," he says. "I have many of the same thoughts bouncing around in my head. Your points are compelling, and I see what you're getting at," he says, meeting my eyes, "but what I can't wrap my brain around is where that leaves us. Let's say we accept your premise, meaning that we can't take action and incite a reaction from Berg...so then what? We sit here and continue to suffer? Wait for Berg to move to another plan that will marginalize us?"

I sit silently, contemplating this question. "Kip, I don't have all the answers. We're trying to figure out the best course of action right now, too. But I can't shake the thought that maybe the reason that every society before us has collapsed into unrest and conflict isn't solely because of poor leadership. Maybe that responsibility lies just as heavily with the masses. With us. The leadership stacks things in their favor to maintain their dominance, but why do we continue to play their game? I think we all recognize that some of our leaders have fallen into the same traps as those in past failed governments—seeking power, control, and personal gain—but we don't have to do the same. Why does one selfish act require another? Maybe this is the juncture where we take a different path, where we refuse to react in the way they expect. Where we change the story."

"It sounds idyllic, but how can we trust that the rest of Tier 2—and more importantly, individuals in Tier 1—will act accordingly?

Especially when—as you stated yourself—fear of displacement in a new system is a strong motivator?"

"Tier 1 has been conditioned for selflessness...we simply need to provide the catalyst. Give them a reason to sacrifice. A rationale more compelling than their fear."

CHAPTER 28

"How DID IT GO?" I ask, waking at the sounds of movement in the dark.

"Shhh, we can talk about it in the morning. It's barely 4am," Eric responds. "I didn't mean to wake you."

"It's okay," I yawn, pulling the incredibly soft blanket to my chin. I wonder if Val would notice if I took this home with me? "Did the boys love it?"

"They did indeed. We got everything started, but it will be a few days before we can test the results. We set up ten different trials, though, with a few variations between groups. I think I might be more excited about it than Tal and Bentley," he admits, a childish lilt to his voice.

"Is that really surprising?" I tease.

"I guess not," Eric sighs, settling on his pillow next to me. "It felt a little too good being in the lab again."

"Live it up while you can," I say, closing my eyes and snuggling close to him.

"How'd you like Kip?"

"He's a lot more calm and reasonable than you led me to believe."

"He must have changed," Eric quips, laughing softly at his own wit.

I smile, my head becoming fuzzy with drowsiness. "I'll tell you more tomorrow," I murmur before allowing myself to drift.

"Yeah you will," Eric whispers, gently kissing my temple.


Val, Eric, and I sit around her table with steaming mugs of herbal tea. Though it's after noon, the boys are still sleeping soundly.

"So that's it," Val says. "If we have this ready to go, then regardless of whether the Committee listens to your research, we'll have our bases covered."

"Exactly," I confirm. "We have to be able to release this to everyone within the Tier system simultaneously in the event that Berg isn't receptive. Which...while I'm hopeful that it will go well, my experience has been that the Director will find some reason to disregard any information that doesn't suit his purposes."

Eric nods. "I know we have to give them the chance to do what's right...but I wish we could just go straight to the back-up plan."

"You never know," I say, "Maybe there's enough pressure from these other Committee members that they'll consider it."

"Doubtful," Eric says, and while I can't bring myself to say it out loud, I wholeheartedly agree.

"So I just need to find a way to have this ready for a blast," Val muses. "I think I can handle that."

"Jessica is going to take care of Tier 1, so if you can get this out to Tier 2, we should be covered," I clarify.

She nods. "I'll get to work. When are you meeting with them?"

"Let's all take a step back and recognize that if the results don't come back the way we expect, we won't have any cards to play—"

"We'll still have information regarding Nick's death—"

"If Jessica finds anything," Eric argues. "Kate, we might wait two days and have nothing concrete."

While I know this is a possibility, I just can't accept it. Something has to pan out.

"I know. I'm not trying to pretend that it's all going to work out perfectly. I just figure one of these avenues has to produce something that we can go off of."

"Are you going to have Jessica arrange a Committee meeting in the hopes of that happening? Or are you going to wait until we know for sure?"

"I don't think we have enough time to wait," I admit. "The longer we are here without moving, the higher the risk that something goes wrong."

Eric nods knowingly.

"I want to set up the meeting. Worst case scenario, we back out and book it back home, hopefully with Berg none the wiser," I suggest.

"And leave Jessica to clean up our mess," Eric states.

"Mmm-hmmm."

"And live knowing that the Tier system is imploding."

"Right."

"So we won't be doing that."

"Nope," I agree.

Val laughs. "You two are hilarious," she comments, standing to put her mug in the sink. "I've got to get back to the office. Food is in the refrigerator for dinner," she instructs. "All I ask is that you save me some." Her hair swings along her shoulder blades gracefully as she slips out the door.

"I see why you liked her," I say softly.

"Kate—"

"No, it's okay. I think she's great," I say genuinely, smiling. "But I'm glad I got you back."

Eric rolls his eyes. "I'm going to take a nap."

"Well I'm going to message Jessica, so that works out," I tease. Then more seriously, I add, "Maybe she has more info on the car."

Eric leans in and kisses my cheek. "I hope so. See you in a few."

## CHAPTER 29

"CAN we do something outside for just a few minutes?" Bentley begs. "I'm so sick of being cooped up in this house."

I did not anticipate that sitting and relaxing would be the most difficult part of our trip, but every one of us is feeling the frustration of doing nothing.

"In a few hours, we'll be able to go and check the results of our trials," Eric offers. "That's something, right?"

Tal nods.

"Hey, I didn't ever hear how you set that up. I assume you couldn't keep everything out in the open, considering that it's a working lab," I ask.

"Right, it was a little tricky, but Val's contact gave us access to a storage room. We put everything on the shelves in there and then locked it. He assured us that it isn't used frequently, and added extra precautions to ensure that they wouldn't be disturbed."

"Perfect," I say. "I'm excited to hear how everything turns out."

Just then, the door is flung open and Val rushes in, her face flushed and panicked.

"Get out!" she shouts, scurrying around and picking up blankets. "You have to go right now, a Tier 1 Committee member is on her way over right now."

"What!?" Eric and I ask in unison, immediately joining Val in her quest to clear any evidence of our presence. Shoving bags, clothing, and pillows in cabinets and under the couch, we make quick work of the space.

"Where can we go?" I ask hurriedly.

"Maybe the park? I can message you when it's safe, I—"

There is a knock on the door. And now it's too late.

Val motions for us to hide in her bedroom with the door shut. We slowly tiptoe down the hall, grateful that Val doesn't have any windows in her entry to give us away.

"The dishes!" I hiss, looking back toward the kitchen.

"I took care of it," Eric assures me, scooting Bentley into the room. Tal has an arm slung over Eric's shoulders, hopping on his good leg. Every once in awhile I catch him attempting to walk on his cast, which I don't think is recommended. But, since he hasn't been needing pain meds, I assume he is just testing his limits and not actually causing more damage. Theoretically.

Closing the door softly, we can hear voices down the hall. Without speaking, I use hand motions to communicate the requirement of absolute silence. Just to be safe, we usher the boys to the other side of the bed. In case we need to hide completely.

When the boys are out of view, Eric flashes me a devilish grin and holds up two glasses in his left hand. Confused, I shrug my shoulders. Motioning for me to come closer to the door, he hands me a glass, then carefully presses his soundlessly against the door. Understanding dawns, and I copy his actions, then press my ear to the bottom of the glass. Immediately, the muffled voices become clear.

"...it's definitely not every day that a Committee member asks to meet in my home," Val laughs, her voice charming.

"I know, I'm sorry for the short notice, but this is a special circumstance."

"Yes, what exactly is going on? I received a notification during my service assignment. Something about new resource allocation?"

"Right, first thing tomorrow, we are going to be instituting changes and we are hoping that you will help us on the production end."

"Well that's exciting," Val says. "We must be doing well if we are upping our variety again in less than six months. What can I do?"

There is a long pause and I adjust my glass, wondering if I'm missing something.

"I'm sorry if I miscommunicated," the Committee member starts. "We aren't increasing anything this time around. There have been some...losses in the system and, in order to compensate for that, we will need to readjust the amounts shipping to Tier 1, and therefore, the amounts left for Tier 2."

"What do you mean, 'losses'?" Val asks, a skeptical tone entering her voice.

"I'm not privy to the details yet," she answers uneasily, "I only know what my assignment is. Here is the official request."

Again, silence fills the hallway and I hold my breath. Losses? Readjusting amounts? This makes no sense whatsoever.

"I'm sorry...but these amounts are far below what is needed to feed our territory. This won't even—"

"I'm aware, but this is how it's always been. For years we've been lucky to have an abundance, but we couldn't expect it to last forever."

"Lori, we haven't seen numbers this low...ever. This is going to cause a complete—"

"Val, there's nothing I can do," she says softly. "Tomorrow morning, you need to hit these sites and readjust the distribution. I have been given assurances that Tier 1 is doing everything they can to minimize the impact that this will have on our population. Personally, I can only imagine that this will be short-lived."

I grip my glass, carefully removing it from the wooden surface and pressing it against my chest so I won't accidentally drop it. My heart pounds in horror as my wide eyes meet Eric's.

"Tomorrow, Eric," I mouth. "Tomorrow Berg is going to get their revolution."

"Not if we get to them first," he mouths back.

Hearing the door shut, our bodies tense until we hear Val's voice.

"It's secure," she says, and immediately Tal and Bentley pop up from behind the bed.

"What happened?" Tal asks, but my brain doesn't even register the question.

"The meeting isn't for another day and a half," I say. "That's too long."

"Move it to tonight," Eric says intensely, gripping the handle of the door and flinging it wide.

"Val, we need to go to the lab now."

"But it's still during normal hours—"

"Doesn't matter at this point," Eric says.


*Jessica, emergency. You probably already know. Meeting needs to happen tonight. Coming to Tier 1 as soon as we can to check lab results. Get us in.*


I am not only asking her to call a meeting with just a few hours notice, but forcing her to get us through the Tier 1 borders unnoticed. With zero prep. If she didn't already regret her decision to work with me, she must be regretting it now. I slip on my shoes to follow Eric.

"You aren't coming, Kate," Eric says.

"What? But I—"

"I agree with Eric," Val interjects. "You need to find Kip. And fast, before this information goes public."

"It probably already has," Eric mutters.

"I've seen the resource numbers," I say. "There is absolutely no way that they are experiencing a shortage. Ridiculous," I reiterate, fuming.

Val's mouth is drawn into a tight line. "I don't know what they'll do to me if I don't order those redistributions in the morning."

"You won't have to," Eric asserts. "Just get that blast ready to go. And get me to the lab. Now."

Val nods, and follows him out the door.

"Mom?" Bentley's voice, small and unsure, calls from the hall.

"You boys need to stay here," I say. "Do not leave under any circumstances. Eat, sleep, and don't bring any attention to yourselves."

"What is happening?" Tal asks, worry written on his face.

"Our plans are being moved up by a couple of days. The bad news...is that we don't have every detail of our plan mapped out. The good news is that it's all going to be over sooner rather than later. Either way, we'll be able to go home knowing we did our best." I move toward the door, but Tal's voice again causes me to pause.

"Mom, how do you know they're going to just let you walk out of there?"

This thought hits me like a ton of bricks. Right. We no longer have time to run through those logistics. But my initial panic at this thought is replaced by a gentle calm.

"You weren't ever planning to walk out, were you?" Tal says softly.

Tears sting the corners of my eyes. "It's kind of all or nothing," I answer. Though Eric and I didn't ever talk about this, I think we both knew that deep down, this was either going to be a success, or it was going to be an utter failure. I guess I just didn't let myself consider the consequences of the latter.

Tal nods, and Bentley squares his shoulders. "If we don't hear from you, when should we start the journey home?" Tal asks.

"Tal, you two can't—"

"Mom, if you and Dad don't come back, we are all those kids have left," Bentley asserts.

"Tal, it's not even possible for you to make that trip on your own right now. We are going to do everything we can to make it back," I assure them, my voice hard, "but if we aren't back and you haven't heard from us by tomorrow at five, make plans with Val to get back to the children. Our home likely won't even be safe anymore—" I begin, my voice catching.

"They're smart, Mom," Bentley interjects. "They'll find a safe place, and we'll figure out where they are."

Is there any chance that Nick removed records of where we ended up? I hope against all reason that this could be a possibility. If Berg doesn't know our exact location, that will at least slow them down.

"I love you both," I say, rushing to them and wrapping my arms around their shoulders.

"Please come back," Bentley whispers.

Taking one last look, I attempt to memorize their desperate expressions. Then I turn and walk out the door.

*CHAPTER 30*

THE LIGHT IS BARELY BEGINNING to fade as I send another message on my sensor. There are only fifteen minutes before Jessica is going to be here to collect me, and so far, no Eric. If he even sent a message letting me know what to expect, this wouldn't feel so stressful. A million possibilities flicker through my mind. None of them good.

Hunkering down behind the trunk of the tree, I wait. There's nothing left to do. Kip has been made aware of the situation, and I can only hope that he is getting the word out to his group before they hit the resource centers in the morning. The timing of all of this is so incredibly tight...one wrench in the works and we are done. Rationally thinking about our plan, I am beginning to seriously doubt our sanity.

Ding. A message from Val hits my sensor.

>*Go without me.*

*Eric? I'm not going to go without you.*

>*Trust me, Kate. Go without me.*

*But I'll have nothing to present!*

>*You'll figure something out.*


I'll figure something out!? Flying by the seat of my pants is not my strong suit, and Eric knows it. If he is putting me in this situation, it must be out of necessity. Before I can panic, a Tier 1 car pulls up along the road and a woman with shoulder-length, auburn hair hurriedly waves me over. Please be Jessica, I think, as I walk toward the vehicle.

"Get in," she instructs. When I'm situated and strapped in, the car resumes its journey and she breathes a sigh of relief, relaxing into her seat.

"I'm Jessica," she says in a high-pitched, breathy voice. Not what I expected from our previous digital interactions.

"It's great to finally meet you," I say warmly.

"Agreed. No time for pleasantries, unfortunately. We need to discuss this meeting now. We'll be there in about fifteen minutes."

"Where is it being held?" I ask.

"The community center auditorium."

My heart stops. I don't know why I expected something different, but presenting in the same room that Nick—I close my eyes and take a deep breath.

"I know," Jessica says softly. "That room brings up intense feelings for me, too." She pauses, waiting for me to re-engage. "I wish I could give you great news, Kate, but I can't. We haven't been able to retrieve specific information from Nick's car—besides the fact that a directive exists, we don't have anything. And that's hardly enough to accuse Berg of foul play."

I nod. I hadn't expected anything where that was concerned. The car must be registered because we don't even have to stop at the border. I don't take for granted the ease of that crossing, considering all of the effort we had to put in to get across with Val into Tier 2. And we got lucky at that.

Around me, homes and buildings begin to appear, and my gaze is drawn to the left. Just a few streets over is Washington Park. Emotions swell within me. Being here and physically seeing this place again is harder than I thought it would be. I miss it and hate it all at once.

"And with having to move the meeting up," Jessica says, pulling me back to reality, "I really have no idea how many Committee members are going to be able to make it in person, but I have prepared the room for people to join us remotely. Again, I just don't know if anyone in other regions will be available. I know that many of them were highly interested in the subject matter, though, so hopefully they'll make an effort."

Discreetly, I flick a few tears from the corners of my eyes. "What did you tell them?"

A sly smile crosses her face as she pretends not to notice my emotional state. "That we had internal info about revolutionary groups in Tier 2."

I laugh. "There's no way our Director will be able to resist that bait."

"That's the goal," Jessica chuckles.

"Do you think they're onto us? Or you?" I ask.

"Oh they definitely don't trust me—or the other Committee members I've been working with, for that matter—but I don't think they have any reason to suspect what I've been up to."

I nod. "I'm dying to know whether they've instituted new policies regarding reversal," I admit.

"Oh they've 'instituted new policies' alright. That's actually why I'm positive that they're not onto me. I would have been dealt with already."

"What do you mean?" I ask, my eyebrows furrowed.

"They've become even more aggressive with their treatments," Jessica explains. "Anyone who is deemed a threat—they find some reason to pull them in. And they aren't trying to be secretive about it, either. It's nearly impossible to expect the population to act any differently, given that kind of threat."

"That makes a lot more sense," I admit. "When you mentioned the apathy of Tier 1, I was shocked. I couldn't believe that they were more concerned with potential placement than doing what's right."

"I don't think anyone really knows what's right anymore," she sighs. "I mean, everyone recognizes that something is very wrong, but it's not like we have any ideas on what to do about it. Right now, everyone is just trying to lay low."

I can't help but put myself in their situation. Would I be able to come up with anything different when my life, family, service assignment, and standing were at stake? For so long, the history that I've written for myself was that our actions in Tier 1 were selfish, but seeing what it's turned into...maybe we were the only ones willing to stand up. Though I'm not convinced that we were acting on anything other than base instinct, that realization builds my confidence.

"Kate, Shari has Beth and Leah. I was hoping that I could find some reason to have them with me, so you could see them, but—"

"No, I totally understand," I answer quickly, ready for this information. Since Jessica hadn't said anything previously, I figured it wasn't good news. "I'm amazed that you even thought about that, given everything else that's going on."

"Of course I did. It's been on my mind since we first made contact. I can't imagine being ripped away from my children..." she trails off, unsure how to finish the thought.

"It was unbearable," I admit softly. Clearing my throat, I move on, "Will Shari be there tonight?"

Jessica nods, watching my face for a reaction. I have none to give. Somehow, knowing she will be there actually fires my resolve instead of weakening it.

"Can I ask why Eric isn't here?" Jessica says.

"You can definitely ask, but I don't have an answer for you."

"We'll be pulling up in three minutes," Jessica states nervously. "What's our play?"

"Stall," I say. "We're going to stall."

CHAPTER 31

I HIDE in plain sight in the hall beside the entrance to the auditorium. Thankfully, many of the people who could potentially recognize me are already seated in the room, per Jessica's stealth observations. Facing the back wall, I pretend to be working on my sensor. Eventually, the traffic into the room begins to slow, and I find myself blissfully alone.

Taking a deep breath, my shoulders relax for the first time in over twenty minutes. Jessica and I both realized earlier that it would be an unmitigated disaster for me to walk in—or be recognized—prematurely. The unfortunate consequence of this plan is that I have no idea what I'm walking into.

"Kate?"

My eyes fling open and dart toward the voice. My breath catches as I recognize the man in front of me. Though he looks at me expectantly, I can't bring myself to speak.

"Kate, is that you?" he asks again softly, moving toward me cautiously.

"Sam," I finally acknowledge. "Yes, sorry, it's me."

Sam smiles, leaning against the wall next to me. Continuing to keep my back to the hall, I look down. "I'm not really supposed to be here," I admit. "I'm going to keep my face hidden if that's alright with you," I laugh, my body tense. While I don't think Sam would turn me in, I don't necessarily want to stake my life on it.

"Nick told me about what happened," he breathes. "I'm so sorry, Kate—"

"You're sorry?" I interject, tears beginning to pool in the corners of my eyes. "How can you be sorry, Sam? I'm the one who ruined Nick's life, who left him alone, and then wasn't here for him when—"

"Kate," he says gently, gripping my arm. "No, stop. That's not true, and I know for a fact that Nick would vehemently disagree with you if he were here. You didn't ruin anything," he assures me, his hand dropping to his side. "Nick's choices were his own. And he was grateful for you."

Tears stream silently down my cheeks. "I'm so sorry he's gone," I whisper. Sam reaches around my shoulders, pulling me close while still preventing my face from being seen.

"Me, too," he breathes. He holds me for a few moments and then steps back, allowing me to collect myself.

"What are you doing here?" I ask, suddenly realizing how odd it is to see him in this building.

"You know. When your son is killed in an accident that shouldn't have happened, you tend to tune in."

"You're attending the meeting?"

"I'm attending all the meetings."

"Berg allows you to do that?" I ask, incredulous.

"They haven't stopped me yet," he says. Before I can ask how he has access to meeting information, or how he relocated to this area, or the other fifty questions that are running through my head, Sam steps away from me and enters the auditorium.

Jessica should be starting the meeting any minute, and I carefully follow him—inching toward the door and waiting for my cue. As her voice wafts into the hall, my heart drops and my hands go numb. *Hold it together, Kate,* I chastise myself. You only have to keep things interesting until Eric gets here. *But what if he doesn't get here?* It's Eric. He'll get here.

Just as I finish arguing with myself, I hear it.

"First, let me present our two different sources—"

Jessica's sentence is cut short as I enter the room. She does a bang-up job of looking shocked as I stride toward the center of the room, directly toward her. Currently, we don't believe Berg has anything to link her to me. We want to keep it that way.

I force myself to stride calmly to the center of the small stage. "I'm sorry to interrupt, but I've come a long way to be here," I start. "Would you mind if I took a few moments?"

Jessica glances from me to the other attendees. I still haven't had the guts to scan the room, but as she moves to the side, I can't avoid facing the seats any longer. The room is approximately half full—faces scattered throughout the seats—but then my attention is drawn to the display set up above the center seats. More faces than I can count appear in small boxes across the projection. Looks like Committee members did, in fact, make time for this.

"My name is Kate—"

"How dare you!" a voice erupts from the crowd, and my head snaps toward the disturbance. The Director is standing in front of his seat, pointing his finger in my direction, and shaking with rage.

"Who are you working with here?" he asks, fuming, whipping his head from side to side. Other regional Committee members glance at each other in confusion, but the people I initially recognized haven't finished staring yet, their eyes still wide with shock. Shari sits just to the left of the Director, and her jaw hangs slack. I am taken aback at her appearance. She looks...awful. Has it only been two years? It looks as though she has aged at least ten.

"I'm not working with anyone," I say, pulling my gaze from her and facing him directly. "Well, not anyone alive, that is," I add, my eyes burning with intensity. Shari puts a hand on the Director's arm, and this seems to at least make him pause before saying something he might regret. *This isn't going to be as hard as I thought.*

Seeing them here makes my blood boil, and my concerns about having the emotional fuel to go through with this disappear. If anything, I'll need to be careful about dialing it back. Before our Committee can do anything else to interrupt, I continue.

"Many of you may remember my pair, Nick, presenting information on reversal a few years ago. I'm not sure if you knew then, but Nick saved my family. I had been treated—against my wishes—and Nick, after seeing many signs of deterioration in our local leadership, took action to put my family back together while pushing for societal change. Through his own personal sacrifice, I might add. I have been living with my pair, Eric, and my children outside of the Tier system for the last two years."

This revelation is accompanied by an audible gasp in the room. I rush on, not allowing an opportunity for the Director to cut me off. "This week, we came back to Tier 1 because we needed to present some exciting—and we think, life-changing—information to leadership here. When we heard about this meeting, we decided it was the perfect opportunity."

I plaster a smile to my face. The room is buzzing, but there's no way to determine whether it's positive or negative chatter. This may end sooner than I anticipated if it's the latter.

"How many of you were here for that presentation with Nick?" I ask, continuing to assume an air of competency. This question seems to catch people off-guard, and a few hands lift into the air. A few more join them until a majority of the room is indicating their presence. Shari and the Director—hands absent—are engaged in a heated discussion. *Eric, please get here soon,* I plead internally, and I can feel a bead of sweat slowly slipping along my temple.

"It seems that a lot has changed since then," I comment. "From what I have gathered since arriving, there appear to be two major schools of thought concerning *what* societal direction we take from here. I know Nick favored integration between the Tiers, but it seems that a majority of people here favor creating a new Tier distribution—again, selecting for the most genetically favorable traits."

"I wouldn't say it's a majority," a woman pipes up in the front row.

"How would these policies be gaining traction without it being so?" I ask, finally getting somewhere.

Silence. The woman who answered looks at the floor.

"When I was in Tier 1—granted, I had little experience with the proceedings within the Committee—but with my limited knowledge, it seemed that everything was determined through majority vote. I guess I just assumed—"

A blinking light on the projection distracts me. I look to Jessica. "Do you know what that means?" I ask. Jessica nods and uses her sensor to activate the square, which becomes large enough in the space above the seats that I can make out a man's face.

"Can you hear me?" a low voice asks, and I acknowledge him, grateful that this unfamiliar tech seems to be working.

"Great, thanks," he says, nodding in Jessica's direction. "To answer your question, I—"

"Sorry, before you go on, would you mind introducing yourself?" I ask, interrupting him.

"Definitely, I'm Tracy Jameson, I am the Director of the Albuquerque territory."

I nod, concealing the shock I feel at hearing such an exotic location. "Go on, thank you."

234 / CINDY GUNDERSON

"We've been concerned about this...process...for quite some time. Votes on large, region-wide initiatives, have always been done unanimously, but talking with people here...the most recent outcomes really don't seem consistent with the general perspective of our area. I've justified this, thinking that other territories must have a completely different take."

"Has this ever been discussed in a setting such as this?"

"We've added it to the agenda a few different times, but there have always been more pressing matters. And honestly, I understand that—we have had some extremely important changes needing our attention, but...well, I guess that makes this issue doubly important," he finishes. His square returns to its previous size and the light diminishes.

"Tracy," a woman starts, directing her voice toward the projection.

Recognizing her voice, I flinch. Grace.

"Your territory has always had a differing viewpoint than ours on any number of issues. I think you are correct in assuming that a majority of Committee members are—" she continues, but is quickly interrupted.

"Grace, you know that these votes haven't been handled properly. There is actual evidence—"

At this, the room erupts. People begin rising from their seats, pointing fingers, and creating a cacophony of sound. Trying to tune into different speakers proves impossible, but I do notice that Shari and the Director have joined the fray. While this type of conflict makes me extremely uncomfortable, I allow it to continue in the hopes that it will buy us more time. Each passing moment builds, and eventually, the energy and noise level in the auditorium reach a peak.

When I am about to make an attempt at regaining control of the room, a disturbance near the door catches my eye. I nearly cry in relief as Eric strides toward me, a definite gleam in his eye.

The noise in the room lessens as the audience begins to recognize our reunion onstage.

"I stalled," I whisper, and Eric laughs.

"Looks like your efforts were effective," he chuckles, kissing my cheek.

"I gave a little about our background and then asked about current thought on how the Tier system should proceed, and then this..." I trail off, taking in the room.

"Perfect." Eric says, leaving my side and stepping toward the center of the stage in order to activate the vocal projection.

"I'm sorry I'm late," he says, and those who hadn't noticed him before turn to acknowledge the newcomer. "If you will all please take your seats...I think you're going to want to see this."

The tone in his voice is provocative enough that people obediently return to their seats, looking slightly more disheveled than before.

"I think Kate gave a short introduction of our family, yes?" Eric asks cheerily, his energy juxtaposed with the general negativity in the room. "If she already covered this next part, let me know. I don't want to bore you with repeated details."

Fiddling in his pocket, he pulls out a drive. "Is there anyone here who could help me load this onto a display? I don't have access to a sensor at the moment," he chuckles, and Jessica stands to assist him. "Thank you," he says, handing it to her, and then facing the audience.

"While she gets that going," he continues, "let me explain. Like all of you, we were raised here in Tier 1, and one belief or premise from our conditioning that has become incredibly problematic for us is this: that the best information can only be shared from the top down. What I mean by that is that our Tier system has completely embraced the idea that Tier 1 individuals, programs, research, and structure provide the best and most complete opportunity for learning truth, which can then be shared with individuals in Tier 2, and previously, Tier 3 who had less capability and aptitude for this kind of truth-seeking. I don't disagree that this system has led to some incredible progress, but how can we be sure that it was the most progress that could have occurred? Could we have made better—or even just different—technological leaps had we adopted another system?" Eric scans the room, pausing for added drama.

"Of course, this is a question that we can't possibly answer with the information we have," he continues. "We would need to create longitudinal studies of multiple systems, and controlling the variables would be an absolute nightmare. We didn't have that opportunity in the infancy of the Tier system, and we don't even necessarily have that opportunity now with all that we are currently faced with. Nor am I even convinced that it would be ethical, but that's an entirely different subject," he smiles, gesticulating with his hands. The Director again begins to rise from his chair.

Almost in an instant, Eric's calm, cheery demeanor shifts. His shoulders lift, his eyes becoming serious as he says, "But we do have new information that is compelling enough for me to risk the lives of my children to find a way here tonight to share it."

Fixing a steely gaze in the direction of the Director—who, upon receiving similar warning looks from those around him, has returned to his seat— Eric motions for Jessica to pull up the display.

"You are likely familiar with Nick's research on integration?" he asks, inciting a low hum in the crowd. "Don't worry, I'm not here to focus on that, but it is imperative that we have a general understanding of it before moving on to my research, so let me just highlight a couple of points."

A chart appears. "If you remember, the participants in one study were tasked with solving challenging puzzles, either with others in a homogenous group—Tier 1 or Tier 2 only—or in mixed company with people from both. The control group was, of course, working the puzzle alone with no other participants. Gender, age, experience, etc. were all controlled for. As a scientist, I was impressed with the level of care that was taken to produce a truly significant result. If you look here, you can see that those participants in the mixed groups consistently solved the puzzles faster than those alone or in the homogenous group."

Turning from the display, Eric again faces the Committee members. "I was kind of floored by this outcome, because when I heard about the study, I actually assumed it would be the opposite. I assumed that there would be communication issues between the two Tiers, possible wasted time in explanation or attempts at inclusivity. This was not an intuitive result. Which brings me to the information I came to share with you tonight."

An image appears on the display and it knocks the breath out of me. Rose and her siblings are in a group—clean, but obviously malnourished—next to our shelter, with bright smiles on their faces. Another audible gasp is heard throughout the crowd. Personal memories like these are not allowed in the Tier system, which is precisely why we knew we had to present one. Even though people are rightly skeptical of this unreliable medium, when coupled with scientific fact, the effect should be powerful. It's a risk, but one we're hoping will pay off.

"These are children that Kate and I recently took in. They are from Tier 3—"

"That's enough!" the Director shouts and I see at least four blinking squares in the projection. The hum from before has begun to build into a low roar. Stomping on stage, the Director approaches Eric, but Jessica launches herself between them. At the sight of physical confrontation, the room becomes silent out of shock.

"I want to hear this," Jessica says, her eyes wide and innocent, as if she can't believe her actions. Composing herself, she says more loudly "I want to hear this, and I'm sure many of you do, as well. I know that we may not agree with or like what is being said, but I'm sick of putting off imperative information because it's uncomfortable," she practically spits. Turning back to the Director, she continues, "Please take your seat. We can discuss when this man is finished."

"You have no right—"

"To be honest, neither do you," Jessica argues, standing her ground. The Director, his face red and fists trembling, slowly returns to his seat.

"Thank you," Eric says softly. "I know this isn't easy. For any of us." As he runs his hands through his hair, I suddenly glimpse the tired circles under his eyes. My heart swells.

"As I was saying, these children are from Tier 3," Eric continues, his tone gentle. "From what we've gathered, when Tier 3 was...released," Eric says pointedly, letting that word hang in the air for a moment, "families scattered, hoping to find a way to survive. A few families survived off the grid, but were either enticed by Berg—or simply became desperate enough—to make contact again, and never returned. These children were left alone."

Any noise that was present in the crowd has completely dissipated at this point. Nobody moves a muscle, absorbing this information. I breathe a sigh of relief at Eric's savvy—giving enough detail to be compelling, but leaving out any identifying information.

"These children survived completely on their own for *years* with minimal resources. If I hadn't seen it myself, there's no way I would believe that Tier 3 individuals—let alone children—were capable of the kind of innovation, cooperation, or tenacity that we witnessed." Eric glances at me, and I nod in agreement. "After stumbling upon this youthful settlement, Kate and I brought them into our home to provide them an extra level of care and protection. It has been an incredible benefit to our own children who weren't swimming in social opportunities," he says, a slightly sardonic chuckle escaping his lips.

"But here's where things shifted," Eric says, pulling up a graph. "Our boys have been working for years on water filtration— attempting to clear toxicity in ways that Berg has been unable to do in the past. I always assumed that Berg had likely solved that problem since we left, but tapping into current research, it seems that it's still an ongoing puzzle."

I smile, knowing that he used that last word purposefully, refer- encing Nick's research.

"These Tier 3 children, upon joining us, immediately jumped in and began contributing ideas to the system we already had going." Eric's face becomes animated as he points excitedly at the graph. "And check out these numbers. Within *five days* of integrating these additions, this is what we noticed." He pauses, zooming in on specific toxicity levels.

"Now, I know what you're likely thinking, because I was thinking the same thing: how relevant are these results, considering they were done on outdated equipment by children?" Eric continues, pulling a few laughs from the audience.

"That's why we had to come here. If this truly was a sustainable— regenerative, even—option for improving water toxicity levels, then we felt we had a responsibility to test it, share it, and present extremely compelling evidence that Nick's research is on the right track. If *children* could make ample strides in solving this incred- ibly challenging puzzle by working together, then what could we accomplish as educated adults doing the same?"

Eric pulls up a new chart and continues, "Of course, you already know what we came up with, or there would be no point to me being here. These are the results from a clinical trial using the best equipment available to us in the newest lab in Tier 2. We were able to complete micro-titration and the water toxicity levels were actually even lower than what we initially predicted."

After allowing the members ample time to inspect the image, Eric turns off the display. When he doesn't speak immediately, I walk to his side and put my arm around his waist. He relaxes into me, and lifts his face to the audience.

"What opportunities are we giving up because we refuse to adapt? Kate and I, of all people, understand how hard it is to jump into something that is completely foreign. But I don't think we can afford to ignore this potential," he finishes, stepping back from the center of the stage, pulling me with him.

## CHAPTER 32

THE DIRECTOR TAKES the stage again, this time seemingly in control of his emotions, but obviously still perturbed. Buttoning his jacket, he approaches the podium.

"That's all fine and well," he begins in a patronizing tone, "but I, for one, have a difficult time envisioning a complete system overhaul because of one or two initial trials. Yes, I agree, this research is promising, but I am still not convinced that it's because of integration. We have years of genetic research backing up the Tier system and the new divisions we are planning to implement. Are we really comfortable throwing that away because we found something that could be—may be—promising? We haven't tested anything longitudinally and there could be plenty of unintended consequences. We just need more time," he says, shooting a placating look our direction. "But thank you for your efforts."

I continue to look in Shari's direction, but she won't meet my eyes. I still can't get over her haggard appearance, but I force that distraction aside. While I would love nothing more than to step up in rebuttal to the Director's comments, I feel compelled to remain silent. A square lights up in the projection and Jessica activates it.

"I can see both sides," an older woman says as her face comes into view. Her perfectly coiffed bob brings out her high cheekbones, making them look almost sharp. "While I am nervous to jump into something that we know so little about, we have also been...concerned...with the direction we are heading. These new—divisions you called them?"

The Director nods.

"I haven't seen any research showing that making our designations more stringent will have a positive effect in the population. Yes, we have plenty of research supporting our current divisions, but as far as I can tell, we are jumping into new territory either way. So, this isn't a comparison of a known entity vs. an unknown, rather it's two unknowns, and I for one would support giving both options equal weight."

As she signs off, I can see the Director stiffen slightly.

"While these new Tiers haven't been as extensively researched—because until now, we haven't had the genetic availability to do so—they are directly extrapolated from our current system. One could reasonably assume that the results would be similar."

I see a few heads nodding in the audience. A man near the back rises from his seat.

"To the point that was made earlier, why hasn't more research been done on alternative options? Especially with so much advancement and the obvious need for change in the Tier system, why is it that the only research being done is surrounding our current model? If we are honestly seeking for truth, wouldn't we want to be sure that we aren't missing anything? That, to me, is an exciting possibility of integration. It would be an opportunity to see differently. Especially because our resource levels are higher— what do we have to lose? If we try it and it isn't working, we would have the opportunity to make new designations at that point. We could even give a specific timeline for reevaluation if that would make everyone feel more comfortable. It seems worth trying," he offers.

More nods. More confused faces on the Committee members within my view. A woman on the opposite side of the auditorium stands and approaches the stage. The Director, surprisingly, moves over to give her space. She must be important to incite that kind of reaction from him. Speaking of importance, where is Carole Berg? I am suddenly very aware of her lack of attendance.

"Thank you all for your input," she begins in a sickly sweet voice. "These are all wonderful ideas, but the fate of the Tier system is obviously not something that can be determined in one evening," she laughs, almost waiting for others to join her. Eventually, the awkward pause stretches to the point that people laugh to avoid the discomfort of the moment.

"I will take all of this back to the main office," she continues, "and we can continue this conversation through messages or in person as needed." She nods her head finally and begins to retreat from the podium. The energy in the room shifts with her movement.

Distress is evident on the faces of those who, I have now gathered, based on their comments, are working with Jessica. But the image that pulls my body away from Eric and forward to center is the slight smile that begins to appear on the Director's lips.

"Wait," I call after her. "Who are you?"

The woman pauses, barely deigning to turn to face me. "I'm Crystal, Carole's assistant," she says, and though her voice isn't picked up by the amplifier, I can hear the disdain in her tone.

"Then you know Nick," I say slowly. "Knew," I correct. "Would you like to know the reason why he—and I—feel so strongly about integration?"

She turns with her arms crossed, as if bored by my commentary.

I steel myself and continue on. "Because even if we don't know exactly where we're headed—even if we don't understand all the ramifications of this new system—Nick, Eric, and I—and I'm guessing many of you—" I add, pointing into the audience, "have seen red flags begin to appear within our current system."

I turn my attention back to Crystal. "We've all done the conditioning. We can recite every warning sign of a failing society at the drop of a hat, yet for some reason, we fail to label them when they're right in front of us. Happening all around us! Somehow, we've convinced ourselves that we're immune to this type of failure because we *logically know* how it happens, and theoretically, how to prevent it," I continue, my voice building in intensity, and my eyes blazing. "I won't sit back and pretend that these signs are anything less than what they are. Berg is withholding information from Tier 1 citizens. They refuse to be accountable, and when they are forced to be, they have created distractions and propaganda to avoid having to take responsibility. Berg is creating fear within our population—fear of missing out on new opportunities, but most importantly, fear of each other. So my reasons for integration? To avoid continuing in a direction that stinks of corruption and reeks of totalitarianism. To change course from a path that I can feel in my bones is wrong. *You killed a man who was attempting to build bridges between our Tiers,*" I nearly shriek. "If that isn't a red flag, I don't know what is. That's why we're here today. We don't even have to be a part of this, we are happy living on our own. We are here because we care about you and feel a responsibility to stand up and do whatever we can to prevent our society from failing like all the others." I finish, pulling in a ragged breath. For a moment I stand there, almost in shock that all of that came pouring out of my mouth. Collecting myself, I see Crystal moving slowly toward me, a smile still sitting on her lips.

"I'm so glad that you brought this up, actually. For a moment, I had forgotten that you aren't allowed to be here," she says, swaying slightly in her approach. "I'm sure we all appreciate your willingness to 'sacrifice' your time to come and try to 'enlighten' us, but you haven't been around for a few years. You know nothing about what you speak," she spits vehemently, the smile finally erased from her face. "I am going to ask you to follow my associates out," she says, her voice sweet once again as she flicks her index finger toward two men near the back entrance.

Suddenly, I feel Eric next to me. "We forgot," he says nonchalantly, "there's one last thing we wanted to show you." He turns his attention to the display as Jessica begins to surreptitiously input information into her sensor. I follow Eric's gaze, not wanting to draw attention to her movements. Before anything begins to appear, I hear them. Dings. All around me, sensors begin to announce a new emergency message, and my shoulders relax. *It's working. Thank you, Val,* I breathe, closing my eyes for a split second before the display lights up.

## CHAPTER 33

Music begins to play as our family comes into view. We are piled together on Val's sofa, though nobody here will recognize that.

*"Hi, I'm Eric, and this is Kate, Tal, and Bentley,"* Eric's voice explains through the video. He introduces us as I watch Crystal and the Director frantically tapping their sensors, then eventually attempting to turn off the projection. A red error message continues to pop up as Crystal attempts different passwords with no luck.

"It doesn't matter," Eric says softly. "This has been sent to every member of Tier 1 and Tier 2. You can turn it off here, but that isn't going to prevent every single person from watching it at their own leisure."

*"We've got some pretty exciting information to share with you,"* Tal says. *"My brother and I have been working on..."*

"What do you think this is even going to accomplish?" the Director hisses. "Nobody is going to pay any attention to what you have to say."

"Then why are you trying to turn it off?" I ask quietly.

"Let it play!" I hear from the audience. Crystal and the Director step back from the display, attempting to conceal their obvious disdain for us and the current situation.

"Alright, we'll let it play, but this is a breach of security that Berg is already looking into. This isn't something we take lightly," she threatens loudly, moving to the side of the stage.

My entire body vibrates as fear, anxiety, elation, and relief flood through me. Truly, we were hoping that we wouldn't have to do this. By far, this is our most dangerous move. Presenting the information was risky enough, but to hijack Berg's communication?

I watch images flash across the screen. While Eric and I were cooped up in Val's apartment, we decided to put this together as a last ditch effort, and I'm pretty impressed with how it turned out. Somehow—I suspect Kip's involvement—Eric was able to dig up old footage and images from the early days of the Tier system through the present—pictures of Tier 1 individuals serving at distribution centers, footage of Tier 2 workers farming and delivering produce to Tier 1, and an endless array of cooperative moments between the Tiers, taken from Berg's security archives.

I absorb the shocked faces of the Committee members. Most likely, very few people in this room have ever seen images like this before —they likely didn't even know they existed. The only pictures that regular citizens have access to are those in old books and conditioning materials, and even those are carefully chosen and distributed. Seeing their reaction rekindles my hope that this just might be enough to spur a change of heart.

The words I spoke when meeting with Kip weren't empty. I believe that we are better than this. Hearing the Committee members speaking tonight nearly tore my remaining hope to shreds, until I remembered all of the effort made by members of Tier 1, Tier 2, and Tier 3 to get us here. We worked together for this moment—connected by a shared ideology and a common goal. This Committee represents such a small portion of our population, and yet we are afraid of them. Why? Because they hold the power? The ability to threaten us? To harm us or our families? So let them.

"Do you think this will work?" Eric whispers into my ear, pulling me close.

"I really don't care at this point," I say. "All I needed was to know that we did everything we could. Do I believe that love is a stronger motivator than fear?" I ask, pressing my cheek against his. "Yes. A thousand times yes," I sigh. "But do I think we did enough to inspire that in Tier 1?"

"We did all we could," Eric echos.

*"This isn't who we are. We are a community that serves each other. Lifts each other. We are no longer in a world where we have to strip resources from one another to survive. We don't hide in our homes, hoping that we'll get the best of what Berg has to offer at the expense of our neighbors. It's time that we opened up our minds and hearts to learn from all people. With all abilities, all genetic codes, all life experiences. We have an opportunity to shift course before we*

*become another failed society. This is the truest test of our condi-
tioning. THIS is the hinge on which societies turn. Can we overcome this insatiable human desire to stay where it's safe? To bury
our heads in the sand? To convince ourselves that it will be fine, in
an effort to avoid personal sacrifice? Can we overcome ourselves?"*
Eric's voice continues as the montage ends. Unable to focus and
knowing that the message is coming to a close, I turn to Eric.

"We need to go," I whisper hurriedly. "We should have found an
opportunity to sneak out while they were distracted," I say, panic
rising in my chest.

"Shhh," Eric says smiling, pointing discreetly toward the audience.
"Look."

The Committee members that I can see are all staring at the
projection with rapt attention. Shari finally meets my eyes with a
sadness in her expression that I can't place. Quickly, she looks
away and, almost immediately, the message is finished. Despite my
anger, I yearn to go to her and fix this. All of it.

"Well, thank you for that," the Director says diplomatically. "I
think we've all had quite enough excitement for one day."

"I have to say," Crystal jumps in, "I am impressed with your
resourcefulness, and I am sure Carole will want to meet with both
of you as soon as possible." Her smile, much like Grace's, doesn't
meet her eyes. The men that were signaled earlier again begin to
approach the stage and I grip Eric's arm.

"Carole will have to wait," Jessica says, striding determinedly
across the stage toward us. "I have orders to take Kate and Eric to
Tier 2 holding."

"Orders from whom? I'm fairly certain that mine trump yours," she says smugly.

"Mine," a voice rises from the back. The man that spoke earlier in defense of integration is standing.

"Mine as well," a woman states, standing next to him.

"And mine," another man says, swiftly rising to join them.

Men and women begin to stand across the room and over a dozen squares are lit up on the projection. My heart squeezes in gratitude for these strangers. Crystal's eyes float across the room, quickly recognizing that she doesn't have the immediate support to squash a group of this size.

The Director clears his throat. "I will make sure that we get them to you first thing in the morning," he says under his breath, but not quietly enough to avoid being picked up through the amplification system. His eyes dart to the side, unsure how to proceed.

"That's fine, it's late anyway," Crystal announces. "Tomorrow will be more convenient anyway."

I breathe a sigh of relief, but any calm I feel quickly dissipates when I catch Jessica's expression.

"Go," she mouths as she rushes toward us. Following her lead, we navigate the stairs and quickly exit the way we came in.

"Where to?" I ask.

"Give that to me," she says quickly, grabbing for my sensor. "They saw you with it."

As I pull it off, she quickly throws it to the floor and crushes it under her foot. "Eric, do you have anything else with you? Files, drives, etc.?"

"Anything I had, I gave to you," he says as we rush to keep up with her frantic pace down the hallway.

"Okay," she nods, all business. I am beginning to question whether I actually sensed any hesitancy from her in the car earlier. *This* Jessica is fearless.

"We can't take my car, too obvious, but I think I have a better option," she says, rounding the final corner and pushing through exit doors near the back of the building.

I halt in my tracks at the sight of her, and Eric seems to be blind-sided as well, given his lack of movement beside me.

"What are you waiting for?" Shari asks. "Get in!"

Even her voice sounds older, more feeble. The vehicle is sleek, and larger than I would have expected for a personal transport, but who knows what Shari uses vehicles for these days. She seems to be close to the Director, and this realization immediately sets off warning signals in my brain. Could this be a trap?

"I...Jessica, are you sure..." I stammer.

"Oh stop mumbling, Kate, and *get in the car!*" Shari commands, sounding much more like herself. "If you haven't noticed, you're in a little bit of a time crunch here."

"But why would you help us!" I blurt out, tears building in my eyes. "You're the reason why we even had to go through all of this! Why would I trust you now!"

Shari flinches at my outburst, but her face remains calm. "Kate, I know we need to have this out, but now is not the time. Please, get in the car and if you don't trust me, I think you trust her. Go with that."

Jessica slides into the front seat, and Eric pulls on my arm. I follow him into the vehicle, searching Shari's face as he closes the door behind me.

CHAPTER 34

THE SUDDEN SILENCE, interrupted only by the comforting hum of the engine, is almost impossible to bear. After the electricity of the past few hours, my body doesn't remember how to calm down. Closing my eyes and relaxing my head into the soft, malleable cushion, I force myself into a deep, slow breathing pattern.

"How do you know this is taking us back to Tier 2?" Eric asks, his voice low. Now that we have left the building, his desire to get back to the boys mirrors my own.

"Because I set the destination while you two were arguing over whether to get in," Jessica mutters.

Unable to contain it, I laugh out loud. "Who are you?" I ask, my voice slightly hysterical.

"What do you mean?" Jessica asks, her face pulled into a scowl.

"A couple of hours ago, we sat in a car and you seemed about to keel over out of anxiety. Now you are commandeering vehicles that aren't yours and commenting on our ineptitude?" I laugh, sneaking a sidelong glance at Eric's baffled expression. "What?" I ask. "It's funny!"

Jessica rolls her eyes. "I'm just good at doing what needs to be done," she says, but I see the corners of her mouth pull up slightly as she turns toward the display.

Eric shakes his head. "Won't Berg be able to track us?" he asks.

"Shari assures me that her vehicle isn't tracked, given her position within the Committee, but just in case..." she trails off, working on her sensor, "...I have deployed twelve other cars to random Tier 2 locations. They won't be able to follow them all at the same time. It should hopefully buy us some time, at least."

Eric smiles. "How in the world were you able to get into Tier 1 communications? With Berg loosening up the reigns in Tier 2, it was relatively simple, but I doubt they have opened up the same loopholes here."

"I am a woman of many talents," Jessica says, a playful smirk on her face. "There's a reason Nick and I partnered up," she comments, a cloud passing over her expression.

"Were you and Nick—" I begin, but then think better of it. "I'm sorry," I say. "I'm sure you miss him."

Jessica nods. "Every day."

"Jessica, we can't thank you enough for your help," Eric states.

She clears her throat. "I am grateful I had the opportunity to participate in this little venture," she says sincerely, then straightens her shoulders, "and, while I appreciate the sentiment, we don't have any more time to chit-chat. I will be dropping you off at a completely random address about six blocks from one of Kip's friend's homes. Val and I decided it would be better to meet in a location that Berg would have no reason to connect to you. I am hoping that you can make it from there?"

My hand subconsciously flies to my now naked wrist.

Jessica notices the movement and nods. "No GPS this time, guys. It's too risky. Here, take a look at my map."

She pulls up a grid of the city and walks us through the directions. It seems simple enough, but I continue to repeat the steps in my head as we drive.

"Val is already there with the boys. She left her sensor at home, as well. It's the best we could do."

Eric nods. "When we get there..."

"You'll need to leave Tier 2 immediately," she finishes his thought.

I swallow hard. My body is already aching from exhaustion—the stress of the day taking its toll on my joints and muscles.

"That part...will be up to you. I haven't had a chance to arrange anything beyond this." Her smile is apologetic.

"Thank you so much," I say, my eyes again beginning to sting at the corners. "I'm going to miss our messages," I admit and she laughs.

"Me, too. But I am hoping I will have plenty more Committee members to talk with after tonight. You know, it'll help fill the void," she comments and I laugh. "Kate, I want you to have these," she says, placing a small, fabric bag into my hands. "They're Nick's."

My breath catches in my throat.

As the car begins to slow, Eric reaches for my hand.

"We won't get to see what happens with all of this," he says slowly. "I don't even know where we'll go, or what we'll do..." he trails off as the vehicle comes to a stop. "Good luck," he says finally. Reaching across the seat, I pull Jessica into an embrace, tuck the bag under my arm, and follow Eric out into the cool night air.

## CHAPTER 35

KNOCKING ON THE DOOR SOFTLY, we wait. Despite the comfortable temperature, I can't stop shivering. Eventually, the door opens slightly, and Val's eyes peek out from behind the edge. Sighing in relief, she flings the door wide and ushers us in. Bentley runs—and Tal hobbles—toward us from a back room and we greet with warm, desperate embraces, attempting to field their questions.

"What happened? Did they listen?" Bentley asks excitedly.

"No, but—" Eric starts.

"Did you have to send the blast?" Tal asks, cutting him off.

"Yes—"

"How did you get out?" Bentley says, nearly knocking Eric off balance.

"Okay, okay!" Eric says, laughing loudly. "We will have plenty of time to talk about all of this, but we need to nail down some logistics first. Can we hold the questions for a bit?"

Tal and Bentley both nod, their faces beaming. For the first time, I notice Kip sitting in the kitchen on a stool. I wave, and he nods in our direction. A deep sense of completion settles over me at having them both present. It wouldn't have seemed right to leave without saying goodbye.

"Val..." I begin, and she smiles knowingly.

"I know, you have to get going," she says. "The boys and I packed up your belongings. If we forgot anything...I'm sorry, but you won't be getting it back," she grins and Eric chuckles. "We also threw in some rations for the next few days. I went over the map with the boys, but I don't think we're going to have time to review it now—"

"It's okay," Bentley cuts in. "I remember the way."

"Dad, check it out," Tal says. "Kip gave me this." He thrusts a small, round object into Eric's hands. "I think it was his grandfather's or something. He showed me how to follow directions with it."

Inspecting it, Eric smiles. "Perfect," he says, handing it back to him. He glances at Kip and nods. Clearing his throat, Kip waves off the gesture.

"I've left everything with Val in the lab," Eric informs him. "Blueprints, instructions, all of it. I wish I could stay to see this out...but since that's not possible, my hope is that you can at least use that technology as a bargaining chip. If Berg refuses to adjust, well...at least you'll have something to motivate them," Eric finishes and Kip nods.

"Thanks for keeping everyone here in check," I add.

Kip stands, moving closer to our near-huddle in the center of the room. "You've given us hope, and that's not easy to come by these days," he says, clapping Eric on the shoulder. Turning, Eric pulls him into a hug, taking him by surprise.

"You've changed my life for the better," Eric says.

Sensing Kip's discomfort with being in the spotlight, I turn to Val. "Thanks," I say simply, then I throw my arms around her and squeeze tightly. "Thanks for everything."

"Will you be safe?" Eric asks her, his voice sounding over my shoulder.

"I have no reason to think otherwise," she says, pulling back from my hug. "I think we covered our tracks pretty well." I step to the side, allowing them to converse without an obstruction.

"Are you sure?" he asks again.

"You know me," she grins shyly. "I'm never sure about anything."

He smiles and pulls her into an embrace. I look away, somehow not wanting to intrude on their moment. Tal and Bentley have already picked up their packs and fastened the straps around their torsos.

"How's the leg," Eric asks Tal.

"Feeling better every day," he answers, puffing his chest out slightly.

"Rose is going to dig that cast," I tease, and he rolls his eyes.

"Mountain trip number two!" Bentley announces, lifting a fist high into the air.

Val laughs as we follow him to the door.

"Any advice on an exit strategy?" Eric asks.

"Just don't get caught," she says, waving as we make our way down the steps and quickly move into the shadows on the opposite side of the street.

"We're going to have to wait here for a few minutes," Eric whispers, short of breath. "I don't think they normally have a night watch on this side of the border, but they must have upped security tonight."

Though his voice is calm, the muscles in his neck are tense. We have walked for what feels like miles through the trees along this fence and haven't found a single section that has been left unattended. I can't imagine that Berg was able to man the entire border, but with only two sides of the Tier 2 border leading into open territory, I guess it wasn't hard for them to anticipate where we'd be headed.

The boys sit down next to us, hidden in the brush. Gusts of wind shake the branches around us, making it easier for us to move without attracting attention.

"What are we going to do?" Tal asks.

"I'm not exactly sure," Eric admits. "While normally I would avoid a designated crossing, it also seems like our best bet. It's probably the last place Berg would expect us to attempt it. And maybe we'll get lucky with vehicles coming in and out—we could use them as a distraction."

Hunched together, we wait. After what seems like an interminable amount of time watching guards milling around the sealed gate, Eric sighs.

"We may have to do this one at a time," I suggest. "Use the trees for cover."

"Or *cause* a distraction," Bentley offers simply.

"What are you thinking, Bent?" Eric asks, his interest piqued.

"There's got to be something flammable around here," Tal suggests.

"You want to set a fire?" I ask, disturbed at how quickly they turned to arson as a potential solution.

"Hey, fire usually catches people's attention," Eric teases. "But, I do think that may be a little suspect. The last thing we need is for Berg to know when and where we left the borders."

I can almost hear the wheels in his head spinning.

"What if..." he starts.

"Way ahead of you, Dad," Tal says, following his gaze.

Though these borders aren't typically patrolled anymore, the fences and gates still stand, serving as a reminder of a time when they were necessary. A time when there was a legitimate outside threat. Next to the main gate, a sturdy branch from an ancient tree protrudes over the guard shelter.

"Do you have the right tools?" I ask skeptically.

"We'll figure something out," Eric says, obviously energized by the challenge. "Bent, wait here with Mom, okay?" Turning to me, he says, "We'll need to double back quite a ways. When I have their attention, you have to get across immediately."

"But what about—"

"We'll go over on our side," he assures me. "Get across and go straight. We'll catch up."

"How will we know it's you?" Bentley asks.

"I'll do my whistle," Tal suggests. "When you hear it, do yours and stay put."

Bentley nods. This is quite the ramshackle plan, but it's the best we've got. The longer we wait, the more difficult this is going to be. And we have to make a lot of headway before sunrise.

"Go," I whisper, waving them off with my hands. "Be careful."

"I love you," Eric says as he turns and retreats into the brush.

"What if they can't get it to fall?" Bentley asks yawning.

"They'll figure something out," I say, but it's been long enough that I'm beginning to worry. I breathe deeply, attempting to portray pure calm to Bentley.

"Mom," he whispers sharply. "Something's happening."

Poking my head timidly from behind the branch, I recognize what he is noticing. That branch is moving significantly more than those next to it, even with the incessant wind. As we stare, it begins to fall through the air, landing with a shockingly loud crack that seems to split the air around us.

"Whoa," Bentley remarks, his eyes wide.

"Whoa is right," I say, pulling him up from the ground. "We need to move. Fast."

The guards buzz around the shelter like angry bees, none of them looking in our direction. While we waited, I was able to scout out our best spot for getting over the fence. About twenty yards to our left, there appears to be some sort of break in the barrier, but it's also completely exposed. With the light from the shelter, it's too risky to chance. Instead, I lead Bentley through the tree line toward the far right section of the fence. Here, the tree branches are dense, preventing much light from filtering through.

Continually glancing over my shoulder, I find the guards still in shock over the massive branch crushing the ceiling of the shelter. *Well played*, I think, moving swiftly toward our exit point, my heart pounding.

"Why are you stopping?" Bentley asks, running into my pack from behind.

My fingers reach the fence and I pause, looking around for the easiest way up.

"Bent, this is where things are going to be a little sketchy," I explain hurriedly. "We can only do this one at a time—it's too exposed at the top, plus, I don't think you're going to be tall enough to reach it on your own. Here's what I'm going to do," I say, pulling myself up into the center of a large oak. "I'll stand here and you climb past me, as high as you can. Then I'll boost you over the top."

"What then?" he asks innocently.

"I don't know what then!" I say harshly, then close my eyes and take a deep breath. "I'm sorry, it's just—I have no idea what it looks like on the other side. There are branches, so my hope is that there's another tree that you can climb down. But just get over, then hide yourself as best you can. I'll come over behind you and we can find the easiest way down."

He nods, his expression serious.

"C'mon," I say, "no time to waste."

Bentley secures his pack and reaches for my hand, then pulls himself up into the tree alongside me. Scampering up the largest branch, he is at the top in a few seconds flat.

"Impressive," I grunt, attempting to follow suit. When I am just below his heels, I reach my hand up and grip his shoe. "Hop over, bud. You can do it."

He hesitates, but only for a moment. Sneaking a quick glance through the trees, I can only catch a few guards in my field of vision. *Faster*. We have to move faster. Bentley's weight lifts from my hands and he slips out of view. *You can do this Kate*, I tell myself, lifting my feet to the final length of branch. Launching myself over the top sideways, my feet scramble for a hold on the opposite tree. Finding something solid, I slowly crouch on the other side of the wall. The complete darkness on this side is startling.

"Bent," I whisper.

"I'm right here," he says softly, directly next to my left ear.

I gasp, nearly losing my grip on the branch above me, my thighs screaming in complaint at my perpetual low crouch. "Don't—gah! You scared me!" I chastise, my heart racing.

"Sorry," he answers sincerely. "In my defense, I don't know how else I could have answered," he mutters under his breath.

I laugh at the sheer hilarity of the situation, and I can practically sense Bentley's grin. "Let's get out of this tree, shall we?" I whisper. "I'm going to go first, then I'll tap your leg when it's safe for you to follow. Don't move until I tell you to, okay?"

It takes some time to reach the ground. The tree we fell into isn't nearly as easy to navigate as the one we climbed, but eventually our shoes hit grass.

"Are you okay?" I ask, brushing myself off. I still can't see more than a few inches in front of my face. The clouds obscure the moon and stars, which is actually quite fortuitous, but also more difficult when moving through foliage.

"Dad said straight," Bentley reminds me.

"You're right, let's walk," I agree.

Bentley yawns again, this time creating a long sigh.

"Are you going to be alright?" I ask, rubbing his shoulder. It has to be nearly midnight. He doesn't respond, but reaches for my hand. I squeeze, and we cautiously move forward through the trees.

## CHAPTER 36

"Mom, I think I hear it," Bentley says as he stumbles along beside me. My steps have become slow and measured to allow him to keep up.

"Hear what?" I ask.

"Tal's whistle. Shhh," he instructs, coming to a dead stop. The clouds opened about an hour ago, allowing the waxing gibbous moon to light our path. Bentley's face looks angelic in the soft, blue light as he tilts his head to listen.

"There it is, did you hear that?" he asks excitedly.

I shake my head, but Bent doesn't wait for my acknowledgment. He purses his lips and sends his signal.

"We have to stay right here now," he commands, lowering himself to the ground, leaning against his pack. Exhausted, I sit next to him. If I don't hear anything within the next few minutes, I'll have to somehow convince him to keep going, but for now...this is a welcome break.

Bentley continues to whistle every few minutes, dedicated to leading Tal and Eric to us. Yet to my ears, the air continues to hold no answer. The wind died down shortly after the moon appeared, and the night air is now cool and calm. Though the temperature felt fine while we were walking, I begin to feel slightly chilled within minutes of sitting down. I reach into my pack and am about to pull out my jacket when I hear it.

I gasp.

"Told ya," Bentley says smugly, and I smile in spite of myself.

"I never doubted," I insist, but Bentley just rolls his eyes.

"Okay, I doubted a little," I admit.

As the sounds grows nearer, Bentley rises to his feet and stretches out his neck to send his call. His whole body seems to work in cooperation to send the notes floating. The trees are thinner here, but the sound still doesn't carry as far as it would on an open hillside.

Eventually, I catch movement on my right and my body tenses. *It's only Eric and Tal*, I remind myself, but I swing my pack over my shoulders just in case. When he sees us, Tal hobbles to me and throws his arms around my neck.

"Took you long enough," Bentley teases, and Tal punches his shoulder softly.

"Maybe you shouldn't walk so fast," Tal banters.

We stand there in a small circle, the sound of our breathing seeming to echo around us.

"Did everything go as planned?" I ask, knowing that it's a dumb question the second it leaves my lips.

Eric grins. "We're here, aren't we?"

"Yes," I respond, "but I want to know what happened. How did you get the branch down? How did you get across?"

Tal seems to puff out his chest at the mere mention of their daring escape.

"Should we talk while we walk?" Eric suggests.

"I don't know how much farther this one should go," I say quietly, gesturing toward Tal.

"I'm doing fine, Mom," he insists, pulling his pack to his shoulders.

"Even so," I say, "I'm winding down. How far do you think we need to go before it's safe?"

"Let's see if we can make it two more miles. That will take us into the foothills and it will be easier to find shelter there. It will also be easier to spot a search party at a slightly higher altitude. Can everyone make it that far?" Eric asks.

Acknowledging our nodding heads, he leads us forward. "Tal, do you want to tell how we got the branch down?"

"Yeah!" he answers excitedly, nearly hopping along the ground. "When we got up there, we realized that the branch was a lot bigger around than it looked from the ground. And we couldn't just use our hatchet—Berg would know it had been done purpose-fully if they took even a moment to inspect it later—so Dad had the idea to use the hatchet as a wedge. I found a great rock, he lodged the blade in the branch, and we started working—"

"Don't forget your contribution," Eric cuts in.

"Oh right, I didn't want the pounding to make any noise, so I rolled up one of my shirts and wrapped it around the rock," he says proudly. "That shirt is trashed, by the way."

"I figured as much," I comment, giving him a sidelong glance.

"It was the best option we had!" he insists, and I laugh.

"I know, I know, I'm kidding. It was a great idea, go on," I say, reaching down to hold Bentley's hand. He's beginning to fall behind.

"It was great, it took a little while to get a really good break in the branch, but then it went pretty quickly. Dad adjusted the position so that it created a jagged break—then when we got about halfway through, the rest of it ripped apart."

"We saw it fall," Bentley adds. "It was so loud."

"It was even louder right above it!" Tal insists. "Dad had to remind me to move, I was just staring at the mess it made."

"We found a good spot to make it up the fence," Eric says. "Obvi-ously you did, too?"

"Yep, we used the trees to boost us over. Bentley went first," I say.

"That's my man," Eric praises, giving him a high five.

"I can't believe we made it," I sigh. "I don't think I've felt that scared...well, since about three hours ago."

Eric laughs as my mind immediately flits back to standing in front of the auditorium full of Committee members, and then—trepidatiously—to that truly terrifying moment a few years ago. My heart pounding as I scanned the line for balloon rides and then locked eyes with Shari...I shudder, and the images fade. My mind continues to wander—revisiting the events of the last few days—as we walk in silence.

After what seems like hours, Eric finally calls it for the night. My eyelids droop as he stumbles to set up the shelter.

"Tal, go break off some long branches. We need to go incognito tonight," Eric instructs. Even though he wasn't mentioned, Bentley follows and begins finding a few branches of his own.

My body aches to lie down, but I force myself to help Eric situate the tent under two particularly luxuriant pine trees. He deftly maneuvers the branches to obscure the shelter as much as possible without compromising the integrity of it.

"Does anyone need something to eat?" I ask, but am met with groans as the boys pull things out of their packs, handing them to Eric for placement in the bear bag.

"I'm too tired to eat," Tal says. "I feel sick."

"Me too," Bentley complains.

"Okay, just go to bed then," I say. "Here, take your sheets."

Reaching for them gratefully, the boys sluggishly enter the tents and settle in for the night. After the initial rustling, the boys are completely still.

"Did they really fall asleep that fast?" Eric asks skeptically.

"I feel like I could do the same," I tease.

"I know, sorry. I just want to make sure we're in a good position so I can actually rest without stressing out," Eric says.

"Do you honestly think they're going to be looking for us?"

"One hundred percent yes. Are you kidding? We just kicked the bees nest."

I yawn. "Yeah, I guess you're right. How long do you think we can sleep before we need to keep moving?"

"My hope is that we can sleep most of the daylight hours. It's only a few hours from dawn."

"Really?" I ask in surprise, scanning the sky. The moon is hanging low.

"Just sleep," Eric insists. "I know my body will wake me up in a few hours and I'll keep watch. When you wake, we can switch off. Hopefully the boys can sleep all the way through. Tomorrow night...it's going to be a long one."

I nod, forcing myself to compartmentalize the tasks ahead of us. If I allow myself to think about any of it with my tired brain, it's going to be my own undoing. Sleep, I remind myself. That's all you need to do right now. Just sleep.

I pull my sluggish body into the tent, careful to avoid knocking the structure of branches above it, and fall into my spot. The uneven ground feels like heaven. I immediately begin to drift, and when Eric's body shifts into position next to me, the last bit of tension in my muscles gives way. I sink into sleep.

## CHAPTER 37

M y eyes fly open, my heart pounding in my chest. Whipping my head to the side, I find Eric's sheet empty and immediately relax. *He's keeping watch*, I remind myself. We're safe. The boys are still snoozing peacefully, and I cautiously stretch, trying to keep my noisemaking to a minimum.

Judging by the light outside, it's got to be mid-morning. Guilt rises immediately at having slept so long, but at the same time...it feels glorious. Still in my clothes from the night before, I carefully open the flap, slip on my shoes, and step out of the shelter. Straightening my shirt, I turn and find Eric sitting on a rock a few paces away. He silently motions for me to follow him.

Birds flit between the branches overhead; a soft breeze whispers through the woods, the strong gales of the night before completely forgotten. When we are a fair distance from the tent, Eric stops and hands me a small, wrapped bundle.

"Breakfast?" he offers, his voice soft.

"Is this from Val?" I ask quietly, mimicking his caution.

He nods. My stomach rumbles gratefully as I open it, the food preservation paper crinkling under my touch. Chicken, mixed with dried fruit and nuts.

"Heaven," I murmur, using my fingers to bring a portion to my lips. "I guess I should have washed my hands first," I mutter, my mouth full.

Eric laughs and shrugs. "There are worse things."

He sits, patting the ground next to him and I settle in. From this vantage point, windows open up between the trees, allowing us a view of the path we walked the night before. Far in the distance, I can barely make out the border fence we crossed. A part of me is impressed with the ground we covered, while another part is terrified that we are still so close. I eat, allowing my mind to cycle through recent events, beginning to process all that I was too overloaded to deal with yesterday. Eric is quiet beside me, a pillar of calm as his gaze follows mine past the trees.

"What are you thinking about?" he asks eventually, leaning gently against my shoulder.

I sigh heavily. "Honestly?" I pause, attempting to gather my thoughts into something coherent. With so many concerns and questions, it's difficult to answer. Especially since I don't necessarily feel like dumping on him right now. There is one that that feels more powerful than the others, so I go with that.

"How I was so close...to the girls, I mean. Shari was right there and I didn't even think to—"

"There wasn't any time," Eric reminds me.

I nod, my eyes filling with tears. "I know," I say, and I do. I know it couldn't have gone any other way. But, it doesn't keep me from replaying it over and over again. Maybe if I had thought to ask Jessica before we met? Maybe she could have had them in the car? Or maybe we could have stopped there before the meeting? That was quite possibly my last chance to see them. *Ever.*

I continue to play out different possibilities in my head, hoping that one will end up with me wrapping my arms around Beth and Leah. Fully aware that finding that option will only crush me because I didn't consider it soon enough. Lose-lose.

"I'm sorry, Kate," Eric repeats for the hundredth time.

"I'm sorry, too, but not just for me," I answer, a tear rolling down my cheek. "For you, for Val, for Kip—for all of them. We get to walk away. They have to keep living and watching this happen."

"You never know. Maybe we shifted something," Eric says. "It's up to them now." He stands, stretching his back. "I left our research with Val," he continues. "She can work with her team and try to get it going. At least, if nothing else, we contributed that."

I smile, holding his eyes for a moment, and the weariness in his face reminds me that he's past due for a sleep rotation.

"Go," I say. "I'll keep watch."

"You got enough rest?" he asks.

"I feel great. Go," I reiterate.

He smiles gratefully and retreats to the shelter. Though I don't relish the idea of being alone with my thoughts, I hope with all the energy of my soul that my own brain is the only thing I'll have to deal with over the next few hours. I ball up the empty paper, stuff it into my pocket, and pull my knees to my chest. Then I watch and wait.

*CHAPTER 38*

FINALLY, we see it. The sun is barely beginning to rise over the brilliantly green trees, a soft mist lifting into the sky. Home. The boys, though thoroughly spent, somehow find the energy to begin running toward the house. Eric reaches for my hand, an obvious bounce in his step.

"You didn't think we'd make it back, did you?" he chides, a grin on his face.

"You mean because we had to backtrack? *Twice?* Definitely made me skeptical."

"Hey, those compasses take practice," he says, slightly offended.

"I'm just glad I didn't have to set the directions. Truly, I'm in no position to tease," I admit. "I was too scared to try it myself."

He chuckles, watching the boys approach the edge of the yard. The setting is aesthetically stunning and both of us—entranced— pause involuntarily, taking the happy scene in.

"Thank you," I breathe.

"For what?" he asks, again pressing toward the house. I stop, pulling on his arm and forcing him to turn toward me.

"For everything, Eric! For being brave enough to push boundaries with your research. For coming back for us. For fighting for us. And then for being willing to sacrifice for social change, yet again. For facing your old life without any complaint, and for being willing to just jump into brand new things at every point of the way to keep us safe," I say, in awe of his constant energy and positivity. "For getting us home," I finish, my voice a whisper.

He pulls me to his chest and I collapse into sobs. All of the pent up stress and tension I didn't even realize I was still carrying floods through me, releasing through my tears.

"It's taken all of us. You, me, Nick, Val, Jessica, Kip—every single one of us. Together," he breathes. "And I don't think that I'm the one who has sacrificed most," he says softly, stroking my hair as I nod against his chest.

Standing there—the tall grasses brushing against my calves—I allow all of it to finally clear my system. Eventually, my breathing begins to normalize.

"Ready?" Eric asks gently.

Pulling back, I nod.

"Race you!" he shouts, and my eyes widen in surprise. Turning on his heel, he runs in a full sprint toward the house.

"Not fair!" I yell, awkwardly chasing him with my pack bouncing against my back. I laugh as I begin to spot little heads moving through the front door and rushing toward Tal and Bentley. We're home. *We're home.*

Later that night, after getting a very long, detailed run-down from Rose about the last couple of weeks and repairing a few odds and ends—including a dislodged beam on one of the bunk beds—Eric and I are settled at the table. The kids have already rushed off to play before bed. We are both resigned to the fact that there's no way we're going to be able to convince them to settle down yet, especially considering Tal and Bentley's currently backward internal clocks. Earlier, Eric and I committed to staying up and suffering through the day, rather than drawing it out and adjusting incrementally. Now, I'm regretting that decision. The boys are overtired to the point of being hyper, and I don't especially relish the idea of carrying out the bedtime routine.

"So," Eric states seriously, letting the word hang in the air as he interlocks his fingers on the table in front of him.

"So?" I ask, my eyebrows furrowed.

"What are we going to do?" he asks.

"About bedtime? You can totally take the lead if you want..." I say playfully.

He smiles, but doesn't engage. "It's only going to be a matter of time, Kate."

I stare at him, confused.

"Before Berg finds us," he explains. "They're going to find us. At best, if they search all of the wrong places first, we'll have a couple of weeks. If they initially guess right..."

"Eric, I think I'm too tired to think about this right now."

He nods. "I am having difficulty not thinking about it," he admits.

Sighing, I resign myself to talking through it, at least partially. I can't leave him alone with these heavy thoughts.

"What if they stop looking?" I counter. "If they don't find any obvious signs of our departure, won't they give up?"

Eric shakes his head. "I don't think that's how it works."

"So...what do you think our best option is?" I ask, falling back into problem solving mode, grieving the loss of my days' worth of internal peace.

"I was thinking about this on our hike yesterday. It seems to me like we have two options."

"Only two?"

"I mean, only two good ones," he teases. "First, we can stay here. We can enjoy the time we have and hope that when they come, the consequences won't be more than we can handle."

"What do you think they'll do?"

"Based on the look on the Director's face? I don't even want to imagine," Eric admits.

I shudder. "Not loving that option," I say. "What's number two?"

"Well, unfortunately, it's not much better," he sighs. "We can pack up and go on the move. But that leaves just as much uncertainty. Maybe more, in some ways. While it increases our likelihood of slipping Berg's search, it leaves all of us susceptible."

"No resources," I state, mulling through the ramifications of this course of action.

"No stability, no home base," Eric continues. "I just...I don't know if that's any better than dealing with Berg. At least with them, I would expect that they would give opportunities to the children."

"All of them?" I ask cynically.

Eric purses his lips. My hands are clenched into fists and a tightness in my chest builds.

"Eric, I don't think I can run again," I blurt out, embarrassed at my weakness. "I don't think I can leave so soon. Just the thought of it...it's too much—"

"We have to leave again?" I hear from behind me and whip my head toward the voice. Tal, Bentley, Rose, and Root stand clustered in the entryway.

"No," Eric explains hastily, "we were just discussing options. We're concerned that...well, that our—this—location won't be unknown to Berg for long."

Searching their faces, I wait for a response.

"I think we should stay," Bentley says simply, and the others nod.

"I've already lost one home," Rose adds. "This one's better," she quickly adds, "and I don't want to lose it, too."

"I know," I respond, my heart aching, "but Berg may take it from us. You don't know what they are capable of—"

"I do," Rose interjects softly, looking at the floor.

I regret my comment instantly. Nodding, I consider carefully before speaking again. "We're worried that if we stay, we might lose everything. Maybe even each other."

"Maybe. But I agree with you, Mom," Tal contributes. "It's too much. We've done all we can. Let's just be done."

I pause, a lump in my throat. "I want to be done," I admit, my nose stinging.

"Can we have a few more minutes to play?" Bent asks, and I nod. They bounce back out into the yard happily, the door slamming behind them.

"How can they just rush off like that after hearing that we might not be safe?" I ask, incredulous.

Eric laughs. "Decision made," he states simply. "No sense in worrying about it anymore."

"I don't know if I can let it go like that," I comment, standing and gathering a few dishes from the table. "Or if I can live with the consequences if something terrible happens. It's like this whole last week. I just keep going back over each moment, wondering if there was a way I could have handled it better. If I would have been more prepared, or thought through things more completely—"

"Kate, you're going to drive yourself mad. Nobody can expect themselves to consider all possibilities in any given moment. You're forgetting that each decision we made was limited by time. Sure, if time wasn't an issue, we could expect complete possibility analyses in every situation, but in the real world? Not realistic. You can let this be," he says, pulling me toward him as I hastily set the dishes on the counter before they fall to the floor. "Let's be done," he says, his voice full of mischief. I laugh at his expression—fully—and it feels like it's been years since I was last giddy. His lips reach mine and I close my eyes, melting into his embrace.

CHAPTER 39

"I CAN'T BELIEVE it's been a week already," I say, listening to the pitter-patter of rain on the roof, wrapped in Eric's arms. The darkness from the morning clouds has prevented the children from waking at their normal hour, and our bed feels cozy and luxurious compared to the chilly air of our bedroom. I don't want to get up yet, and the rain will prevent any real progress from being made on our projects anyway. Based on the fact that Eric isn't pushing to leave either, it seems that we've both silently agreed to remain relaxed and wrapped in our blankets.

"I'm not going to lie, there is a little seed of hope germinating within me," I admit, using my hands to mime a tiny seedling sprouting from the ground. Eric laughs and tickles my ribs.

"Crush it, Kate," he teases. "You know they're going to come."

"But what if they don't!" I insist. "Maybe things have changed and they don't care about us anymore. Maybe everyone in Tier 1 banded together and political change is in the works."

"It's a lovely thought," Eric agrees, "but I don't want you to be devastated when it isn't true."

"It could be true," I insist stubbornly.

He rolls over and presses his lips to mine. "If I kiss you, it means you have to stop talking," he says between pecks.

"It's not going to work," I say, laughing and pushing him away, kneeling on the bed.

"Shhh!" he says, "You're going to wake the kids!"

"Why would that be a problem?" I ask churlishly. He lies back on his pillow, his arm above his head, and looks at me in defeat.

A smile breaks my sullen expression and I pull the covers over us, lying next to him. "I'm kidding," I whisper. "I don't want the kids to bother us either."

He looks at me skeptically.

"I won't bring it up anymore if it makes you nervous," I offer.

"It's not that it makes me nervous," he sighs. "It's more that...I just don't want you to be disappointed anymore."

"I know," I say, kissing his cheek. "You know that none of this is your fault right? We shouldn't regret past decisions and all that?"

"Theoretically..." he says slowly.

I kiss him more intensely, cutting him off. "I hear that if you kiss someone, they have to stop talking."

"Hmmm, we should probably test that theory," Eric whispers, pulling me close.

CHAPTER 40

"THANKS FOR HELPING," I say gratefully, attaching the last few shirts to the drying line. "Now go play!" I insist, waving Rose off to join the others. The boys won't be finished planting for another hour or so, but the younger children have been peeking around the side of the house, just waiting for Rose to finish. We had to take advantage of the small break in weather to avoid drying clothes in the house. The clouds in the distance are ominous, making me hope that I won't have to bring these right back inside in a couple of hours.

In such a short amount of time, we've already reached a certain level of normalcy. All of us have slipped easily back into routine, making our time in Tier 2 feel hazy and dreamlike. After deciding to stay, Eric and I joked about doing nothing at all. No food storage or gardening, no preparations for the year ahead. We could just throw caution to the wind and do whatever we wanted for a few weeks.

I pick up the empty basket and walk toward the house. As it turns out, that's simply not who we are. So we're doing laundry. And planting. And Eric and the boys are aiming to implement our new filtration system by the end of next week. While we're continuing to work as usual, we did all agree that we could afford to indulge just a bit for mealtime. While I was initially missing the fresh food of Tier 2, our dinners of late have left nothing to be desired.

Our little homestead is full and rich, abounding in energy and joy. No skirmishes, no complaints. I couldn't have dreamed up a better way to spend this time. Every morning, I awake to an empty, quiet yard more grateful than the day before. *One more day.*

Back inside the house, I finally begin the task of organizing and emptying out our packs. Though I meant to deal with them initially, there were too many other distractions. I had forgotten how much work it is to cook for this many people, let alone cleaning up after them. With our meals for today already prepped, thanks to the older children, I line up the gear and begin to sort everything into piles.

It goes more quickly than I had anticipated, likely because we used up everything perishable and came home with less than we took initially. I quickly wash the camping sheets and hang them to dry with the laundry, then set up the shelter to air out. I'll sweep it out later, when everything else is put away.

Reaching into the bottom of my pack, I find something unexpected. A bundle that feels unfamiliar beneath my fingertips. Pulling it out, I freeze, staring at it. I can't believe I forgot that

Jessica handed me these. The moment must have gotten lost in all the other demands that were more pertinent at the time.

Retreating to my bedroom, my heart beats faster as I carefully open the sack and pull out its contents. Notebooks, Nick's favorite hat, a baseball...my fingers trace the thread, remembering the many times he played with the boys at the park. Then, my hand closes around something that I have difficulty forcing myself to remove. Just feeling the smooth wooden handle causes my face to contort and tears to stream down my cheeks. With shaky movements, I pull the rattle from the bag and stare. *This was Leah's.* Her favorite toy. At least, it was when she was little. I can't believe he kept it. Holding it to my heart, I will it to remind me of her face each time she played with this. The memories are slipping a little more each day and it kills me.

Standing, I blow my nose with a cloth on the dresser and take a few deep breaths before returning to the bed. Placing the objects to the side, I open the first notebook.

*Kate is beautiful.*

I read this sentence three times before forcing myself to move on. What are these?

*Her stomach is getting larger by the day and I can physically see the little kicks against her skin.*

. . .

Are these his personal journals? I didn't know Nick kept a journal, though it doesn't surprise me. He was religious about keeping notes on his trials. I continue to read, my curiosity peaking.

*I met with the Committee tonight. It felt great to report our success with the program so far. Bentley and I are getting along great. Being with Kate is...well, more than I could have hoped for.*

I turn the pages. More notes on our life, more moments that I'm not sure I want to remember. Though some of it provides fresh perspective, Nick and I discussed most of this at one time or another. Near the end, however, I find something that catches my eye:

*"At least I know why that dream was so persistent for her."*

What? What dream? I flick back a few pages and begin reading.

*"Kate continues to struggle with this dream—about her mom. Though I obviously haven't seen it myself, her description is disturbing. Like her mom was desperate to tell her something. I'm going to dig into this and see what I can find."*

. . .

*Good luck*, I think, then laugh at the ridiculousness of the thought. This has already happened, and I have already spent days upon days searching any of my mom's files that still existed. If there was anything there, I would have already found it.

Turning the page, I continue reading.

*Found something today. It was restricted, but as if that ever stops me...haha.*

I laugh in spite of myself, shaking my head.

*Kate's birth records aren't consistent with her health records. When I traced it back, I found a discrepancy that didn't sit right with me. Seemed to be a clerical error, but...I don't know. It stuck out to me and I want to look into it.*

My heart stops. Could there have been something I missed? I don't remember having to bypass any restricted files in my search. But maybe I already had access as her progeny? Tracing the page, I blur through the sentences, trying to find another revelation. He explains Berg's edict to place children with fit parents, to rehabilitate those who struggled after birth—*yes, I know all of this*, I think impatiently. What does any of it have to do with—

. . .

"Mom!" Bentley calls and my head shoots up. The front door slams, and seconds later he is racing through my bedroom door. "Mom, Dad says you have to come see this."

"Can it wait just a minute? I—"

"No, you have to come right now!" Bentley insists, his eyes wide with excitement.

"Alright, I'm coming," I laugh, setting the journal down on the bed, still open to the page. *This better be good,* I think, following him to the yard.

Bentley leads me to a grove of trees on the other side of the garden.

"Ta-da!" Eric announces as I round the corner, pointing at a structure in the trees.

"Whoa! Is this what you guys have been working on all morning?" I ask in awe. A platform stretches between the trees with steps nailed into the bark. Tal stands in the center of it with his hands on his hips, his cast protruding from his pant leg.

"I'm super impressed," I admit, inspecting it from below.

"We're going to add walls, and a window—Dad says we could even connect another one in that tree over there," Bentley explains exuberantly.

"With a rope bridge," Eric adds.

"I thought you guys were doing chores..." I tease.

"We were," Tal says, "but then Bentley had this idea and it was too good to waste."

"I love it," I say. "Where are the little ones?"

"They're playing tag," Eric answers, and Bentley rushes off in search of the game.

"Thanks for coming to check it out," Eric says, turning to me and putting his arm around my shoulders.

"I was kind of busy," I admit playfully, turning to walk back to the house, pulling him with me.

"Yeah?"

"I was emptying our packs—remember that bundle Jessica gave me?"

Eric looks confused.

"She gave me some of Nick's things," I explain. "I found some old notebooks in there. He discovered something odd with my birth records, but it doesn't seem like it led him to anything substantial."

"Huh," Eric says, his eyebrows furrowed.

"Want to come read the rest of it with me?" I offer.

"Sure," he says, "Just let me put these tools in the shed."

I nod, watching him go.


"I'm over here!" Bentley shouts, racing behind the cucumber trellises.

"That's not fair!" Tal exclaims as he hobbles in his cast, attempting to find a way around that prevents him from escaping.

I laugh, carefully sidestepping the soft earth along the garden.

"They are going to be so muddy," I comment to Eric as he pops out of the shed.

"Yeah...but at least they're enjoying the weather now that the rain stopped."

"A small consolation," I mutter.

Suddenly, Eric's head shoots skyward, searching the horizon.

"It's definitely going to rain later. Those clouds are moving closer by the minute," I comment. When he doesn't answer, I search his expression and immediately tense.

"What is it?" I ask, but he holds out a hand, silencing me.

"Kids!" he shouts across the yard, "get in the house."

*It's happening.* Though I can't hear or see what he's noticing, I can feel it. The energy in the yard has shifted. Someone's coming.

## CHAPTER 41

ERIC and I wait in front of the door, the kids hiding in the back room. They know the drill: remain silent until one of us comes to retrieve them. We assume that Berg will at least allow us the courtesy of comforting them before we have to leave. I had honestly convinced myself that we were past having to worry about this. *I was so sure...*I sigh, my eyes misty.

"It's going to be okay, Kate," Eric says softly.

"We don't know that."

"I know. But it feels like the right thing to say," he whispers, his arm again around my shoulder, squeezing me tight.

The vehicle stops, exactly where the transport parked when we first arrived here. This truck looks more heavy duty—I doubt the road here was as easily passable as it was the first time around. While it's similar to the truck Val used to sneak us into Tier 2, it has a covered back end and visible interior seats.

"Those would have been nice," I mutter, and Eric looks at me confused.

Before I can explain, the passenger door opens and my jaw drops. I'd recognize that bob anywhere. My hands clench into fists, my fingernails pressing into my palms as rage, hurt, and frustration coalesce into an explosive concoction within me. I take an angry step forward—

"No," Eric says, pulling me back. "Wait a second, I think—"

Instead of walking toward us, Shari moves to the back seat. Opening the door, she pulls something—a tiny person with vibrant, blond hair—into the sunlight. Setting her on the ground, she reaches in a second time...

Ripping from Eric's grasp, I run, nearly tripping on a rock near the steps. Closing the distance, a thought occurs to me. *I look like a crazy person! They don't even know who I am!*

Slowing, I attempt to pull myself together, but my shaking hands are a lost cause. Shari meets my eyes as I round the front of the vehicle. A deep sadness fills her expression, but she quickly engages with the girls, her tell-tale mask of confidence replaced upon her face.

"Beth, Leah, this is Kate," she explains, squatting down next to them and pointing my direction.

Two pairs of brilliant, shining eyes search my face. Beth smiles first. "You knew our daddy?" she asks, her voice innocent and sweet.

I nod, tears streaming down my face. Crouching down, I open my arms, hoping beyond anything that they'll choose to run into them. Beth looks at Leah and grins playfully, then rushes toward me.

As they both hit my chest, I'm careful not to squeeze too tightly, but it's difficult to restrain myself. The smell of their hair warmed by the sun, their soft shoulders, their chests rising and falling with each excited breath—it all nearly undoes me.

As quickly as it began, the girls pull away and inspect my face.

"Why are you sad?" Leah asks sincerely.

I laugh at her boldness. That's exactly like Leah. "Because I'm so happy to see you," I choke out, forcing my face not to break.

"Can we go play?" Beth asks, glancing over my shoulder, yearning to explore the yard.

"Yes, of course. If you ask the man by the door really nicely, he can tell the other kids to come out to play, too," I whisper, as if sharing a secret.

"There are more kids?" Leah asks, her eyes wide. I nod, and they race toward Eric, holding hands.

Standing up, I lean against the vehicle for support before facing Shari.

"Shari—" I start, but can't get the words out initially. Trying again, I choke out, "Thank you for this. I know you're here to take us, and I'm definitely not excited about what will happen after that point, but thank you *so much* for letting me see them—"

"Kate, I'm going to stop you there."

I look up, embarrassed. Clearly, I don't understand the protocol here. "Okay, I'm sorry, I just thought—"

"So dramatic," she huffs, pulling her bag out of the car. "You don't need to apologize. I know this is probably overwhelming. Let's go inside and talk," she commands, stalking toward the front door.

Confused, I follow her back to the house. The kids are already pouring back into the yard and Shari stops, taking them all in.

"You've...multiplied," she comments, then continues up the steps.

After settling us at the table, Eric rises to fill three glasses of water.

"I'm good," Shari says, and Eric obediently puts one glass back in the cupboard without comment.

"Kate, you know I've never been good with...sharing my personal thoughts—" she starts, but I cut her off.

"On the contrary, I think you're typically more than happy to share your opinions about most things," I tease, my voice laced with a slight undercurrent of hurt.

"I mean, I'm bad at sharing my feelings. Is that better?" she asks, her voice surprisingly tender.

I nod, taking a deep breath.

"The truth is, ever since you left...I've been second guessing a lot of things. I watched Nick's trials with great interest, and was horrified when—well, you know, when he had his accident."

I raise my eyebrow.

"I'm not going to comment on that, just hear me out," she continues in a rush. "I'm going to be honest, I don't want to give up my comfortable life. I really like having the flexibility to do what I want, and I know you probably think that makes me a terrible person, but it's true. That being said, I do actually want our society to succeed. The Director..." she sighs. "He's been on the wrong path for a long time. I kept hoping that we could find a happy medium, but you both saw how he responds to new information," she chuckles.

"Is that why you helped us that night?" I ask softly.

"Kate, I've wanted to help you for—" she purses her lips and her eyes squeeze shut. *Is she going to cry?*

Just as quickly, her face returns to normal and she clears her throat. "I've wanted to help all of you for a long time. After Nick's death, I took the girls in and tried to find some information on where Berg had left you. That trail was difficult to trace, let me tell you," she laughs. "Nick covered his tracks well."

"But you found us." Eric states.

"With Jessica's help. She was able to pull up coordinates from your messages."

"Why would Jessica help you?" I ask sincerely.

"We've been talking on and off for the last few months. She never mentioned her communication with you, which...I guess I understand why. Though it would have been helpful and could have possibly saved us all some trouble."

"Shari, I'm really glad that you've recognized all of this, but I need to know what happens now. Eric and I assumed that our time here would likely be short lived. These kids—they're our family now and we will do whatever we need to in order to make sure they are taken care of."

"Kate, some of these children are Tier 3," Shari states, her eyes focused on the table.

"All of them are," Eric says. "As far as Berg is concerned, I'm sure our kids don't qualify as Tier 1 anymore either."

"I don't know if that's really true," Shari comments. "But luckily, it doesn't really matter either way." She raises her eyes to look at us. "A lot has happened over the last few weeks. I don't know if it was because of your presentation, or just the sheer fact that so many Committee members were able to witness Carole's representative and the Director collectively lose their minds at you being there, but the Committees are in the process of being...restructured."

I look at her in surprise. "What does that mean?"

"Look, I'm not going to promise that full integration is going to happen anytime soon—"

"But it's being considered?" I ask, my voice shrill.

Shari nods. "Investigations are being carried out at the request of a regional Committee majority and inter-region discussions about integration are on the table. At least for now, our region will be equally distributing resources between both Tiers."

Eric reaches for my hand.

"This is monumental, Kate," she continues. "The infrastructure alone—it's going to take time."

I nod. "No, I understand. I'm thrilled to hear that it's moving in the right direction, though. Even the fact that they are considering —I can't even imagine what this will look like..." I trail off, pondering. "We've learned a lot being here, Shari. It hasn't been easy by any stretch of the imagination, but it's been incredible. I believe we need to give more attention to the power that struggle has to benefit us. That's where our research teams need to look next. If we could—"

"I don't think it's going to be an easy sell to study struggle," Shari interjects. "But you two need to figure out whether you want to be involved in any of this. Or not," she says, abruptly standing and reaching for her bag.

"What do you mean?" Eric asks, standing alongside her.

"I'm going to be frank. Berg isn't going to bother you anymore. You've suffered enough, and the Committee members recognize that. The Director and Carole—they have enough to worry about without trying to track you down. You can stay here, or, when the dust settles, I'd be happy to help you resettle in Tier—well, whatever it ends up being called at that point. It's up to you."

My eyes are misty, and relief floods through my shocked system. I can't even process what I'm hearing well enough to respond appropriately.

Eric takes a deep breath. "I think we're happy here," he states simply. "I know it isn't perfect, and we'll likely have to re-evaluate at some point, but for now, I can't imagine going back. And I doubt anyone there would be thrilled to see us. What do you think Kate?"

I nod. "We've built a fantastic life," I say, proud that when the words leave my lips, I believe them to the core. "It's not something I want to walk away from. And honestly...I don't know if I could handle stepping into all of that."

Shari nods, shifting her weight.

"I'll go call the girls," I offer reluctantly, my heart already aching at the thought of them driving away. Maybe I can spend a few moments with them outside before they have to go. Even now, I can tell that this visit is only going to make things harder. And yet, I would never take it back. Just seeing them—knowing for a fact that they are vibrant and thriving, alive and well cared for—has lifted an immense burden from my soul.

"Kate," Shari says softly, reaching out to touch my forearm. "They're here to stay."

I stare at her, unable to comprehend her words. My whole body trembles.

"But Berg—they're Tier 1. And they don't know—" I stammer.

"Berg has approved it," she assures me. "I didn't really give them a choice, to be honest. And I've talked with the girls. They know enough," she says, opening my hand and setting my old sensor in my palm. "If you change your mind," she whispers, then turns and opens the door.

"I've got one for you, too, Eric," she adds, almost as an afterthought. "I'm going to go get the girls' things out of the back. Can you help me bring everything in?" she calls as she walks down the steps.

Eric follows her, and I am left alone—numb—standing in the kitchen.

## CHAPTER 42

As soon as the dust settles after Shari's visit, I spend the afternoon playing with the children in the yard. So far, the clouds have been kept at bay, and I couldn't be more grateful.

The girls, understandably, are exhausted and worn out before any of the others. They probably needed a nap earlier in the afternoon, but I'm so beyond this stage of life that I didn't even think about it. After putting them to sleep, directly following an early dinner, I finally have an opportunity to return to the journal. Though Eric isn't immediately available, I can't force myself to wait any longer.

Plopping myself on the bed, I flip the journal over and begin to scan where I left off. My finger freezes when I see a sentence that stops my heart in my chest.

*I don't think Kate's mom is her birth mother.*

What!? That can't possibly be true. Anger rises and chokes my throat. How could he even postulate something so ridiculous? He doesn't have any evidence to come to that conclusion. Though frustrated and confused, I continue reading.

*In fact, I'm sure of it. Tracing her genetic markers, it's basically the only plausible explanation. I have more markers in common with Kate than the woman who raised her. Running a trace on her code, was able to find a few options in Tier 1 who could potentially match. Many of them I was able to rule out based on age and location, leaving me with only a handful of potential candidates.*

My heart pounds, causing my vision to blur slightly, and making it difficult to read the words on the page clearly.

*I searched through records on these few remaining individuals and came up with something very interesting. One woman matching Kate's code was taken in for rehabilitation in the same month of Kate's birth. She was only nineteen at the time, has never paired again, has never had more children as far as I can tell. But she has remained in Tier 1, and has actually been a big part of Kate's life.*

Before I finish the paragraph, tears fill my eyes. It's not possible.

*I'm convinced that Shari is Kate's birth mother, the timing is just too perfect. I wasn't able to find exact records from her time in rehabilitation, but I've seen plenty of patients like her. My guess? She had hormonal imbalances after birth and they weren't able to get them under control soon enough to place Kate with her again. By then, she had likely bonded with new parents and it wasn't ideal to remove her. I haven't been able to find out anything about Shari's pair. I'll have to keep searching. The worst part about having this knowledge is that I have no one to share it with. There's no way I can bring this up with Kate, not with how tense their relationship is now. It would make no sense and it would absolutely crush her. And Shari? There's no way I can ask about this. With how deeply I had to search to find her records, I can only assume that she wants the information buried. Though I can't help but wonder—why didn't she share this with Kate as an adult? Was she embarrassed? There's absolutely no shame in what she went through, and I know Kate would have understood. But now? It seems too late.*

Completely in shock, I stare at the pages, reading the words over and over again. What was in the dream with my mom that spurred Nick's investigation? *Was she even my mom?* I can't remember it! Those images haunted me for years, and now that I could finally attempt to make sense of it, I can't pull it back. I remember agreeing to be treated, but I had no idea...How could Nick have kept this from me? *I watched my mother die!*

I breathe deeply, my system in complete shock. Think, Kate. Shari is only eleven years older than you. This is not even physically possible. And of course our markers match. That's the point of being matched with a mentor, right?

But...my thoughts begin to spin.

*What if that wasn't her real age.*

This thought hits me like a brick. She looked so much older...the other night, she looked like she had aged ten years...What if she was placed as my mentor as a consolation? Because she wasn't able to raise me? What if that's why she chose to never have more children? Unable to process, I continue to the next entry, hoping to distract myself.

*Worried about Kate. The dreams are getting worse. Beth did the funniest thing today—*

I skip a few pages. Can't handle that right now. What if the reason Shari was so insistent about me being willing to sacrifice was that she had already lived it? If, back then, she had admitted that what Berg was asking of us was unreasonable, she would have had to re-examine so much of her own life. Was it actually in my best interest to be removed from her permanently? Should she have fought against that decision? Could she have?

*Kate.*

Again, my heart stops. Is he writing *to* me?

*Kate. I don't know how all of this is going to go down and I can't say anything to you right now, so I'm putting it here in case I don't get to say it later. You know that funny thing you do with your nose when you laugh? I love that. Or the way your eyes light up when you watch the kids? It's the absolute best. I'm walking out this door tonight knowing that I might not see that again and it's kind of killing me. But you know what? I am also so sure that what I'm doing is right. We—society, not us—are heading in the wrong direction. I can feel it, and now I have evidence that my gut feeling is correct. I know I haven't made all of the right decisions. In fact, I've made some fairly terrible ones. I keep telling myself that I can't judge my past actions with today's information...I don't know if that's actually true, but it makes me feel better. Acting now is the most exhilarating thing I've ever done.*

I grin, wishing that he could have participated in my discussion with Eric on the same topic.

*I cringe at the thought of you seeing these notes someday. When I wrote all of this down, I thought I was helping...but looking back over this, I'm not sure that's true either. I should have told you about Shari. Over the last few weeks I have judged her harshly. How could she put her own daughter through all of this after what she's experienced? I think at least I have a small understanding now. I was so entrenched, so convinced that what I was fighting for was right and true. I supported Berg 100% and acted in blind faith. I can see Shari doing the same. Especially since she lived it. She lives every day with that sacrifice, so how could she admit—to herself—or anyone else that it was a waste? Or that the leadership that made that decision for her could have been wrong? Anyway, I hope you'll understand. I mean, really I still hope you'll never have a reason to see this...but I digress. Wish me luck? I love you.*

I stare at the pages in complete shock. He did get to tell me at least in part how he felt, and that moment on the transport will forever be seared in my memory. Could all of this be true? Even as I sit here, pieces begin clicking into place, and it's becoming harder to explain away. Shari's willingness to watch the kids at all hours of the day and night, her commitment to being there for me—well, until I began to push her away. I always thought she was just conscientious. Her inability to pair, her agitation whenever I brought up her inability to have children...

But if this is true...frustration builds and my shoulders tense. She knew what it was like to lose someone she loved. A literal piece of her. To be treated without consent and held against her will. I echo Nick in asking how she could put me through that? Why wouldn't she have supported me in standing up for an alternative? Maybe it wasn't as painful for her? *Was it simply easier for her to give me up?* To see me with new parents, to miss being that person in my life?

No, it couldn't have been. Nick is right. Shari has always been completely dedicated to Berg's objectives. I just never knew she was *that* committed. Here I assumed that, as a Committee member, she was along for the ride for all the perks she received...selfish and unfeeling. But now I think she just might have earned them.

I set the other notebook aside for later and return to the kitchen, still unable to form fully coherent thoughts. Grabbing the soap roughly from the edge of the sink, I begin to wash the few dishes left from dinner. I didn't get to hear this when I could have done anything about it. Not in Tier 1, not when Shari was here. How could she not mention this to me even now! I didn't have the opportunity to talk to Nick about this, or about his integration trials, or about his vision for the future. I *won't* ever get to talk to him about any of it. Ever. Shari apparently lived her whole life lying about who she truly was. *Lying to me.* Both of them were denied a chance of finding a true pair and they didn't get a chance to experience this—all of this—for real. *Nick missed out on Beth and Leah,* too, I think, and Shari...Shari missed out on *me.*

How did I not know this only mere hours ago? I could have brought it up—gotten some answers. Or even just looked at her differently in that moment, instead of envisioning her again as someone so far removed from—I jump back as the dish I was holding shatters against the sink. Folding to the floor amidst the pieces, I wrap my arms tightly around my shoulders, close my eyes, and rock.

CHAPTER 43

THOUGH IT'S ONLY BEEN a few days, the girls have completely settled into their new life. They run from sun up until sun down, only sometimes commenting on our lack of their favorite foods. Every morning and evening I sit, simply watching them play. I don't think I'll ever take for granted a single moment. Even as I think it, I laugh internally, and leave the window. If only that could remain true.

Picking up a stack of clean, folded clothes, I move to our bedroom to place them on the shelves. As I turn to leave, something catches my eye. Sighing, I walk over and tuck the edge of Nick's notebook back in with the others. I know Eric's been reading them, which I really don't mind, but it's funny that he tries to hide it. Especially since he never puts them back in exactly the right position. We still haven't talked about any of it. I don't think I'm ready to yet, and Eric respects that enough to leave it alone.

Turning to exit the room, I think better of it, and sit down instead. Disturbing the now tidy stack, I pull out the last notebook. Not for the first time, I wonder why he chose to write these on paper instead of logging them on his sensor? They could have so easily been damaged or lost and all of this would have been lost on me.

Brushing my hand along the smooth surface of the book, I wonder —would it have been better that way? Am I glad to know any of this? Would it have been easier to keep my current view of Shari and my family? Would I take it back if I could?

*So many questions,* I think, tapping the book on my leg. I haven't had the courage to open these last pages. Mostly because I don't know if I can handle it's contents, but also—if I'm honest—because I don't want it to end. I don't want to know that I've seen all there is left of Nick. That there's nothing more just waiting to be discovered. As long as this book remains closed, I can convince myself that he's just gone for a time, waiting until I'm ready to come visit again.

I stare at the cover for a long time. And then, timidly, open to the first page.

Slowly, I walk back into the kitchen, my eyes filled with tears, and the notebook hanging from my hand. I jump when I see Eric seated at the table, clipping his nails.

"Gross," I comment, wiping my nose. "We have a porch for that."

Eric lifts an eyebrow and glances at the notebook in my hand. "I wondered when you were going to get to that one," he says smiling, continuing on to the next finger.

"You've read it?" I ask softly.

He nods.

"Eric—"

"I'll call Shari. We can start preparations in the morning," he says, scooping his cut nails into his palm and moving toward the compost bin.

I stare after him. "That's all you need? Me, standing here—a complete mess—and suddenly you're ready to leave our home, move our kids into the complete unknown. Into a system that is likely in turmoil, where we won't know what to expect for years?"

Eric smiles broadly, his eyes twinkling with excitement. Moving close, he tenderly kisses my cheek, then places his hands on my shoulders.

"That's all I'll ever need, Kate." Giving a gentle squeeze, he turns and walks toward the door, happy, playful voices wafting in as he pushes it open and steps into the yard.

OUR LIFE ISN'T PERFECT. In fact, it's far from it. There is still so much progress to be made, and sometimes it's all quite overwhelming. Especially when I feel like there's so little that I can actually do to catalyze change. Our society is so big and convoluted at this point, that even the smallest shifts take an incredible amount of work and patience. Knowing enough about myself now, deep down I recognize that I wouldn't be satisfied with my own apathy. But, in my darkest moments—when I want to give up and run back to that shelter in the woods—I reflect on Nick's words and remind myself that *I make a difference.* One person makes a difference.

*I've come to believe that every community needs caretakers. People who have a larger perspective, who see something that others are oblivious to. Maybe it's life experience, perhaps it's a struggle that is unique to them, but however that wisdom comes, it's their responsibility to lead those who haven't had the opportunity to find it. Without guides like these, it's just expected that we will eventually fall back into what's easy and comfortable. And 'easy and comfortable' don't ever lead to progress or growth. I don't know that I necessarily qualify as wise, but I am more confident now that my struggles have built something I can offer. And if I'm not offering, then what's the point, really?*

*I have to take care of this imperfect, precarious system that we've built. Limits need to be set, and I need to be there to guide that discussion. Our trajectory desperately needs to be corrected, and I need to be there to point it in the right direction.*

*Despite our shortcomings in recent years, we have overcome impossible odds and built a society that has experienced peace. If we who truly see can't bring ourselves to fight to protect that, then who will?*

## ALSO BY CINDY GUNDERSON

Tier 1

Tier 2

Yes, And

I Can't Remember

Let's Try This Again, But This Time in Paris

Holly Bough Cottage

The New Year's Party

www.CindyGunderson.com

Instagram: @CindyGWrites

Facebook: @CindyGWrites

Cindy is first and foremost mother to her four beautiful children and wife to her charming and handsome husband, Scott. She is a musician, a homeschooler, a gardener, an athlete, an actor, a lover of Canadian chocolate, and most recently, a writer.

Cindy grew up in Airdrie, AB, Canada, but has lived most of her adult life between California and Colorado. She currently resides in the Denver metro area. Cindy graduated from Brigham Young University in 2005 with a B.S. in Psychology, minoring in Business. She serves actively within her church and community and is always up for a new adventure.

Made in United States
North Haven, CT
17 September 2023

41678606R00195